+ Veronica!

Shattered

Jennie Marsland

ISBN: 978-0-9877832-1-9

Editing by Pat Thomas

This is a work of fiction. All references to real historical events, places or people are used fictitiously. All other names, places and events are products of the author's imagination, and any resemblance to actual people, places or events is purely coincidental.

Cover Art by Kim Killion, Hot Damn Designs

Jennie Marsland can be found on the web at jenniemarsland.webs.com and jenniemarsland.blogspot.com

Dedication

In honour of those who served, in memory of those who fell.
Then and now.

Acknowledgements

My fellow members of Romance Writers of Atlantic Canada have provided invaluable encouragement, insights and support through the last three years of my writing journey. Thanks for the laughs and inspiration. In particular, Michelle Helliwell, Julia Smith and Deborah Hale took time from their own writing to read my manuscript and offer suggestions.

Editor Pat Thomas gave generously of her time and knowledge. Her sharp eye and good judgment have been priceless, as is her friendship.

Lucinda Campbell took the mysteries of formatting the e-book version of *Shattered* out of my technology-challenged hands with efficiency, and was a pleasure to work with.

Kim Killion at Hot Damn Designs produced a fabulous cover. Thank you, Kim.

My Grade Five teacher, Mrs. Ashley, planted a seed when she told me after I'd scribbled a poem, "You'll be a writer someday." I never forgot her words, and I've tried to pass on her encouragement to my own students.

Artist, musician and friend extraordinaire, Kathy MacGillivray, has been there through thick and thin. When the going gets tough, she reminds me of why I write – for the joy of it.

Finally, my partner Everett, who's grown used to me spending hours at my computer and has learned not to worry when I go around muttering to myself. After all, normal is a relative term. Love you, and thank you for putting the music in my life.

Other Books by Jennie Marsland:

McShannon's Chance

Trey McShannon survived the carnage of the Civil War, only to discover that the deepest wounds are those to the heart. A traitor to his home state of Georgia, Trey has built a new life for himself in the untamed Colorado Territory. Now it's time to find a wife to share the future he's worked so hard for – but can he free himself from his past?

McShannon's Heart

When Rochelle McShannon accompanies her father to his old home in Yorkshire after her mother's death, she thinks she's leaving everything that matters behind her – including the man she expected to marry. When tested by the divided loyalties of the looming Civil War, she can't choose love over her bond to her family. Chelle wonders if she's even capable of the kind of love that can overcome bitterness and grief, the kind of love that lasts a lifetime.

Chapter 1

Halifax, Nova Scotia
September 1917

"K-K-K-Katy, b-beautiful Katy,
You're the only g-g-g-girl that I adore…"

The three singing sailors lurched along Brunswick Street, trailing liquor fumes in their wake. Liam Cochrane caught his companion by the waist and pulled her out of the men's path, into the darkened doorway of a closed pub. One of the three looked over his shoulder with a good-natured leer and snapped off a salute as limp as his wilted uniform. Giggling, Georgie pressed into Liam's arms, edging him further back into the shadows.

"Liam, my head is spinning. If I have any more to drink I'll be as tipsy as those three. It's time to go home."

She snuggled against him. Her curves fit his hollows to perfection. When Liam bent his head to kiss her, she rose on her toes and tangled her fingers in his hair. A brief, fierce moment later, Georgie rested her head on his shoulder. With her pressed warmly against him, her lips grazing his neck, going home was last on the list of things Liam wanted to do. He tucked a finger under her chin and turned her face up to his.

"You sure you're ready to call it a night?"

Georgie's smoky green eyes glowed with invitation while her fingers ran lightly along his spine. "No one will be home. I didn't say anything about calling it a night."

She reached for his mouth. She tasted of youth and life, heady and potent as the whiskey in his blood. Liam kissed her again, hard and deep.

"I like the way you think, lady. Let's go."

They had a walk ahead of them, all the way from Brunswick Street north to Richmond, but the bootlegged rye they'd shared during their picnic in Point Pleasant Park had loosened up Liam's bad hip. As for Georgie's inhibitions, after three evenings together he knew they didn't need much loosening. Girls like her had been rare in Halifax before the war, but not any longer. Peekaboo blouses and skirts that showed the ankles were only surface ripples on the current of change.

They started north past Citadel Hill, walking hand in hand. At the foot of the slope the squat base of the town clock lay in shadow, but the late sun gilded the face on its round, domed column. Half past eight. A stiff sea breeze snapped the flags that flew from the old fort on the hilltop. Beneath, the grey stone reflected the pink of the twilight sky. Later, fog might roll in off the Harbour, but for now the stored heat radiating from buildings and cobbles kept it at bay.

Halifax wore a grim face in the grip of winter, a drab and ghostly one in rain, but on a fine, end-of-summer day like this the city and its people smiled. Even the brick and stone of the industrial waterfront looked brighter and more welcoming, the bustle of wartime business a little less serious. The long evenings drew people out of blacked-out homes and barracks to stroll, socialize and look for trouble, always easily found around the Hill. This part of town catered to the two greatest wants of men just in from the sea, one of which was drink.

They passed another pub, once Liam's favourite, now

locked and shuttered under prohibition. Damn shame, but with the Harbour full of ships from all over the world, a man didn't have to settle for the rotgut served in the 'blind pigs.' He'd cultivated his sources since being invalided home. A bottle of forgetfulness didn't cost too much if you knew where to find it.

He avoided the eyes of the people they passed and concentrated on keeping himself and Georgie upright. After six months back in the city, he still hadn't learned to bear the respectful or pitying glances of strangers. When a thin, greying woman smiled at them and exchanged a knowing look with her rotund husband, Georgie wrinkled her pretty nose.

"I'd rather be dead than old and stodgy."

Liam let out a bark of laughter. "Stodgy isn't in your nature, Georgie."

She tilted her chin at him. "I hope it isn't. I don't like nosy people. Why can't they mind their own business?"

Liam tightened his arm around her. The busybodies just plain embarrassed him, the more so since he and Georgie weren't a couple in any way that mattered. She was mercifully sensible about that. He couldn't resist teasing her.

"If you don't like nosy people, why are you working for *The Herald*?"

She glanced up with a coquettish smile. "Because the pay's half-decent and working for a paper is a lot more interesting than selling nightgowns at Simpsons. Besides, the advertising editor likes me."

"Are you sure he doesn't like you too much? Perhaps that's why he's hired you on permanently."

That was why they were celebrating tonight. Georgie arched a carefully-groomed brow. "Jealous, Mr. Cochrane? Perhaps you should be. My boss isn't an unattractive man."

Liam thanked God for straightforward women. Georgie flirted with the same frank honesty she applied to everything, and he asked for nothing more.

"Miss O'Neill, you were born to trouble as the sparks fly upward. If I were smart, I'd stay away from you."

Georgie's eyes widened before she dropped her lids. Then she met his gaze with a coquettish grin. "Do you disapprove of me?"

Liam considered the question seriously. There'd been a time when he would have thought Georgie very forward, but he no longer felt any need to judge.

"No. Why shouldn't a girl have her fun? I saw little enough laughter on women's faces in France."

Her grin turned mocking. "Why don't you stay away from me?"

"Look in the mirror, Georgie." Neat and trim in her new, cornflower-blue skirt and lacy white blouse, she had no reason to wonder why she drew men's eyes, and Liam knew she was well aware of it. With tension settling in the pit of his stomach, he edged away from her. She held his hand and kept her silence. No one could say Georgie lacked perception.

Half an hour later they reached Richmond, with Liam's hip giving him hell. *Idiot, why didn't you get on a tram? You'll pay for this tomorrow.* Thankfully, Georgie had sobered up enough to walk without his support. She kept pace with him as he limped down Russell Street toward her home.

"You should have brought your cane."

"I didn't plan on walking home, but we both needed the exercise." The shrapnel-torn muscles in his left hip might never be much stronger, but coddling them wouldn't help. And he was thankful for the wound, in a way. His 'blighty' had been his ticket out of the trenches. He knew too many others who hadn't been as lucky. Michael-John—

Don't. He focused on Georgie to dispel the image of his dead brother's face. "How's your head feeling now?"

"Better. It isn't spinning anymore. Now you know I'm a cheap drunk."

At the bottom of the hill The Narrows glimmered under a lopsided moon, the sparkling water showing here and there between leafy branches. The maples lining the broad street whispered in the breeze. *Let Me Call You Sweetheart* drifted from a Victrola on someone's porch; the tinny melody blended with laughter. The carefree sounds left Liam cold.

Richmond had been a good place to grow up, almost country, with room for gardens and backyard hens, for ball games in summer and shinny in winter. Of course, in the last three years it had changed like everything else. People no longer took notice when a car rattled by, and electric lights glowed from many of the windows. Perhaps that was why this didn't feel like home anymore.

Liam gathered Georgie in his arms when they reached her family's rambling white Victorian. He forgot his pain in anticipation of having her on his lap in a darkened room, until he noticed the light shining from the kitchen window.

"Are you sure nobody's home?"

After a moment of teasing contact she pulled free. "Mother and Dad are in Dartmouth visiting friends for the weekend, and Alice was going out with Stephen Mitchell. She must have left the light on. Come on."

Liam breathed a sigh of relief. He didn't know Georgie's family well, and he had no desire to end the evening with small talk. She led the way up the walk, fumbling in her purse for her key. Before she found it, the door opened. Georgie paused with the key in her hand, her back stiff with annoyance.

"Alice, you're home. I thought you were going out with Stephen tonight."

Georgie's voice showed no sign of tipsiness now. Its sharp edge caught Liam by surprise. She'd been so bubbly and easy-going in the time they'd spent together.

Where chestnut-haired, rosy-cheeked Georgie was a study in contrasts, Alice had subtler colouring. Liam hadn't seen her up close since he'd returned home. She'd never been around when he called for Georgie. He remembered Alice vaguely as a skinny kid, mousy-haired and quiet, not the kind of girl boys noticed, but in the past three years she'd grown into her tall frame. Her yellow linen dress suited her willowy shape, and her hair had darkened to cinnamon, or perhaps it only appeared darker against the pallor of her skin. Liam wondered if she'd been ill. She looked at Georgie with amber eyes that seemed too big in her oval face.

Alice reached for the door jamb as if she needed support. Was she trembling? "I cancelled. Georgie, Carl's home."

Georgie dropped her purse and swayed on her feet. For a second, Liam thought he might have to catch her. She grabbed his hand and regained her balance. "*What?* When?"

Alice darted a look over her shoulder. "About an hour after you left."

Georgie lowered her voice to an angry hiss. "Why didn't he give us some warning? If Mother had been home—"

"He said he wrote from Liverpool, that there must have been some mix-up with the letter, but I don't believe him. It's like him to decide to surprise us. He never did think before doing anything." Alice sounded as shocked as she looked. Only now did she appear to notice that Georgie had company. "Oh, I'm sorry. It's good to see you, Liam. Has Georgie told you that Carl was missing in action last fall?"

"Hello, Alice. No, I didn't know." Strange. Liam didn't think Georgie had ever been particularly close to her brother, but he'd have expected her to mention a thing like that. Then again, he hadn't asked. By unspoken agreement, they didn't talk about the war at all.

"We haven't heard a word from him since. It turns out he was wounded and captured. His shoulder. He says it's healed well. He managed to escape from a prison camp. He's upstairs asleep now."

Colour flooded back into Georgie's face. "What a day. First work, and now this." She released Liam's hand. "You've been on your feet too long. Come in and sit down, and I'll make coffee. We could all use some."

She sounded like herself again, but for Liam, the glow had gone from the evening. He'd never cared for Carl O'Neill, and both of the man's sisters seemed more taken aback than overjoyed at his return.

"Thanks, but you girls won't want company tonight." He kissed Georgie's cheek and cursed Carl's timing. "Nice to see you again, Alice. Say hello to Carl for me." He turned away.

"Alice, lock up, will you?"

Alice stepped aside to let Georgie in, then stood in the doorway while Liam's form merged with the darkness. A few uneven steps and he'd disappeared. She cast a glance up the stairs, closed the door and tiptoed across the creaky hall floor to the front room, where only a few modern touches lightened the look of the heavy, worn Victorian furniture. They'd put in electricity last year, and Alice still noticed how the stronger light washed out the muted stripes in the ivory wallpaper. Georgie sat under the lamp in the overstuffed armchair, with the drawer of the table beside her open, a pile of papers in her lap.

"It wouldn't surprise me if that letter's in here somewhere." Georgie leafed through the papers without looking up. Alice found a lumpy spot on the horsehair sofa under the window.

"It isn't. I looked after Carl went upstairs."

Georgie glanced up, eyes full of contempt. "Waste of your time."

Alice let her sister's tone roll off her as she'd learned to do years ago. "I know a military letter when I see one."

Georgie ignored her, scanned the envelopes one by one and tossed them on the floor. In the tense silence, Alice stared at the cover of the magazine on the coffee table. *Good Housekeeping*. The only one Mother took. To Alice, the title was a meaningless jumble of lines and curves. No one had managed to teach her to read, in spite of countless punishments for lessons left undone and examinations failed.

Georgie gathered up the mail and crammed it back into the drawer. As always, her temper cooled quickly. "Well, it isn't here. Drat Carl. There's no excuse for him coming home on the sly like this. What did he have to say?"

Alice recalled what she could of her awkward conversation with her brother, blurred as it was by shock. "We only talked for a few minutes. He didn't have much more to say than what I told you outside. He did say not to send for Mother and Dad, to let them have their weekend away."

"How does he seem?"

"He looks healthy enough, I guess, but tired. Older." He'd given Alice no time to form any deeper impressions, no time to get an idea what the reckless, angry boy she remembered had become, other than a man. She shot a glance full of misgivings at Georgie. "You know what the doctor said about Mother back in March. She nearly broke her heart over Carl when he went missing. If he breaks it now—"

"Don't borrow trouble, Alice." Georgie leaned over and fussed with the mail, straightening the envelopes before she pushed the drawer closed. "What did you think of Liam?"

For a moment Alice's head spun as it had when she'd opened the door to Carl, but only for a moment. She'd had a lot of practice at hiding her feelings.

How many Sundays had she watched the back of Liam's head and listened to his voice responding through Mass, with no thought of what her penance would be if she confessed it? Secure in the certainty that he'd never notice, she'd woven her adolescent dreams around him and made sure her family got no hint of it. Even on his first Sunday back in Halifax, she'd managed to hide her pain when she saw him in church with his family, twenty pounds thinner than he should have been and leaning heavily on his cane.

He'd have forgotten long ago, but the day she'd quit school Liam had come across her on his way home from the rail yard. She'd been loitering at the bottom of Russell, afraid to go home. He stopped to ask why she'd been crying.

"Alice, what's the matter? Has somebody hurt you?"

"No. I just had a really horrible day at school."

Liam's brash young face had tightened in a frown. With an awkward, half-guilty movement, he glanced around as if afraid of being seen, then brushed a tear from her cheek. "I had more than a few days like that myself. Don't let it get to you. Hearing you sing in the choir on Sundays, I don't think you need to worry too much about math and history." He gently swiped her other cheek to make her smile.

Five years later, Alice's skin still prickled with the memory of his touch. Had she kept her secret all this time only to give it away to Georgie by watching Liam from the door like a lovesick schoolgirl?

"I'd say he's changed, like Carl. He couldn't help it. The better question is what do *you* think of him, Georgie?"

Georgie bent to pull off her shoes – or was that just an excuse to hide her face? "My feet are killing me. I wouldn't have worn these if I'd known we were going to walk all the way across town. Liam's a lot of fun when he wants to be, but losing his brother hit him hard."

A brutal hand seemed to close around Alice's heart. In her shock over Carl's return, she'd completely forgotten. Michael-John, the youngest of the three Cochrane boys, had been killed at the Somme last summer. This was the first time she'd spoken to Liam since he got home, and she hadn't even thought to say 'I'm sorry for your loss.'

"I'm sure it did."

"He's learned to like his liquor, and I suspect he's got a roving eye." Georgie massaged her arches, then rose with a sigh. "I'm going to make that coffee. Is there any sugar left?"

"No, we can't get any 'til next week."

After her sister left the room, Alice moved to the piano and let her fingers drift softly across the keys. She couldn't play much of anything, just some hymns, a few silly ragtime pieces and the occasional snatch of melody she'd composed herself. Tonight she couldn't play at all, not with so much discord around her – and inside her.

Georgie was falling for Liam. She hid it well, but the signs were plain enough to anyone who really knew her. And she hadn't answered the direct question Alice had asked.

Carl had come home, with a restless look in his eyes and only a few terse words to say after two years away.

Grow up, Alice. The whole world's changed. She left the piano, closed the front room door behind her and climbed the stairs to bed.

Chapter 2

The screen door crashed, followed by a shout. "Mum, the hay man's here!"

"Why don't you yell a little louder? Nan and Gramps might not have heard you across the street."

"All right, I will."

In his room at his older brother's house, Liam still lay in bed listening to the voices of his sister-in-law and nephew coming up through the heating grate in the floor. He pictured seven-year-old Drew getting ready to shout again. His mother Ruth scolded him, her voice stern but with a hint of laughter.

"Andrew, don't you dare. Your uncle's still asleep. Here's Mr. Haines' money. Go and get Della's breakfast."

The screen door crashed again. Liam swung his legs over the edge of the bed, poured a glass of water from the pitcher on the nightstand and rinsed the taste of stale whiskey from his mouth. His head ached dully, but he'd discovered over the last few months that he wasn't prone to long hangovers. Some food in his stomach and he'd be all right.

Nolan had already left for work – no Saturdays off for him these days – and Ruth would want to get breakfast cleared away. Liam got to his feet, bracing himself for the searing bolt of pain that shot down his bad leg. He really overdid it last night.

As he washed and dressed he heard four-year-old Emily run downstairs. Already a vain monkey, Nolan's daughter had his black Irish good looks and knew how to use them. Her brother

Andrew was blond, with a strong resemblance to his grandfather Cochrane, a resemblance Liam shared.

He ran a wet comb through his hair, found his cane and slowly negotiated the stairs. In the kitchen – everyone's favourite room in the house – Ruth had a smile for him. A lighter blonde than her son, with easy curves and warm blue-grey eyes, she filled the house with her good humour. Nolan was a lucky man.

"Morning, Liam. I thought you might sleep late today, though that isn't easy with my pair of young whirlwinds in the house."

"I woke early. Thanks." He took the cup of coffee Ruth handed him, turned his back on her warm yellow and brown kitchen and stood by the window, watching neighbours pass on their way to work. The familiar faces reminded him of mornings at the rail yard. Liam had dropped by there to say hello in the spring and hadn't gone back. Half the men were new, and the ones who remembered him were too busy to talk about yesterdays. The scarcest commodity in Halifax now was time.

Emily climbed onto her chair and made short work of a slice of cinnamon toast, only pausing to toss Liam a fetching, buttery grin. He looked away. Seeing Michael-John's dark eyes in his niece's face hurt as much as seeing them in Nolan's.

Andrew ran in from feeding the family Jersey, kicked off his shoes and scrambled to his seat. He waved his slice of toast as Liam sat beside him. "Want to walk up to Needham after breakfast, Uncle Liam?"

Ruth put a glass of milk in front of her son. "Your uncle might want to stay close to home today."

A familiar leaden weight of frustration settled on Liam. Drew liked nothing better than to take his father's binoculars up to Needham Hill and watch the ships in The Narrows and Bedford Basin, but the way Liam's leg had wobbled coming downstairs, he knew he wouldn't be walking anywhere today.

"Sorry, Drew. Maybe tomorrow."

The boy took it as a matter of course. He didn't remember Liam as he'd been before going overseas. Drew only knew his uncle as a near-cripple. He didn't seem to remember Michael-John at all.

"I can tell all three classes of cruisers now. Arethusa, Diadem and Apollo. And I know the minesweepers, too. I wish Dad could take me out with him, but he isn't allowed to." The self-satisfied grin on his milk-mustached face turned to a frown.

The weight of Liam's frustration grew. As a ship's pilot, Nolan did a job only eleven other men on Earth knew the Harbour well enough to do, while Liam no longer belonged anywhere. "He will be when the war's over. At this rate you'll get your pilot's papers younger than your dad did."

Ruth shook her head as she handed Liam a plate of scrambled eggs and toast. "Not if he doesn't pay more attention in school, he won't. Want some cinnamon, Liam?"

"No thanks. Looks just fine."

"Just watch me, Mum." Drew finished his milk and slid from his chair. "Can I go ask Artie Jessom if he'll go up to the hill with me?"

"All right. Bring Artie by for some lemonade afterwards." Ruth pushed aside her nasturtium-patterned curtains and watched from the window until Drew was out of sight. "Liam, we got a letter from Celia yesterday. She wanted you to read it." She laid an envelope on the table. "Emily, go and wash up. Your face looks like a piece of cinnamon toast."

Emily squirmed down from her chair and ran upstairs, dark curls flying. Liam pulled the letter from the envelope. Celia had married and moved to Ontario last year. Now she was running her husband's general store while he was overseas. Liam couldn't picture his flirtatious kid sister as a grown woman, let alone a wife.

I had a letter from Matthew last week. He was on

> *leave in London when he wrote and said he was well. He seems more worried about me coping with the store on my own than about himself. I'm managing, but I certainly could use some help and there doesn't seem to be any to be had here in Uxbridge. Everyone else is as busy as I am.*
>
> *Ruth, you wrote that Liam is feeling somewhat better and starting to get restless. Do you think he'd consider coming up to give me a hand for awhile? Use your own judgment. If you think he's ready, show him this letter. If not, don't say anything. I don't want him to feel obliged...*

Ruth stood by the sink sipping her coffee, watching him.

Getting restless? Liam guessed she'd been watching him more closely than he'd suspected over the last few weeks.

"Sounds like Celia's got her hands full."

"Yes, it does. It's been hard on her, so far from home with Matthew at the front and you here."

And Michael-John not coming back. She didn't get to say goodbye to him either. Liam and Celia had both missed the memorial service, the support from neighbours, the chance to mourn.

"I miss her, too." Missed Friday nights at home with Celia entertaining an admirer in the front room, the banter floating upstairs while Michael-John got ready for a university dance and Liam cleaned up for a night out with friends from the yard. Nights from a different time. Could he be any more of a stranger at Celia's place in Uxbridge?

He felt Ruth watching him as she began gathering up the children's dishes. "We all miss Celia. Liam, Nolan and I have been more than glad to have you—"

"And I've been glad to be here."

"We know, but you're at loose ends."

Loose ends? He'd seen the glances Nolan and Ruth exchanged when he came home smelling of liquor, when he radiated anger and frustration in spite of himself. Had they had enough of him? If they were eager to see Liam move on, whose fault was that?

Not long before he'd left for Europe, he'd overheard a neighbour talking to his father coming out of church. "You can be proud of your boys, Jack. Nolan's a solid, steady man now that he's settled down. Michael-John is clever, and Liam's like you – not one for books, but a worker. No grass will ever grow under his feet."

The clever one and the dogged one. The fallen hero and the returned misfit – or was coward the better word? Why didn't he have the guts to pull himself together and move on?

"Yeah. I'll write to Celia. Ruth, you and Nolan weren't up when I got home last night so you likely haven't heard. Carl O'Neill's home. Arrived yesterday."

Ruth set the dishes in the sink and turned around. "You don't say. I thought he was missing in action. I've never heard a word about him coming home. Did you?"

"No. I didn't even know he'd been listed as missing. Georgie's never mentioned him."

A wrinkle appeared in Ruth's forehead. "I heard the O'Neills were having a time with Carl before he shipped out. Your mother said Frank O'Neill was no angel when he was young, and the apple hadn't fallen far from the tree. Finally they told Carl to start behaving himself or move out, so he enlisted. It devastated Mrs. O'Neill when he went missing. Probably thought they drove him to it. She hasn't been well since."

Liam saw Alice's pale face again, amber eyes wide with shock. "He never let them know he was coming. Pretty shabby of him, I'd say. Has Alice been ill? She was there yesterday when I took Georgie home, and she looked like she'd seen a ghost. I know Carl turning up was a shock, even if she was glad to see him, but I wondered."

"I haven't heard that Alice has been ill. I think she had a

rough winter with her mother, and I don't imagine her father's a joy to live with, though I don't think he drinks much anymore. With Georgie working, Alice bears the brunt of things at home. She more or less runs the house."

Liam ate his breakfast and finished clearing the table for Ruth, then refilled his coffee cup and settled into one of the wicker chairs on the front porch. Another fine morning, the fifth in a row. In Halifax, a streak of good weather like that at any time of year brought on something akin to paranoia. The other shoe had to drop soon.

On the surface, Kaye Street looked much as it always did at the end of summer – green lawns a little sun-baked, clay streets dried to a fine powder and lines of laundry fluttering, bright against the sky. Saltboxes and Victorians, the homes hadn't changed since Liam's childhood. Now, with the wartime boom, people had work and most of them kept their places up.

Children's voices floated from backyards. Across the street, Liam's mother stepped out on her front porch and waved. She'd be over later to help Ruth do some canning. Not every mother and daughter-in-law could be neighbours and still be civil to each other, but his mother and Ruth managed it. They were actually good friends.

Liam shifted to ease his hip and leaned back in his chair. Going to Uxbridge made sense. Something to keep him busy until he knew what he wanted to do with his life, and more to the point, what he'd be able to do. Twenty-six was too old to be aimless. Perhaps in a new place his wrenching sense of disconnection would fade. It never left him, except when he was with Georgie. She had a way of blocking out the world.

It was too quiet here. His mind rushed to fill the vacuum, not with the din of the battlefield – he'd learned to shut that out – but with other memories. The voice of a street vendor early in the morning, drifting up to the window of Beatrice's flat in Chelsea. The sound of the elderly couple who'd lived downstairs, bantering companionably. The rhythm of Bea's soft breathing as she slept beside him.

Shame lanced through him before he pushed the thought of her away. He'd been stupid, but at least he hadn't come home like Carl O'Neill, unannounced, to a family that didn't know how to feel about his return. And when it came to women, he'd learned his lesson. He should be grateful to Bea for that, and grateful that Georgie seemed to understand.

"So, there's a social next Friday." Carl glanced at the church bulletin on the coffee table. "Are they worth the time these days?"

Alice glanced up from the skirt she was hemming. "Depends on what you consider worth it."

"Are you going?"

"Probably."

Carl looked her up and down, casually dismissive. He sat with his arm across the back of the front room sofa, looking more than a little dangerous in worn uniform pants and an undershirt that revealed the good-sized scar on his shoulder. His dark hair was uncombed, the dark circles under his eyes obvious. He looked away when Alice tried to hold his gaze. She focused on her sewing again.

"I've been seeing Stephen Mitchell for awhile. He's stationed here right now with the military police, but he's expecting to be posted overseas soon." She wouldn't bother to tell Carl about her cancelled date last night. He hadn't been home a full day, but Alice already knew that would mean nothing to him.

"MP? That would be your style. Power without danger. So tell me, who else is around?"

She bit her lip. Responding to Carl's baiting had only made it worse in the past, and she didn't want a quarrel. Her parents were coming home tomorrow. For her mother's sake, she'd keep the peace if it were possible at all.

She searched her memory for names of Carl's friends. Most of the crowd he'd run with before enlisting were still overseas. Alice wasn't in touch with the few who were in town. In the end, she rhymed off the first three names that came to mind. "Liam Cochrane. Tom Harris. Dennis Mahoney."

Down the street a door slammed. Carl jolted upright, stalked to the window then spun on his heel. Alice hadn't seen him sit still for five minutes all morning. He shrugged and dropped onto the sofa again, but he didn't relax.

"Dennis is all right. I'll likely find more of the old crowd downtown." His lip curled in a sneer as he looked at her. "For Pete's sake, Alice, what's wrong with you?"

Her eyes had filled with tears of anger and disappointment. Had it been too much to hope that Carl's time overseas would give him some appreciation for his family? She straightened her back and put steel in her voice. She wanted to keep the peace, but her days of meekly accepting his insults were over.

"Carl, you didn't let us know you were coming home. You're surly and you pace like a cat on a hot tin roof. I can't imagine what you've been through, but I'm a grown woman now and you aren't going to treat me like dirt under your feet. And I'll tell you something else. You didn't bother to ask last night, but Mother hasn't been well. She blamed herself when you went missing. If you upset her or treat her badly, Dad will send you packing just like he did before."

Carl got to his feet slowly this time, fists clenched. As a boy, he would have lashed out. Alice half-expected him to now, but when she looked into his familiar blue eyes they were different. She saw a stranger.

"If you think Dad could handle me now, you're no brighter than you ever were."

He took one long stride toward her. Alice's mouth went dry.

"Carl, what are you doing?"

She braced herself for a blow, but at the last second he turned on his heel. He glanced over his shoulder as he left the room. "I don't know why I bothered coming back here. I should have stayed in Montreal or gone West."

The front door slammed behind him. Alice slumped on the piano bench and let the tears come. All she could think of was the hurt on her mother's face when she discovered that her son was here but that he hadn't really come home to her at all.

Silence filled the house. Georgie was working, but she'd phone the news of Carl's arrival to Dad so he could prepare Mother. Alice drew a few shaky breaths and pulled herself together.

Was Carl shell-shocked? Did that account for the change in him? Perhaps, but he'd always been difficult. She should ask Stephen for advice, but she'd never talked about her family with him and something in her shrank from doing it now. Too personal – and too humiliating.

Patience. She had nothing else to offer. Could dealing with this changed, explosive Carl be worse than the grief they'd all suffered during the winter when they'd thought he was lost to them?

An image from that time came back to her. Liam's mother in church before Mass, lighting a candle for Michael-John, stark pain obvious in her eyes. What a lot of sentimental tripe people spouted about Silver Cross Mothers and the ultimate sacrifice. No words could take away the pain of losing a child.

For a moment, the man Liam had become filled Alice's mind. What was he doing now? Perhaps he slept late. She pictured him asleep, his bronze-gold hair tousled, his short, slightly darker moustache and beard softening his jaw, framing his mouth. That picture made her breath catch.

She'd tried not to think of Liam when he shipped out because it hurt too much, but she hadn't been able to help herself. Every time she saw a recruiting poster, every time she heard her mother read the war news in the papers, she saw him. Now that he was home, thinking of him was a pointless indulgence – or perhaps not entirely. It might be silly, but knowing he was only a block away on Kaye Street brought her some comfort, or it had until he started seeing Georgie.

Alice let herself dwell on Liam for only a few seconds before facing reality again. Stephen had next weekend off. If he asked her to the social, as he probably would, she'd tell him about Carl and how his return was affecting her family. Stephen did have a heart beneath his tough MP exterior, and she knew she'd crept into it.

Life's short, Alice. Take what it offers, and don't waste your time reaching for what you can never have.

Chapter 3

"Well now, Ruth, look at you." Nolan held his hands out to his wife as she stepped into the kitchen in her crisp new navy poplin, her honey-coloured hair falling to her shoulders in soft waves. Liam didn't wonder at the appreciation in his brother's eyes. Ruth batted her eyelashes at Nolan like a movie vixen.

"Like it?"

"I like it." He drew her into his arms for a hug that no doubt would have been a kiss if they'd been alone. "Any woman who can cook a dinner like we just had and then come in here looking like this... maybe we should stay home."

The restlessness riding Liam prodded him sharply. Six months. Had he already been here too long?

The knocker on the front door rapped. Ruth eased out of her husband's embrace. "That'll be Carol. Should I tell her we'll be home at eleven?"

Her grin held just a hint of mischief. Nolan's hand lingered on her arm. "No later." His eyes followed Ruth as she left the room. Liam grinned at him over the rim of his lemonade glass.

"Nolan, no one would guess you've been married for close to nine years."

Nolan leaned against the sink as if it were a ship's rail. After years spent at sea in all weathers, his long, lean frame was at ease anywhere. "I suppose not. Remember when I used to say I'd never settle down?"

At the table, Liam drank the last of his lemonade and wished for something stronger. Nolan had a bottle of good Scotch in the pantry, a gift from the captain of a Royal Navy cruiser, and Liam could almost taste it, craved the mellow burn to warm away the tight ache in his leg. He'd gone downtown Tuesday night and found that a couple of his own sources had disappeared, probably closed down by the police. It had happened before. They'd be back, but he hadn't wanted to risk making another trip too soon. He refilled his tumbler from the cut-glass pitcher and took a deep swallow.

"I remember. Nolan Cochrane, merchant seaman, with a girl in every port. All you ever had to do was turn those bedroom eyes on them and they melted. When I was sixteen I couldn't wait to follow in your footsteps. And Michael-John was in awe."

"The kid was always shy."

"Yeah. Then Ruth came along and you got your wings clipped."

"Only by choice, Liam."

"If you say so."

The taunt only made Nolan grin. "I'm looking forward to the day when it happens to you."

Liam shook off the picture that formed in his mind of Bea's sexy crooked smile, the tilt of her head with its halo of dark curls. "Don't hold your breath."

"Just wait. Are you meeting Georgie at the hall?"

"Yeah. She told me not to bother coming to the house." The warm evening brought out beads of sweat on the back of Liam's neck under his white collar, but a sullen chill settled in the pit of his stomach. He hadn't been to a church social since coming home, though there seemed to be one every other week in aid of the war effort. His leg made a convenient excuse, but the truth was he had no taste for crowds and chatter, questions and condolences. It had been decided that the whole family was going to this one, though, and he didn't want to rain on their parade. Besides, Georgie had made it difficult to say no.

Nolan summed him up with a glance. "You don't look like a

man headed for a good time. Need something to grease the wheels?"

"You won't have to twist my arm."

Liam forced himself to sip the fiery Scotch slowly. The smile left Nolan's face. His next words seemed to come with a struggle.

"Liam, I wonder sometimes. Do you still really enjoy a drink, or do you drink because you need to?"

Before he could answer, the door knocker rapped again and noise erupted in the front hall. Drew and Emily shouted a greeting to their grandparents and Ruth was talking to Carol, an older neighbour who watched the children occasionally. Liam's father's voice rose above the commotion as he laughed at something Drew said.

Liam downed the rest of his drink in one swallow before they all crowded into the kitchen. He stood up for a hug from his mother. With a quick swish of her skirt, she wrapped her arms around him and pecked him on the cheek. He didn't miss the flash of concern in her eyes when she smelled the whiskey on his breath, but she didn't mention it.

"I was afraid you might back out on us. Nolan, how did you do it?"

Nolan clapped Liam on the shoulder. "I didn't. Thank Georgie O'Neill, Mum."

His mother's dark eyes took on a teasing glint. "Hmm. I see. Maybe I will." She checked her reflection in the polished door of the stove's warming oven and smoothed her bobbed near-black curls, still only sparsely mixed with grey. She looked closer to forty-five than her actual fifty-five, but the past three years had added to the fine lines around her eyes and mouth and given her a patient look in quiet moments – she who had never been known for patience. She lifted a brow at her husband's pointed glance.

"Don't worry, Jack, I'm not going to pester Liam about

Georgie. I'm just glad he's coming with us."

Dad pinched her arm. "Did I say anything, Meg?" Liam couldn't help smiling. He'd inherited his father's big-boned six-foot frame, and hoped to age as well. Thirty-five years on the docks had kept Dad fit, and he'd greyed so young that no one really noticed anymore. He'd always been the kind of man who would fight you in an alley and drink with you afterwards, and that youthful carelessness still showed through the lines on his face, dimmed but not extinguished by the loss of his youngest boy.

St. Joseph's Church Hall was a stone's throw away on the corner of Russell and Gottingen. The Cochranes edged their way into the hot, crowded hall and stood by an open window, where a wisp of a breeze blew through. There were no seats to be had, with the parish out in force to raise funds for Belgian relief.

The band was already on the platform tuning instruments. Liam laid his cane on the window sill and leaned against the wall. His shirt was already sticking to his back. Posters beckoning recruits and urging families to can food for winter filled the spaces on the walls, between photos of parish events and the decorating committee's red and white crepe paper flowers. One wall held a row of photographs of young men from the parish, all in uniform. Liam's picture hung next to Michael-John's. He'd looked very much like Nolan. The banner above the photos read 'For King and Empire', as did the brass memorial plaque in the church.

Yeah. Is that what a man thinks about when he goes over the top? When he sees a brother cut in half by machine-gun fire? He'd never told, would never tell his family he'd seen that, any more than he would tell them about Beatrice. Overseas he'd held back in his letters home, waiting for the right words. Now there were none.

It served you right. You should have kept your pants buttoned. Liam's heart started to race as the noise and humid air closed in on him. His head swam with the whiskey he'd bolted.

A hot summer night, a dance floor packed with couples. A dizzying mix of perfume, aftershave and sweat on the air. Bea in his arms, her midnight blue eyes looking into his.

"So, Canada, what's your name and where are you from?"

Home had been a distant memory, blotted out by her nearness. For a few hours that night nothing had existed but her. At Bea's flat after the dance, he'd lost himself in her kisses while the storm broke. The pounding of his pulse had drowned out the thunder, and while flashes of lightning cut the darkness, she electrified him with her touch.

An ocean away, he jumped when his mother touched his arm. "Liam, are you all right?"

"I need some air." He turned from her worried face and pushed his way toward the door. When he was almost there he spotted Georgie across the hall, scanning the crowd, obviously looking for him. He couldn't run off without speaking to her.

His breathing settled and his head cleared as he watched her make her way toward him. She wore a light dress of a gauzy, pale green fabric that clung to her curves and flowed to emphasize the alluring sway of her hips. When she reached him she took his hand, her palm soft and warm. Real.

"You're here, Liam."

For now. Until time tricked him again. Liam kissed her cheek and closed the door on his memories. "Yes. Come and say hello to the family."

When his mother saw him returning, her eyes lit up with relief. Liam smothered his guilt and led Georgie to her.

"Mum, here's Georgie. How long has it been since you've seen her?"

His mother's gaze lingered on him for a moment before she took Georgie's other hand. "Too long. You look lovely, dear. Are your parents here?"

"Thank you, Mrs. Cochrane. No, Dad and Mother decided to stay home. She minds the heat these days. I'll tell her you were asking after her, though." Liam didn't doubt her sincerity, but it made him a little uncomfortable to see Georgie become the proper young woman speaking to an elder. He'd never seen that side of her. Was she that anxious to impress his family?

His mother responded to Georgie's sincerity. After fifteen years of meeting her sons' girls, she read them well. "Thanks. Liam told us your brother's home. How is he?"

"Carl's lucky. He was wounded, but not seriously. He spent six months in a German prison camp, but he says he wasn't mistreated. He's been given six months' leave, then he'll likely be posted back to the front."

"Oh, let's hope he's not."

"Yes." Georgie spoke to the others, then laid a hand on Liam's shoulder. "Liam, Stephen and Alice and I have seats over by the refreshment table." She included the whole family in a smile. "It's nice to see you all again."

Liam followed her back across the hall. Tall and rather formidable in his MP uniform, Alice's escort, Stephen, stood and held out his hand. "Good to see you safely home, Liam. Mentioned in a couple of dispatches, I hear. I hope I do as well when my turn comes." His obvious respect set Liam on edge, bringing back the urge to leave.

"Thanks, Stephen, but here's hoping your turn doesn't come." To quell his restlessness, he turned to Alice. "Hello."

"Hello." Her shy amber eyes only looked into his for a moment, but that moment left him tongue-tied. She certainly had grown into her looks. The other night at her home she hadn't been dressed in her best, but how had he missed noticing those soft, ripe lips?

When Stephen took Alice's hand a hint of colour crept into her cheeks. He missed it, as he'd turned his attention back to Liam. "Doesn't look like there's much chance of it being over that soon, does it? Got any advice?"

He'd have to be one of the persistent ones. Liam reacted

without thinking. "Yeah. Don't take any promotions. Better a live private than a dead officer."

A flush crept up Stephen's neck. As Liam took his seat, Georgie laid her hand over his. He pulled away. This was why he'd avoided these functions. He couldn't dissemble well enough, not with the truth still so fresh in his mind.

All right, Cochrane, time to take your foot out of your mouth. He squared his shoulders and smiled as if what he'd just said was a joke. "But why are we talking about the war when we're sitting here with the two best-looking ladies in the room? Alice, what happened to the little girl I remember?"

When she smiled, her eyes sparkled like sunlight on a rippling brown brook. "Three years happened, Liam. I thought Nolan was the talker in your family."

"He thinks so, too. After I saw you the other day, I wondered why I haven't seen you all summer. Then it occurred to me that you aren't in the choir anymore."

"No. I gave it up almost three years ago."

"Why?"

She glanced down. "I was needed at home, and they had enough sopranos."

The band finished tuning and struck up a quick ragtime number. Stephen led Alice onto the floor. Georgie reached for Liam's hand again and leaned back in her chair, one sleek tan pump tapping the floor as she watched the dancers.

Liam followed her gaze and found Alice, a picture of lissome grace as she moved with Stephen among the other couples. They kept a reserved distance between them, unlike three or four other pairs who pushed the limits of propriety. When the music changed, another khaki-clad young man asked her to dance and Stephen returned to the table.

"Liam, may I borrow Georgie for this one?"

"Sure."

Georgie's dress became a bright whirl of colour as she gave

herself up to the music. She would have done the same with any partner, but Liam found himself fighting an urge to punch Stephen. He closed his eyes and rolled his shoulders. *Why shouldn't a girl have her fun?* He certainly didn't expect Georgie to sit here with him all evening.

When the band began a waltz Stephen brought her back, nodded his thanks and returned to claim Alice. Liam looked into Georgie's expectant eyes. He should be able to handle a waltz without falling on his face. He took her hand. "Care to go back out?"

"Of course." She grinned and squeezed his fingers.

As they circled slowly at the side of the dance floor, Georgie ran her hand across his back. Without a word, she found the tension there. She pressed at the knot between his shoulder blades with gentle fingers.

"You're upset."

"No, just a bit uncomfortable. I'm out of practice."

Her touch sent his heart racing again, with a different kind of tension. Georgie moved a little closer and smiled up at him, the smile that told him she wouldn't say no to some passionate kisses and maybe a little more when the dance was over. Liam didn't doubt that she had her limits – Georgie was no fool – but he was quite certain he hadn't discovered them yet.

Her fingertips brushed the back of his neck. "This is the first time we've danced. Did you realize that? You're a good dancer, Liam."

"You're kidding me."

"No, I'm serious. Maybe you aren't up to a fast dance right now, but I can tell."

"It helps to have a beautiful partner."

They stopped talking and relaxed into the music. As they swayed in the shadows at the edge of the floor, Liam caught sight of Alice in the crowd of couples, her oval face just above Stephen's shoulder. There was no laughter in her eyes now. She looked thoughtful, even a bit sad. Then she seemed to catch herself, looked up at Stephen and said something that made him chuckle. He didn't appear to notice her somber mood. There was a couple headed for the rocks, if Liam had ever seen one.

The waltz ended. An old acquaintance of Georgie's asked her for the next one, and Liam, pleased he'd at least managed not to stumble, tapped Stephen on the shoulder. "Fair exchange?"

"Sure. I'll go get us some punch." Stephen ran a hand down Alice's arm before walking away. The possessiveness of the gesture grated on Liam after what he'd just seen on her face. He shrugged the feeling off. Jealousy, that was all. He wasn't used to being on the sidelines.

He took Alice's hand and drew her into his arms. Dancing and the heat had brought the blood to her cheeks, and her eyes sparkled like running brook water again. Although she blushed, he sensed no shyness in her body. She fit naturally in his arms, as if she belonged there.

Yeah. She sure isn't a kid anymore.

Then, like a bolt from the blue an image flashed into Liam's mind of Alice dancing close, nestled in his arms with her head on his shoulder. *Jesus, Mary and Joseph, where did that come from? She's Georgie's sister!* He loosened his hold on Alice but that didn't dull his awareness of every slender curve, of her light floral perfume. Worse, he saw in her eyes that she felt the awareness between them, too.

Before he could make an excuse and abandon her, the band ended the waltz with an extra flourish. The leader bowed to the crowd. "Catch your breath, ladies and gentlemen, while the chair of your Social Committee says a few words. I give you Mrs. Frances Henneberry."

Everyone returned to their seats, Liam with a sigh of devout thanks. He angled his chair to put Stephen and Alice out of his line of sight. *As far as I'm concerned, friend, she's all yours. Good luck keeping her.* Thin, sharp-faced Mrs. Henneberry stepped onto the platform with a self-conscious smile and cleared her throat.

"Ladies and gentlemen, it's wonderful to see you all here, supporting our parish's efforts to ease the suffering of helpless civilians overseas. There is more than one person here tonight who could tell us first-hand just how severe those sufferings have been and what our sons and brothers have sacrificed in the effort to end them. The least we here at home can do is—"

"Shut up. That's the least you can do."

The words carried clearly from the corner nearest the O'Neills' table. Every head swiveled. Georgie blushed deep red. Alice's face blanched pearl-white. In the shadows just beyond the lighted platform, Carl leaned against the wall, his face flushed with heat and liquor. No one at the table had noticed him come in.

An older, heavier Carl than Liam remembered, with a harder face. The tough kid had grown into a tough man, with an added belligerence. One look at his glazed eyes told Liam Georgie's brother was a loose cannon.

He and Stephen got up at the same instant and started toward the corner. Stephen got there first and planted himself in front of Carl.

"You've said enough. Your sisters are here."

"I'm not leaving 'til I make my point." Carl pushed Stephen back and raised his voice again. "That old windbag hasn't got anyone at the front. She doesn't have a clue."

The scathing words on Liam's tongue died there. Up close, Carl reminded him too much of men he'd seen in hospital, men who woke in the night screaming as he'd done more than once. Men who spent their days looking at the world through vacant eyes. And Mrs. Henneberry annoyed the hell out of him, too.

"You're right, Carl. She doesn't. This isn't the place for either of us. Come outside and get some fresh air."

Fists clenched, Carl took a step forward. "Don't bullshit me, Liam. I'm not going anywhere until I'm good and ready. Who do you think you are, anyway? Your little brother isn't the only one who's been killed overseas, you know. Just—"

Liam didn't hear the rest of the sentence. Rage blotted out his compassion, rage and the memory of Michael-John's wide, sightless dark eyes. His first punch landed hard in Carl's belly. The second hit his jaw, knocking him backward and throwing Liam off-balance. They hit the floor, fists flying. The next thing he knew, Nolan was dragging him to his feet while his father and Stephen pinioned Carl. Liam shook his brother off and dove at Carl, only to have his bad leg collapse and land him back on the floor. Nolan helped him up again and got a firm grip on his arms.

"What the hell? Liam, stop it!"

The girls stood nearby now. Georgie's eyes sparkled with anger, but the strain on Alice's face did more to clear the haze from Liam's mind. He stopped struggling with Nolan, took a deep breath and swallowed. The metallic taste of blood in his mouth made his stomach churn.

"The son of a bitch made a crack about Michael-John."

Nolan released his hold and took a step toward Carl, putting himself in the man's face. "If I ever hear of you mentioning my brother's name again, I'll finish what Liam started. Dad, Stephen, get him the hell out of here."

Still winded from Liam's first blow, blood trickling from his nose, Carl didn't offer much resistance. Liam figured he'd gotten the worst of the encounter himself, a split lip and what would likely be a magnificent shiner. A couple of older women were on the platform trying to soothe Mrs. Henneberry, who looked on the verge of tears. He should go and say something to her, but at the moment he couldn't find the words. He shrugged Nolan's hand from his shoulder.

"I'm leaving. Apologize to Georgie for me, will you?" Without waiting for an answer, Liam walked out.

Alice stood silent beside Georgie while Nolan made Liam's

apology. When he walked away, Georgie gathered her handbag and shawl. "I'd best go home and see if I can keep this from getting worse. I never dreamed Carl would show up here."

"Neither did I, but something like this was bound to happen sooner or later. I hope Liam's all right." Alice wasn't thinking of his bruises, but of the look she'd seen in his eyes before he jumped Carl. As much pain as anger. It didn't help that she could still feel Liam's arms around her, unconsciously drawing her closer as they danced. Or had she moved closer on her own?

"I don't imagine he'll want to see anyone tonight. I'll talk to him tomorrow." Georgie craned her neck toward the door. "There's his father and Stephen back now. I'd better be going."

Across the hall, the older Cochranes were preparing to leave. Jack picked up Liam's cane from the window sill on the way out. Alice's fingers curled into fists as she watched them go. She'd look like a complete fool running over to the Cochranes' now, but it took all her will not to follow and see for herself how badly Liam was hurt.

Father MacManus stepped onto the platform, his face more troubled than disapproving. "Gentlemen, if you please, let's have some more music." The band struck up a waltz. Stephen reached Alice's side and took her hand.

"We saw Carl halfway down the street. He was starting to cool off. Has he been like that since he got home?"

Concern and more showed in his eyes. Alice squirmed inwardly with shame. She was going out with this man and letting him develop feelings for her. She should be thinking of him, but the image of Liam staggering up from the floor, his mouth bloodied, still filled her mind. She couldn't discuss Carl with Stephen – not now.

"Not as bad as that. Stephen, I don't think I have the heart for dancing anymore tonight. Please stay and enjoy yourself. I'll see myself home."

He kept his hold on her hand. "Alice, I'm not letting you go home alone if Carl's going to be there in that condition."

She tried to pull away. "Look, I think white knights are lovely, really I do, but it's only three blocks and Mother and Dad and Georgie will be there. It really would be easiest if I go alone."

A muscle tightened in Stephen's jaw; a sullen light flared in his eyes. "All right, if you say so."

Alice stood on tiptoe to kiss his cheek. "Thank you. Stephen, I'm really sorry about all this. Please stay and have a good time. Goodnight."

Outside in the dark, Alice took her time walking down the hill. When she reached home she stopped on the sidewalk. Step into the latest confrontation between Dad and Carl? No, she'd give them some time to get through the worst of it. She hesitated a moment, then walked on, down to the bottom of the street where it met Campbell Road.

The rail yard stretched between Campbell and The Narrows, separated from the street by a gated fence. The noise of box cars being shunted together mingled with men's voices. They raced the clock twenty-four hours a day now to keep up with the extra war-time traffic. Barely visible in the shadows outside the glow of a streetlamp, a man stood near the gate. Even in that light, Alice knew him.

The driver of a passing wagon stared as she dashed across the road, heels flying, the skirt of her dancing dress floating in her wake. Liam didn't hear her until she was right beside him.

"Liam."

He started and took a step back, his face still hidden. "Alice, what are you doing out here? Why aren't you back at the hall?"

"I didn't feel like staying and I didn't feel like going home, so I took a walk. Looks like you did, too." He still had on the black trousers and pinstriped grey shirt – now spattered with blood – that he'd worn to the dance. He obviously hadn't been home.

He moved into the light. His lip was still bleeding and he had the beginnings of a black eye. "Yeah. Do you know if Carl's all right?"

"No, but it looks like you got the worst of it. Here, you could use this – or maybe not." Alice felt herself blush as she held up the handkerchief she'd pulled from her purse. The silly, lace-edged affair looked utterly useless for mopping up after a fight.

Liam grinned with the undamaged side of his mouth, pulled his own handkerchief from his pocket and held it to his lip. Alice lifted a hand. "Over to the left – right there."

Her fingers hovered inches from his mouth. Cheeks flaming, she pulled her hand back. "I can't believe you're asking about Carl after what happened. Liam, what did he say to make you jump him like that?"

Liam had managed to stop the bleeding. He wiped his face with the clean end of the handkerchief, wadded it up and stuffed it in his pocket with a shrug. "It doesn't matter what he said. I'm asking about him because I'm more like him than you might think. Six months ago I would have told off Frances Henneberry myself."

"Perhaps, but I don't think you've ever been much like Carl."

"Oh? What makes you say that?"

Alice took a deep breath of moist night air. She should just turn around and go home, but the ache she sensed behind Liam's words kept her there, made her answer.

"Liam, do you remember the time you found me down here, five years ago? I was upset about school and didn't want to go home. You noticed that I'd been crying and stopped to make sure I was all right. Carl would never have done that."

"No, I can't say I remember." Liam looked at her as if seeing her for the first time. "I remember Celia saying once…" He placed his hands lightly on her shoulders. "Alice, I'm sure you don't need me to tell you, but you've grown into quite a woman. Don't let the past hold you back."

Alice held his gaze. If nothing else, she'd earned his respect. And that meant more, much more than she would have expected.

"Georgie said she'd see you tomorrow. She went home to try to keep the peace between Dad and Carl."

"That'll give her time to cool off. She didn't look too pleased with me back there."

"She was furious with Carl, not you. Georgie..." Alice almost put her hand to her mouth when she realized what she'd been about to say. *Georgie cares for you.* "Georgie's always had a quick temper, but it doesn't last."

"Yeah. Well, I'll stop by tomorrow. I need to talk to her. Nolan got a letter from Celia last week. Her husband's overseas and she's wearing herself out running their store. I'm going to go and give her a hand for awhile. I may stay up there if things look promising. You'll let me tell Georgie though, won't you?"

A chill wind seemed to blow over her, through her. She had no right to concern herself with Liam's comings and goings, but here he was, standing close enough to touch, only a few steps away from where he'd stood the only time he'd touched her. Before tonight. Out of selfishness, out of desire, out of a need to give back the comfort he'd once so casually given her, Alice reached out. She brushed her fingers across the plane of his cheek while her thumb caught the soft edge of his beard.

His jaw tightened and his good eye widened in surprise. She couldn't hold back a smile. The tears would come later, in private.

"You look like a ruffian. Of course I'll let you tell her. Good night."

She walked away. Halfway home, she swung around to look down the hill. He was gone.

Chapter 4

Alice closed the front door softly, switched on the hall light and stood still, listening. Her father's and Georgie's muffled voices came from the front room, but she heard nothing from upstairs.

She dropped her purse on the hall chair, stepped out of her French-heeled pumps and sighed with relief as the floor cooled her feet through her silk stockings. When she opened the front room door, Georgie looked up from her magazine.

"You're home early."

Alice watched her father out of the corner of her eye as she entered the room. He looked relaxed enough. Apparently there'd been no confrontation yet.

"I didn't feel like staying at the dance."

Georgie lifted a shoulder. "You might as well have. Carl didn't come home."

"Maybe that's for the best. Is Mother still up?"

"No." Curled up in the armchair, Georgie tucked her legs more securely beneath her and turned back to her reading. Dad hadn't raised his gaze from his newspaper. Georgie would have already said everything worth saying, so Alice pulled the bench further from the piano to make more room for her long legs, then perched on it and ran her eyes over the sheet of music on the ledge.

Beautiful Dreamer. Mother's favourite piece, one of the three or four she still played. She'd played it that afternoon before supper. Her mother's fingers still flowed over the keys as easily as her younger daughter's. She'd taught piano before her marriage, but it had made no sense to try to teach music to her own child, a child who couldn't even master the alphabet. She'd encouraged Alice to amuse herself at the piano, but her formal lessons had ended when she was seven or eight. She'd learned to play and sing on her own, by watching and listening.

Alice followed the rise and fall of the notes on the page as she sang the lyrics in her mind. She didn't know the technicalities of reading music, but the pattern on the page made much more sense to her than letters and words. She found a brief refuge in a private world of melody until her father spoke.

"Why didn't Stephen come in?"

His blue eyes held no warmth. Over the years they seldom had when he looked at Carl or Alice. Only Georgie knew how to make them sparkle. Alice had accepted that a long time ago.

"I told him to stay at the dance. I saw no reason to spoil his evening because I felt like coming home. It is only three blocks."

"You'll lose him if you aren't careful."

She responded with silence. Stephen had looked hurt as well as angry when she'd left him. Then erratic footsteps sounded on the walk. Georgie dropped her magazine. Alice's heart lurched. Her father rose, threw his paper down and stalked to the door. He kept his voice low, but she heard the venom in it.

"Christ, look at you. You're a soldier on leave, not a waterfront thug, but no one would know it. You aren't welcome here in this condition."

"That's rich. Seen you come home in worse condition."

The door thudded against the wall as Carl shoved his way through, then again as his father pushed him back against it. "I said you aren't welcome here."

A hand struck flesh, then Alice's purse plopped onto the floor, followed by a crash as the chair toppled. Georgie breathed a quick 'Damn!' and jumped up. Alice followed her out into the hall.

Carl leaned against the wall, smiling, as his father scrambled up from the floor. "Want to try again, old man? I'm not fourteen years old anymore."

The girls put themselves between the men, Georgie facing her father, Alice facing Carl. Facing the same memories she knew Carl faced, of lying in bed trying to close her ears to the shouting downstairs when Dad came in late. The tense silence between her parents at breakfast. Going lightly around the house for hours afterwards. The times when a glance from Dad had sent her scurrying to another room. Times she thought were behind her. She blinked away tears and tried to reach her brother through his anger.

"Carl, if you keep on like this, you're going to find yourself in prison. Just go upstairs and go to bed. Please."

Blood from his nose had run over Carl's mouth and chin and was drying there. The hollows in his cheeks had deepened since he came home, and underneath the unnatural flush his skin was a poor colour. He sagged against the wall and she watched his rage dissolve, leaving only pain in his eyes.

"Jesus. Some things never change."

Alice pleaded with him, as helpless against his demons as he seemed to be himself. "Carl, please."

Her knees weakened with relief when he pushed himself away from the wall and started up the stairs. Behind her, Georgie took Dad in hand – skilful as always.

"You know Mother's awake and listening to all this. Now isn't the time. Leave Carl alone until he's sober."

Dad muttered something under his breath, stomped into the front room and banged the door shut behind him. Alice mastered her shaking legs and followed Carl upstairs. She waited in her room until she heard him come out of the bathroom and close his bedroom door, then she crept across the hall to wash off the little make-up she'd applied before the dance.

She patted her cheeks dry. Her clean face looked back at

her, all shades of cream, warmed by the golden brown of her eyes and deeper colour of her hair. Not an unattractive face. As Liam had said, she didn't need to be told that, but what else did she have to offer? Alice closed her eyes and pictured Liam washing his face, going lightly over his bruises. She almost felt the warmth of his skin under her fingertips again and turned away from the mirror. He was leaving. He'd slip out of her ken – as he must sooner or later – whether he left or stayed.

It was ironic that, as the daughter of the manager of the sugar refinery – one of Richmond's biggest employers – many of the neighbours would consider Liam beneath her. The Cochranes were a solid working-class family, a cut below her own by some standards – but not in drive or intelligence. Nolan had a good job. Celia had always been on the honour roll at St. Joseph's. Michael-John had finished his first year at Dalhousie before enlisting. People said he'd wanted to be a doctor. Liam preferred physical work, but he'd inherited his father's shrewdness. Even if Georgie wasn't the one for him, he'd never settle for an illiterate woman.

No sound came from Carl's room. Likely he'd just fallen on the bed and passed out. Alice slipped on her nightgown and climbed into bed. By then, silly, childish tears rolled down her cheeks, just as she'd known they would when she left Liam at the bottom of the hill.

Liam made his way up Kaye Street slowly and painfully. Damn it, his leg seemed to be getting worse instead of better. Perhaps he'd wrenched something rolling around on the hall floor.

A light shone from his parents' kitchen window. So they'd left the social and come home to wait for him. Across the street at Nolan's, the reading lamp was on in the front room. Carol was still there, minding the children. Nolan and Ruth must have stayed at the dance.

Rather than walk in on Carol looking like he'd been in a street brawl, Liam struggled up the steps of his parents' porch and down the hall to the kitchen. They were both at the table, still in their good clothes. As usual after a night out, his mother had set out a pot of tea to go with a plate of sliced bread and butter. Mum shook her head at the sight of Liam's face.

"Nolan was always the adventurous one. Michael-John was the quiet one, and you've always been the one with the temper. You're going to be something to behold in the morning."

As might be expected of a mother of three sons, she sounded more rueful than upset. Liam tried to recall the last time he'd been in a fight. He'd been… what? Sixteen? Eighteen? His father hooked a chair with his foot and pushed it back from the table.

"No lectures tonight, son. Sit down."

This room had looked more or less the same for as long as Liam could remember. The walls were green now instead of white, and they'd replaced the old stove with a new Enterprise just before Liam went away, but those were only surface things. The ugly red hooked mat an old aunt had given Mum still lay by the door, and the square maple table bore only a few added scars to mark the years.

Richmond people lived in their kitchens, and there'd been so much living done in this one that the walls had soaked it up. Nolan had proposed to Ruth here. The whole family had sat together here the night before Michael-John and Liam sailed for Europe. They'd greeted Liam here with tears of grief and gratitude when he arrived home, alone.

The stabbing pain in his hip gave way to a familiar ache when he took the weight off it. "No serious harm done, but I'll probably look worse than Carl tomorrow."

His father looked him over, searching beneath his bruises, reminding Liam of the sleepless nights they'd spent here together during the first couple of months after he returned home. He'd told Dad more than he'd told anyone else, even Nolan.

"Maybe, but that boy is in a bad way, and I don't mean from what you did to him."

"Yeah, he is." Regret took strong hold in the emptiness left by Liam's anger. "But I'll punch him again if he doesn't keep his mouth shut."

"If I don't beat you to it." His father met his gaze in a moment of shared grief. Mum caught the look, shared the moment.

"What *did* Carl say, Jack?"

Dad touched her arm, a small gesture of comfort. "It doesn't matter. He's been paid for it. Liam, Nolan told us he got a letter from Celia the other day, that she said she could use your help."

"Yeah. I'm thinking about it. It's time I was doing something."

Mum's gaze held his, full of concern. "No one's rushing you, Liam. Give yourself time."

But time wasn't doing much for him – physically, or in any other way. Not like it had for Alice. She'd grown up and learned to carry herself as well as Georgie. But then something else told Liam that inside, Alice felt as out of place as he did. He had no idea why.

That impulsive touch of hers… She felt sorry for him, of course. Those amber eyes were a window to a soft heart, and that disturbed him. One thing he could say about Georgie, she'd never shown him a trace of pity. Georgie. If only he could hold her right now, bury his mouth against her soft skin and lose himself, lose these stray feelings. Georgie, or another shot of Nolan's whiskey.

"I don't know, Mum. I just know I have to do something. I can't listen to the likes of Mrs. Henneberry anymore."

The corners of his father's mouth quirked in a grin. "I've

never seen such a look on Frances Henneberry's face as when Carl told her to shut up. She does love the sound of her own voice, when it comes right down to it."

Mum rested a hand on Liam's – hers protective, maybe a little bit possessive. Her protectiveness was new since he'd come home, like her patience with him. "I feel sorry for poor Helen O'Neill. I don't know what I'd do if you'd come back like Carl."

I did. I just had a fraction more control. The clock above the icebox chimed ten. Liam had talked enough for tonight. He stood and reached for his cane that leaned against the wall. He'd forgotten it completely when he left the hall. When would he learn his limits?

"I feel sorry for her, too. I might as well stay here tonight, Mum, if you'll have me. Ruth wouldn't thank me for scaring the kids with this face at the breakfast table."

"Your bed's made up as always. Goodnight, Liam."

He listened to the distant rumble of the rail yard as he waited for sleep. It brought back the street sounds of London on a rainy night, the last night of his last leave with Bea. Holding her after they'd made love until they were spent, with the light of the streetlamp slanting through the blinds and onto the bed. Her hand touching his face while the clock ticked relentlessly toward morning.

"Don't think about tomorrow, love."

But when he closed his eyes, it was Alice's cool fingers he felt on his cheek. He tried to be angry with her, to scorn her for her pity, but he couldn't. The gesture had been too genuine.

Liam turned onto his side, scolding himself. He had no right to be thinking of Alice at all.

Drew scrambled up the incline behind his father, then lay on his stomach at the top of Needham Hill. A stiff breeze ruffled his hair as he peered through Nolan's binoculars. In the distance to his left The Narrows opened into Bedford Basin, dark and churning with whitecaps. In precise formation, a sea-going wolf pack of twenty-five or thirty lean grey ships rode the waves.

"There's the *Highflyer*! You didn't tell me she was going with this convoy."

Nolan lay on the grass at his son's side. "I didn't have to. Good thing you aren't a German spy, Drew."

Drew, with the binoculars still trained on the Royal Navy flagship, wriggled forward to a better vantage point. He'd been fascinated by her since she'd arrived in port, to be hailed for sinking more than one enemy vessel.

"I can see her guns. Can she really make twenty-one knots, Dad?"

"She could when she was new, and Captain Garnett tells me she can run yet. I wouldn't be surprised if she's still close. She's seen some action, and I expect she'll see more."

Liam sat on Drew's other side, his bad leg stretched out in front of him, his cane beside him. He shook his head when the boy rhymed off the names of five or six other vessels.

"And the Navy worries about crews of neutral ships landing. Maybe they should arrest all the little boys in town if they're concerned about spies." He leaned back on his hands and scanned the convoy, with flags at full stretch in the fresh breeze.

Georgie worked at the paper until noon on Saturdays, so he was spending the morning here on the windy hilltop, as he had so many mornings when he was Drew's age, when Nolan had been the one watching the ships in the Basin while Liam climbed trees or teamed up with Michael-John to annoy their big brother.

Nolan sat up, yawned and curled his arms around his knees. He'd slept on board three different ships through the week, to be ready to guide them out of port as soon as the submarine booms at the mouth of the Harbour were opened in the morning. He'd earned himself a rare Saturday off. He could have slept in, but Liam knew Nolan's time with the children was rare and precious.

Liam wondered for the hundredth time about one of the ironies of this war. He and Michael-John had gone overseas with a Canadian Expeditionary Force battalion full of merchant seamen and fishermen's sons, while Nolan said the Canadians he met on Royal Navy vessels were mostly Prairie farm boys. Nolan took the binoculars from Drew and looked in the other direction, along The Narrows and toward the Harbour. With another sigh, he passed the binoculars back to his son.

"Sometimes I wish I was still on a merchant vessel and didn't have to deal with military brass bickering about who's in charge. Our Navy, the Royal Navy, the port authority. I wish they'd make up their minds."

Yes, Nolan looked tired, from a combination of stress and long hours. One of the reasons Liam was staying with Nolan and Ruth instead of his parents was to take up some of the slack with the children while his brother was working so hard, but he couldn't replace their father.

"But you have some control over your own destiny now. You're the one giving directions when you're on board."

"Yes, but—"

"Itchy feet?"

Nolan tousled his son's hair. "Not me, Liam. Drew, did you see that little yacht down there beside the *Highflyer*? I did, and she looks like a beauty."

Drew trained the binoculars where his father pointed. Liam turned his bruised face up to the sun's warmth. He'd miss times like this, with Nolan and the kids and his parents, more than he wanted to admit if he went to help Celia.

"Guess I'm the one with itchy feet these days."

Nolan swung around to face him. "So you've made up your mind?"

"Yeah. After last night, I think it's time." So why was it so difficult to say so? "I'm going to write to Celia this afternoon."

"She'll be tickled pink to see you, Liam. It's been a big load for her to carry at twenty-one – running the store and worrying about Matthew."

"I'm sure it has. Once I learn the ropes, maybe I can take over for awhile, so she can come home for a visit." Liam shook off a sudden chill. What if he found himself alone in a strange place and discovered he couldn't cope, physically or emotionally?

Nolan picked up on his doubt. "That won't take you long. You know, Liam, growing up I always thought you had more ambition than I did."

The words were meant to be encouraging, but they hurt. Six months of trying to find his drive, waiting to want something again, to care, and still… nothing really mattered. Not storekeeping. Not Georgie. Only the family, and Liam was about to leave them behind. Again.

"I don't know. I gave up early on the idea of following you to sea. I never felt the way you did about it." Truth be told, though he'd had his dreams of seeing the world, he'd always expected to end up right here.

"No, but you were doing well at the rail yard. You'd have been a foreman by now if you'd been able to stay. You're good at managing people."

Liam reached for his cane, rose and tested his weight on his bad leg. It protested. He swore under his breath. "Maybe. I liked being outdoors at the yard. I guess I could drive a truck or clerk in a warehouse. If my leg was stronger, I'd talk to Jess about going back to the boat shop." Liam had worked with his cousin Jess in Prospect Bay the summer after high school and enjoyed it, even though he hadn't been there long enough to do much more than fetch and carry. The rail yard was closer to home and paid well, and at seventeen he'd been content with that.

"It'll be good to see Celia again, and who knows? Maybe I'll be a natural at storekeeping."

They whiled away the morning on the hill, then trooped into Ruth's kitchen in time for lunch. Afterward, she and Nolan took the children downtown for a treat and Liam headed for the O'Neills' to talk to Georgie.

As he approached the house, his heart started racing. For himself, he didn't give a damn if Carl was home. He'd be happy to land another fist in the man's face, but Liam didn't want to make things harder for Mrs. O'Neill or for Georgie and Alice. And what about dealing with their father? From what he knew, Frank could be as hard to handle as his son. It wasn't as if Georgie were sixteen, but Liam probably should have acknowledged her father before now.

He got a glimpse of Alice through a kitchen window, a slender shape in a blue cotton print, standing by the sink. Better talk to her and see how the land lay first. Liam limped around to the back door. When he knocked, Alice jumped and nearly dropped the plate she was drying. She opened the door a crack and kept her voice down.

"Liam. Georgie's not home yet. She must have had to work late."

Her eyes were wide and anxious, her shoulders tense as if expecting a blow. The protective urge that came over him took Liam by surprise. He eased the door out of her grasp and stepped into the kitchen. Alice darted a frightened glance over her shoulder, but she didn't ask him to leave. Following her lead, he spoke in an undertone.

"Was there trouble when you got home last night?"

"No, not really. Carl arrived after I did and there was a bit of a scene, but I convinced him to go to bed. He hasn't come down yet. Mother is still upstairs, too, and Dad has gone downtown."

She'd retreated until her back hit the table. Her obvious nervousness short-circuited Liam's common sense. Georgie had given him no idea things were so tense at home. No woman deserved to live in fear like that. Instead of doing the smart thing and getting out, he moved toward Alice and took her hand.

"Relax. I'm in no hurry to tangle with Carl again. Alice,

who's his commanding officer?"

"He hasn't said." Colour rose in her cheeks as she glanced down at their joined hands, but she didn't pull away. Neither did Liam, though he knew damn well he should.

"Then I'm going to find out. He needs help."

"Yes, but he's already spent months locked up in a prison camp. More time in a cell isn't going to help him."

The sadness in Alice's voice tugged at him more than her fear. "No, but it's the military's responsibility to see that he gets the help he needs."

"And how good a job are they doing at that these days? How good a job did they do for you?"

She had Liam there. He'd had good doctors, but he'd also dealt with others who didn't believe in wounds they couldn't see, and too many among the military brass agreed with them.

"It's his only chance, Alice. And what about you? You're afraid of him. I can see it."

"Liam, I—"

Footsteps sounded on the stairs, too quick and heavy to be Mrs. O'Neill's. Alice pulled her hand from his and raised it to her mouth. Liam let his cane clatter to the floor and curled his hands into fists as he faced the figure coming down the hall.

"Afternoon, Carl."

Chapter 5

Carl stopped in the kitchen doorway, eyes blazing in his bruised face. "You've got a hell of a nerve showing up here."

"I came to see Georgie. As far as I know, this is still your father's house, not yours." Liam braced himself, but Carl didn't come at him. Instead, he took a slow, menacing step toward his sister.

"Why didn't you send him packing, Alice?" He smirked when he saw the blush on her cheeks. "Got a thing for Georgie's beau? You'd be better off with Stephen. He'll step into his father's business when he's through playing soldier. Liam's got nothing."

Alice faced him with her amber eyes snapping. "That won't be true in a year's time. Where do you think you'll be in a year, Carl? In jail or dead?"

By the look of him, dead was the best guess. Liam knew his own demons too well not to recognize them in the eyes of another man. He moved to put himself between Alice and the violence radiating from her brother, but before he could get there Carl lashed out with his right. His open palm snapped against Alice's cheek, throwing her back against the table. Liam launched himself at Carl in the same instant. With quickness fired by rage, Carl spun, kicked and caught Liam high on his weak leg. Pain exploded behind his eyes as he went down. Then the back of his head struck the floor and the pain winked out like a cinder, leaving nothing.

"Liam!" Oblivious to her stinging cheek and the sharper pain in her back where she'd hit the table, Alice threw herself down beside him, undid the top button on his shirt and laid her hand on his chest. It didn't move. His face was dead still, mouth slack. Panic choked her as she looked up at Carl.

"He's not breathing."

Carl's anger deflated so fast he seemed to shrink with it. He met Alice's horrified gaze for an instant, then sprinted out the kitchen door, leaving it swinging open behind him. Alice turned back to Liam and pressed her fingers to the side of his neck, frantically searching for a pulse. She found it, fast and erratic.

"Breathe, Liam. Please." After the longest moment of her life, his chest lifted. A few seconds later he opened his eyes. Slowly, they focused on her.

"Damn."

"Thank God. Here, lean on me." Alice got her arm beneath his shoulders and helped him sit up, just as her mother appeared in the doorway.

"I heard shouting. What – Oh, no. Alice, where's Carl?"

"Gone."

Her mother's face paled with shock at the sight of her marked cheek. "He hit you."

"It's nothing serious, Mother. Liam stopped in to see Georgie, and Carl came down and lost his temper. Liam got the worst of it trying to protect me." Alice scrambled up from the floor. "Liam, can you stand?"

He gripped the edge of the table with one hand and pushed himself up with his good leg. When he tried to put weight on the other, it buckled. When he leaned on Alice to keep from falling, his sudden weight almost toppled her. She helped him to a chair and brought him his cane.

Her mother still stood in the doorway, taking short, shallow breaths, a hand to her chest. Alice hurried to her. "You came downstairs too fast. Sit here."

She led her mother to a seat. Liam's eyes were closed, his face tight with pain, his skin an awful shade of grey where it wasn't bruised. Alice called Ruth Cochrane, got no answer and called a cab. She hung up the phone and stood with her hand on the receiver. If she were to go to Liam and take him in her arms, feel his heart beat and be sure he'd be all right, what would happen?

You couldn't be that forward. Can't you just see Georgie walking in? This is a big enough mess already. Alice crossed the room and laid a hand on Liam's shoulder.

"I'm taking you to the hospital. You need to see a doctor."

He squinted up at her. "There's not much point. It'll do me as much good to go home and rest."

Behind the pain, warmth flared in his eyes, just as it had on the dance floor last night. Her hand slid along the hard curve of his shoulder while her mind followed its own wilful course.

"No arguments. You hit your head, and there's no one home at Nolan's. You're not going to take any chances." Alice moved to the window, so she could watch for the taxi and keep some distance between them. Mother looked a bit better now, with more colour in her face, but her shoulders slumped.

"What's going to become of your brother, Alice?"

Alice put an arm around her mother's shoulders. Wouldn't it be better to be Liam's mother, mourning for Michael-John, a son she could be proud of? "No one can help him unless he decides he wants help. I think he will, sooner or later."

"He's going through hell right now," Liam said, "but he isn't a coward, I'll say that for him. If he was, he wouldn't have survived what he's survived."

They waited in silence, her mother's thoughts, she knew, focused on Carl while Alice's thoughts were wrapped up in Liam.

You can't lose something you've never had, Alice. You can't change things with your brother. She'd never been close to Carl, and her dreams of Liam were just that. Dreams. So, both were on their way out of her life – Liam halfway across the country to his sister, Carl on a short path to destruction, it seemed.

When the cab arrived, Liam rose, leaning hard on his cane. "You stay here with your mother, Alice. I can manage."

Mother sat up straight. "No, Alice, you go with Liam. I'm guessing he won't go to the hospital at all if you don't, and Georgie will be home any minute. I'll be fine."

Liam rolled his eyes when Alice told the cab driver to take them to Camp Hill. She grinned at him.

"Save it, Liam. You're going."

He snapped off a mocking salute. "Yes, sir." With a sigh, he tilted his head back against the seat and closed his eyes. "Georgie isn't going to be pleased about this."

Alice retreated to the corner of the seat, a safer distance. Georgie would be in a rare temper when Mother told her the news, and why not? She had a right to be upset, far more right than Alice.

"Georgie will know who to blame. This won't hurt her the way it will Mother."

For a heart-stopping moment, Liam's gold-flecked eyes searched hers. "Or you. Carl doesn't know how lucky he is. Neither does Stephen."

Dry-mouthed, pulse skipping, Alice looked away. It wasn't fair that a few words from him could do this to her when he didn't really care. "Growing up, Carl was always closer to Georgie, as close as he was to anyone. She stood up to him early on, and he respected that."

"And she never even told me he was missing."

Alice kept her gaze on the passing traffic as she chose her words. She couldn't let slip that Georgie's feelings for Liam were growing past flirtation. "Georgie isn't heartless, Liam. Far from it, but she's strong. She knows the difference between things she can change and things she can't."

"You're strong, too, Alice. You showed it when you put Carl in his place today."

The warmth in his voice drew her gaze again. She couldn't help it. "I was angry."

The normal side of his mouth tugged upward. "Me, too."

Alice shared the smile. There was something endearing about Liam's temper, quick to flash and just as quickly over, with no grudge held. Like Georgie in a way. She'd seen it years ago, and though he'd changed so much, that part of him hadn't.

The new veterans' hospital stood on a knoll overlooking Halifax Common. While a doctor examined Liam, Alice fidgeted in the waiting room, looking out over the expanse of bright green grass fringed by trees beginning to turn colour with autumn.

As much as he'd tried to hide it, she'd seen the pain it cost Liam to get out of the cab and into the building. How much damage had Carl done? How long would Liam suffer for defending her? When he left, would he only remember the pain she'd caused him?

There he was now, on crutches, swinging down the hall with practiced ease. Oh, Lord. He joined her in the waiting room, frowning, but with a contradictory light in his eyes.

"I need to call Ruth. She should be home by now. They want to keep me."

Keep him? That couldn't be good. "What did they tell you?"

Liam touched the back of his head and winced as he found the lump there. "That it's a lucky thing I've got a thick skull. Dr. Gregg also said he thinks I still have shrapnel in my hip, and that's why it's giving me so much trouble. They're going to x-ray it, and if he's right, he wants to open it up again on Monday."

A spark of hope glimmered behind his dour look. Alice refused to fan it just yet. "And afterward— "

"He says that if he finishes the job they started at the hospital in England, I'll be a lot better. He says that once I'm healed I shouldn't even need a cane."

"Oh, Liam." In the next instant Alice had her arms around him. A quick hug and she stepped back, tingling from the contact. "That's wonderful." Heat blossomed in her cheeks.

Balanced on his crutches, Liam looked down at her. The light in his eyes had brightened to a warm glow that made her blush hotter still.

"We'll see. Alice, you might as well go home. I'll give you money for a cab."

The last thing she wanted to do was leave him, but what excuse did she have to stay? Liam should be resting and she should be worrying about Mother, not standing here playing with fire – about to make a fool of herself. "Thanks, but I've got money. Good luck on Monday, Liam. I'm sure Georgie will be in when you're ready for visitors. I'll – I'll see you around."

As Alice hurried up the front walk, Georgie opened the door. "You're back. Mother told me what happened. How's Liam?"

"He's going to be fine." Alice studied her sister's face while her breathing slowed. Georgie was angry, no mistake about it. "In fact, this might be a blessing in disguise. He's going to have more surgery, and his doctor thinks it'll make a big difference."

"That is news. When?"

"Monday. How's Mother?"

"She's all right. I convinced her to go back to bed after she told me what happened."

Georgie stepped aside to let Alice in. Dad stood in the hall. His eyes blazed at the sight of Alice's bruised face.

"Carl had better not show himself here again."

His anger wasn't really for her. Like Carl's drinking, her bruises were a source of shame for the family. Alice glanced at her cheek in the hall mirror. The mark would be with her for awhile.

"Dad, Carl's sick. That's not just an excuse. It's the truth."

Her father snorted. "Sick? How can you defend him? He's been a bad lot since he was fourteen. I'm through with him, and so are you girls. If he shows up here you aren't to let him in. Is that clear?"

Without waiting for an answer, he turned his back and strode into the front room. Alice's eyes stung with tears, but she forced them back. They'd only earn Georgie's contempt as well as her father's.

"I'll go up and see if Mother's awake. She'll want to hear about Liam."

Sunlight filtered through the drapes and brightened the white knitted spread on her parents' bed. With its pale green ivy-patterned wallpaper, Mother and Dad's room always made Alice think of summer. Mother was awake. She sat up and lifted a hand to Alice's bruised cheek when Alice sat beside her.

"Carl used to be protective of you when you were small. Do you remember?"

"Not really."

Mother gave her a sad smile. "You've always been shy, Alice. More than once Carl chased off other children who tried to bully you."

"And then he started trying to bully me himself. Oh, he didn't succeed very often," she added when hurt showed in her mother's eyes. "Dad didn't let him." Another reason why her father dismissed her. He didn't respect people he had to protect.

Alice looked down at her mother's other hand on the bedspread. Mother's hands had always been beautiful, even more now that her long, slender fingers were no longer roughened by housework. Alice's hands had the same delicate bone structure, the same flexibility, in spite of dishwashing and laundry. A musician's hands, if only she weren't so slow-witted.

Mother reached for her hand and squeezed it gently. "Alice,

you remember what your father was like when you were small. Carl's his father's son. He'll straighten out, just like Frank did."

Alice bit back a retort. Dad didn't drink anymore, but that was the only way in which he'd 'straightened out.' The years hadn't softened him any. Would time do any more for Carl? "I hope so."

Mother's fingers pressed hers again. "You deserve a home of your own, dear. You'll make a good wife and mother. You and Stephen—"

At the mention of Stephen, Alice started. He hadn't crossed her mind once since last night. She kept her gaze down as shame scorched her cheeks. She'd never deceived him, but she'd let him deceive himself.

"Stephen and I aren't making any plans. He'll be shipping out in a month or two."

"And when he comes back—"

"He hasn't said anything about when he comes back."

Mother's tone turned stern. "Stephen cares for you. You must know that. You'd be a fool to refuse him. How could you do better?"

"I don't want better, Mother. I want more." Alice rose from the bed. Big words. Who did she think she was? As Dad never hesitated to remind her, she wasn't for every market. Mother said the same thing, a little more gently.

"Alice, what do you mean? You aren't like Georgie, able to make your own way. Do you want to grow old here, waiting on me and your father?"

Alice's throat constricted with the same dread that sometimes haunted her late at night. Dread that life would never be anything more than a grey monotony of days filled with nothing that mattered. She stiffened her spine and held her mother's gaze. There were worse fates.

"If it's that, or grow old waiting on a man I don't love, what's to choose? And if Stephen and I had children, who knows if they'd be like me? You need me, and I'm content, or would be if not for Carl. I can forgive him for hurting me, but not for hurting you."

Her mother coughed the small chronic cough that went with her weak heart. She studied Alice's face for a moment and sighed. "You feel that way now, when you're twenty and the mirror is still your friend. You'll sing a different tune at thirty-five, but it'll be too late then."

Thirty-five. Would she even have Mother then, fifteen years from now, or would she be completely alone? Alice recalled that brief moment with her arms around Liam, felt his solid warmth again. She would be alone if she kept thinking that way, if she didn't get him out of her mind. Her soul.

"Maybe it's always been too late. Now let's get you dressed and downstairs for dinner."

She helped her mother into a house dress and held her hand as she took the stairs, pausing for her mother to take a careful breath at each step. She heard her father and Georgie in the kitchen, talking as Georgie started supper. Alice saw Mother settled on the front room sofa, then slid onto the piano bench.

A book of practice exercises stood open on the ledge, next to the score for *Beautiful Dreamer*. Looking at the repetitive, rising patterns of notes in the exercises, she ran her fingers along the keys.

"What do you call the first scale on this page, Mother?"

Her mother glanced up briefly from her magazine. "It's a major scale. Why?"

"Which one?"

"G major."

Alice examined the pattern of lines and notes on the page more closely. "So if it starts on the second line from the bottom, it's G?"

"Yes."

Something clicked in her mind. She ran her eyes over the

next scale on the page. "This next one starts on a space. What's it called?"

"A major." Her mother rose and slowly crossed the room to stand behind her. Alice looked down at the keyboard.

"What key does it start with?"

Mother leaned over her shoulder and pointed. "This one."

Alice glanced at the page again, frowning. "So G is one note lower?"

"Yes." Their eyes met. Mother's held something new – respect, tinged with a little surprise. "Move over a bit, Alice."

Mother joined her on the bench. "Don't worry about the names of the notes. Just look at the keys. You might remember this from when you were little. This is middle C – this key here." She played the note, then pointed to a note on the score of *Beautiful Dreamer*. "Here it is, right in the middle, between the treble clef and the base clef – the right-hand and left-hand parts."

Alice studied the score. The lines and spaces looked like stair steps, going up just as the notes on the piano rose in pitch. It made perfect sense. She placed her finger on a note two steps above middle C and played it two keys above the note her mother had played. "Is that right?"

"Yes, it is." Her mother laid a hand on her shoulder and pointed. "Alice, the melody starts here. You know what it sounds like. Now follow the notes and try to play it, just your right hand first. That's it."

Alice's fingers trembled on the keyboard.

I'm reading.

Chapter 6

Liam tried to writhe away from the pain tearing at his leg, but hands on his shoulders held him down. An English man's voice spoke in clipped tones. "Get that mask on him, nurse, quickly."

No. Let me die. I can't go home, I can't face them. *Liam tried to knock away the nurse's hands as she put the anaesthetic mask over his nose and mouth, tried to tell them, but he didn't have the strength. The doctor spoke again, sternly.*

"Lie still and take your medicine, lad. We've other men waiting."

Bea. I'm sorry, Bea, I should have—

The nurse pressed the anaesthetic mask to his face and said something soothing, only it wasn't her voice any longer, it was Mum's.

"Wake up, Liam. That's it, wake up."

He opened his eyes. Slowly his mother's face came into focus, and he remembered. He was in Halifax, not the field hospital, and he'd had surgery this morning.

"Mum."

Liam's whole body throbbed in time with his head, and when he shifted, blinding pain rocketed down his bad leg. His pulse pounded in his ears and his breath came quickly, as if he'd been running.

Sitting on the edge of his bed, his mother leaned closer, tears wetting her cheeks. Her voice trembled.

"It's all over. You came through with flying colours."

She faded in and out of his ether fog. Why was she crying?

Mum had always been a rock when anyone was ill. Liam swallowed against a wave of nausea and reached for her hand. "Then what's wrong?"

"You've been talking." Her voice dropped to a whisper. "Michael-John… you saw it happen, didn't you?"

Wonderful. As if his family didn't hurt enough for him already. He closed his eyes, not trusting himself to look at her.

"Yeah, I saw it."

Running. Running until his lungs were ready to burst, through a cloud of smoke and dust kicked up by bullets, lit by the strange flashes – like summer lightning – of far-off artillery fire. Mum's voice dragged him back.

"He was caught in barbed wire and you tried to get to him, but you couldn't. Not in time."

Michael-John's familiar figure struggling on the wire. Then the rattle of machine-gun fire.

Liam squeezed his eyelids tighter, took a slow breath and willed his voice to stay steady.

"No. Not in time."

Her question came out quiet and calm, without a trace of judgment. "Why didn't you tell us?"

Liam opened his eyes. He'd never been able to fathom his mother's strength. Since coming home, he'd learned that she'd always been the glue that held the family together. Now here she was, holding him together. Why couldn't he have kept his memories to himself?

He gathered his strength and sat up, braced on his hands, holding himself hard against the pain. "I told you he died in an instant, Mum. That he didn't suffer. When – when it actually happened, that was true. What would have been the point in saying anything else?"

"Oh, Liam." Mum got her arms around him as he wrapped his around her, both of them clinging and supporting at the same time. The only time he'd ever seen her need support. "No, he didn't suffer. You're the one who's suffered. You don't have to be strong for us, son. We've told you that before."

"I know." He blew out a shaky breath and leaned against her, his cheek resting for a moment against her hair. Only now, as his burden slipped from his shoulders, did he understand how crushing it had been.

When he lay back on his pillow again, she gave him a teasing smile through her tears. "That's not all you told me, you know. You've been asking for someone."

Bea. Had to let that cat out of the bag too, didn't you? Liam dredged up a grin and rolled his eyes. "Georgie. For heaven's sake, have a heart and don't tell Nolan or Dad."

His mother shook her head, stroked his hair. "No, not Georgie. I think the name I heard was Bea. Was she someone you knew overseas?"

"Yeah."

"Very well?"

"Not as well as I thought."

He was fully awake now, and hurting as much as he'd hurt when he was wounded. Good. Concentrating on the pain meant he couldn't focus on anything deeper.

His mother sat up straight, dark eyes flashing. This was the Meg Cochrane her children knew.

"That's for the best, then. There are plenty of girls for you closer to home."

Before Liam could think of a reply, Dr. Gregg came in, brisk and efficient. "You're awake. Welcome back, Liam. You're rid of a few pieces of metal I'm sure you'll be much better off without. Mrs. Cochrane, we'll be moving your son back to his room now. He needs something for pain and he could do with a few hours' sleep."

Liam's mother kissed his cheek. "You rest. Your father and Nolan will be in later." Before straightening up, she whispered "Your secrets are safe with me."

There was nobody like her. "Thanks," he whispered back. "Now get out of here."

When the door had closed behind her, Dr. Gregg gave Liam his shot of morphine. Groggy and sore, he lay back and waited for the drug to pull him under.

Plenty of girls closer to home. But it wasn't Georgie's vivid face that came to him in this last waking moment. He drifted off on a vision of Alice's soft-lipped smile.

Alice sat at the kitchen table, her pen awkwardly poised over a blank sheet of staff paper. "Sharps. Father Charles Goes Down And Ends Battle. F, C, G, D, A, E, B." She repeated the phrase twice before marking the key signatures on her paper. When she finished, she held the sheet up to the sunlight slanting through the back window. Her sharp symbols were all different sizes, with different slants. She started to crumple the sheet, then caught herself and smoothed it out again. Music was beautiful on the page as well as to the ear, if it was written beautifully.

Someday, Alice.

She checked the clock on the shelf by the stove. Georgie should be home any minute, and she'd planned to stop at the Cochranes' to see how Liam's surgery had gone this morning. All afternoon Alice had kept busy, but the time still crawled. If only she could phone Ruth and ask. Was he in a lot of pain? Did the doctor still think he'd see a big improvement? She smiled at a vision of him walking freely, without pain – but sadness followed. The faster Liam healed, the sooner he'd leave. And she couldn't think of him now without thinking about how he'd ended up in the hospital in the first place.

There'd been no word from, or of Carl since he dashed out Saturday afternoon. Likely he was hiding with one of his friends downtown, but if he'd been frightened enough to run any distance, he might end up charged with desertion, unable to ever return home.

Just as Alice picked up her pen again, Georgie walked by the side window of the kitchen on her way to the back door. Alice reined in her feelings and kept her voice casual when her sister came in.

"You're home. Were you as busy as you expected today?"

Georgie let the screen door swing closed, sat and kicked off her shoes. "And then some. We got the advertising circular for Wednesday almost finished, though. I stopped to talk to Liam's mother on the way home. She says he's in some pain, but the surgery went well. I'll drop in to see him tomorrow."

"Say hello for me." Alice gathered up her staff paper and took it through to the front room so her sister wouldn't see her face. Georgie still didn't know Liam was planning to move. Would he tell her tomorrow? How much would that news hurt her? A chilling thought took the glow from Alice's relief. She might not even get to speak to Liam again before he disappeared from her life for good.

She set her staff paper on the piano ledge, leaned down and stroked a key. The sound rang softly and died away.

Liam stared at the ceiling, mulling over how good it would feel to tear a strip off someone. His hip and leg hurt like hell, and just being in the all-too-familiar confines of a hospital room set him on edge. It had only been twenty-four hours since his surgery, but it felt like days.

His last shot of morphine was wearing off, and he'd tired himself hiding his discomfort from his mother when she dropped in earlier. Yesterday had passed in a drugged haze, but today had been tough and tomorrow would be worse – when they stopped giving him medication. They wouldn't replace it with liquor either, as they had in England.

The whole situation reminded him too much of the weeks

he'd spent in hospital overseas, waiting to hear from Bea. He'd written to her shortly after his first surgery, then again when he came to his senses after the bout of infection that followed. A few weeks after that, when he'd gotten no word from her, he'd written to her parents. Just before he was transferred to the convalescent home, their reply came.

A newspaper clipping that showed a smiling Bea in her wedding gown, her new husband beside her. She'd married less than three months after Liam's last leave. The terse note that accompanied the clipping said she'd asked her parents to convey her apologies. Liam didn't believe that; he guessed she didn't even know they'd sent the clipping. It would be more like her to let him judge her by her silence. And he had. He'd said 'good riddance' and come home without a backward glance – and now here he was in hospital again, still thinking of her.

At least for now, he had the luck to be the only patient in his four-bed room. That had its good and bad points. Easier at night, but the hours dragged during the day. He dozed and dreamed until he lost track of time and reality. Bea's face blended with Georgie's, England with home. But when he was awake and coherent, he found himself thinking most often of Alice.

It made no sense, this pull between them, but the way her gaze softened when their eyes met told Liam she felt it, too. As if he'd act on an attraction to Georgie's sister. Even if he hadn't decided to go to Celia, he was through being stupid with women.

Someone knocked softly. Georgie's head appeared around the edge of the door. "You're awake. Hello."

Liam sat up and watched her as she crossed the room. She had a fresh colour from her walk to the hospital, and the wind had played with her hair like a lover's fingers. No man with eyes could deny how fetching she was.

"Hey."

She sat in the chair by his bed, crossed trim legs under her chocolate-coloured serge skirt. "How are you feeling?"

"I've been better. How do I look?"

"Tired."

She looked so warm and vibrant. Had he been a bit in love with her after all? If so, it was all the more reason to walk away. "You look great."

"Thanks." Georgie grinned, then sobered as she reached out to touch Liam's cheek. "Carl really let you have it, didn't he? But from what Alice told me, it seems he did you a favour."

"Maybe. Dr. Gregg seems to think so. I'm not going to be running races anytime soon, but he says I should be able to get around pretty well once I've healed."

"I'm glad, Liam. You deserve it."

Saying what he had to say was harder, a lot harder than he'd expected. "Georgie, last week we heard from Celia. She needs help in her store, and she asked me to join her in Ontario. I think as soon as I'm able, I will. If it works out, I'll probably stay. I'm not – I can't seem to settle in here."

Though she covered it with a smile, regret came through in her voice. "I see. Well, we've had a good time, haven't we, my friend?"

Oh, yeah. Liam took her hand. "Georgie, I'm not going to forget you."

She leaned down for a quick kiss. "Nor I you."

Thank God for sensible women who didn't ask for more than he could give. He should have known Georgie would take it like this. Liam didn't give much attention to the hollow ache that tinged his relief.

"I haven't hurt you, have I?" He watched her face.

She squeezed his fingers. "Of course not. Now close your eyes, Liam. You're tired. I'll just sit here for a few minutes, until it's time to catch the tram."

So that was over. He'd be able to leave knowing he'd done the right thing. Liam closed his eyes and drifted off in spite of his pain. When the nurse came in with his shot, Georgie was gone.

Alice picked out the melody line of *Beautiful Dreamer* slowly, playing from memory while she kept her eyes on the music. Instead of focusing on each note she tried to see the whole pattern, how it rose and fell as her fingers shifted on the piano keys.

The kitchen door shut, followed by Georgie's quick footsteps in the hall. When she stepped into the front room, Alice closed the piano.

"Georgie. I haven't started supper yet. Dad's working late, and I didn't expect you this early. I thought you were going to see Liam."

"I did, but I didn't stay long. He was tired." Georgie combed her fingers through her hair to tidy it, took off her sweater and tossed it on the armchair. "We did talk, though. He told me he's leaving to work in his sister's store as soon as he can. So…that's it for us, I guess."

Faint as it was, Alice caught the note of disappointment. She glanced at Georgie out of the corner of her eye. "Are you sorry?"

In the past, when she'd broken off with anyone, Georgie had laughed it off with a witty comment that would make the man's ears burn if he heard it, but not this time. "In a way. Liam knows how to treat a girl, but he's not an easy man to get to know. I guess I didn't manage it. Come on, let's get supper."

While they worked, and later while they ate, Georgie kept up her usual chatter about her day, but her animation didn't quite ring true to Alice. After supper, Georgie left to pay a call on a girlfriend. Alice finished washing the dishes and took the mending basket out to the back doorstep.

The days were still long, most of the leaves still green, but the faint chill in the air spoke of fall. Alice picked up one of her blouses, threaded a needle and started stitching a tear in the ivory lace edging the collar.

Her breath caught when a man's shadow edged forward past the corner of the house. His footsteps made no sound on the earthen path. She stood, expecting to face Carl. She started breathing again when Stephen rounded the corner.

He froze in his tracks when he saw her. "Alice, what happened to you?"

Alice laid her blouse in the mending basket and rose to meet him. He'd be sure to hear though neighbourhood gossip anyway, so she told him the truth.

"I'm not trying to excuse Carl, but if you'd seen his face when he left… I feel worse for him than I do for Liam or myself."

Stephen put his hands on her shoulders. "So you haven't seen Carl since then?"

"No." Alice looked into his eyes. If only she could respond to the glow she saw there. "Stephen, will you do something for me? If he's picked up by the military police, will you do what you can to see that he gets help?"

Stephen drew her a little closer. "Help? I'd like to flatten him. If I hear that he's been arrested I'll suggest that he be examined by a doctor, but face it, Alice, Carl has always been difficult. I remember what he was like at school as a kid. As far as I'm concerned, he deserves whatever he gets."

What else could she expect? In the time she'd been keeping company with Stephen, Alice had learned that he saw the world and people as either good or bad. She gathered her resolve and said what she should have said weeks ago. She hadn't wanted to hurt him, but from the moment she'd seen Liam getting up from the floor at the dance, his face bloodied, she'd known she had no choice.

"Stephen, we need to talk. I haven't been fair to you."

"Oh?"

Alice felt his body stiffen before she stepped back. She tensed in response. She'd never had to hurt anyone like this before, and Stephen really was one of the nicest men who'd taken her out.

"No, I haven't. I've thought for a few weeks now that you… feel differently… about me than I do about you. You deserve better."

The angry flush on his face deepened. "I agree. You know, I was going to give you a ring before I shipped out. I guess I can save the money and my time."

His voice rang with injured pride. His face radiated it. And she'd actually thought she cared for this man. Why hadn't she seen his sense of self-importance before?

A lot like Dad.

Alice shuddered. If anything frightened her more than the idea of growing old with no roots of her own, it was the possibility of ending up yoked to a man like her father.

"I'm sorry, Stephen."

He marched off without answering, so stiff and angry Alice actually giggled once he was far enough away not to hear. Poor Stephen…

Guess you'll be saving your time, too, Alice.

Chapter 7

Alice kept her eyes on the left-hand part of the Schubert Étude as she played, the right-hand part already solid in her memory. Her phrasing needed work, but every time she practiced it sounded a bit better. She'd done little else in the days since breaking up with Stephen.

The usual Saturday chores waited, but the house was quiet now with her parents out and Georgie not yet home from the paper. No need to hurry. Alice didn't look up when she heard someone at the front door. It was time for the mail.

Then the caller knocked again, louder and more insistent. She sighed and rose from the piano. An icewater chill ran through her when she opened the door to a military police officer.

"Is this Lieutenant Carl O'Neill's home, miss?"

Stomach sinking, Alice opened the door wider to let the man in. "Yes, it is. I'm his sister, Alice O'Neill. Has something happened to Carl?"

Grave-faced, the M.P. took off his cap as he stepped inside. "I'm afraid so. He was in a fight downtown early this morning – a bad one – and he was hurt. I don't know how seriously, but I was with the patrol that picked him up and…" the young man shifted from one foot to the other. "He's at Camp Hill. Someone ought to go to him. Are your parents at home?"

Oh, God. It didn't take him long, did it? "No. I'll go. I'll call a cab right now. Thank you."

Alice made the phone call, then checked her reflection in the hall mirror while she marshaled her shaken wits. The marks Carl had put on her face still showed, but a little make-up would cover them. Her father wouldn't be pleased if she left the house without it. She ran up to her room, applied some foundation and powder and hurried down again. If only she could leave a note… She shrugged off the old, familiar shame. There wasn't time for it.

The smartly-uniformed young woman at the hospital reception desk gave her a pleasant, inquiring smile. "How may I help you?"

"I'm here to see my brother, Lieutenant Carl O'Neill. He was admitted early this morning."

The receptionist referred to a list. "Yes. Come with me. I'll tell his doctor you're here."

Alice followed her to the same room where she'd waited for Liam, all cool walls and dark, heavy leather-upholstered chairs. She sat and clasped her hands together to steady them. Pictures of Carl as a rambunctious little boy, as an angry, distant young man, revolved in her mind. When the same doctor who'd seen Liam appeared, her tongue stuck to the roof of her mouth. Smiling, he tucked his clipboard under his arm and shook Alice's hand.

"Miss O'Neill, I'm Dr. Gregg. Pardon me, but have we met before? You look familiar."

Alice nodded. "Yes, I was here with a friend a week ago."

"Ah, now I remember." His smile faded. "Well, Miss O'Neill, I treated your brother Carl when he came in this morning. He's a lucky young man. He's got a cracked collarbone, a couple of broken ribs and a concussion, but nothing worse. He'll live, but he's been in a fight he'll never forget."

Alice released the breath she hadn't known she was holding. She wouldn't have to break the news to her mother that Carl was gone. "Oh, thank God. May I see him?"

"Yes, but only for a few minutes. Let's say ten. I must warn you, he's been given medication for pain. He won't be awake."

"I understand."

"Fine. Before I take you to him, we need to complete his paperwork. We haven't received his personal information from the military police yet." Dr. Gregg handed her the clipboard and fished a pencil from the pocket of his white coat. "If you could fill in his birth date and the names of his next of kin—"

Alice had learned to deal with these situations years ago. She took the pencil, poised it over the paper, then shook her head, blushing. "I'm sorry, Doctor. I'm too shaky at the moment. The officer who came to the house made me think I'd find Carl dead when I got here. I'll give you the information, but you'll have to fill it in for me."

Dr. Gregg wrote down the facts she gave him, then took her up a floor to Carl's room. The curtains were drawn, shutting out the bright afternoon sun. After her ride in the warm cab, the cool air made Alice shiver. She held tight to what the doctor had told her as she stepped quietly in and stood by Carl's bed.

He lay in a deep morphine-induced sleep. She looked down at his battered, swollen face. She wouldn't have known her tough, good-looking brother.

"You've never belonged anywhere either, have you, Carl? Why can't you see how much alike we are?"

She shivered again, sat on the edge of his bed and took his hand. She could only hope that on some level, he knew she was there – but if he did, what comfort would it give him? What comfort could anyone give him?

A few minutes later she glanced around the room. When her gaze touched the man in the only other occupied bed, her chill evaporated in a rush of warmth from deep within her.

Liam.

What kind of impish chance had put Carl in Liam's room? He lay still, eyes closed, a pair of crutches leaning against the wall close at hand. All the stern lectures she'd given herself forgotten, Alice tiptoed across the room and eased herself into his visitor's chair.

His mouth looked almost normal now, and the bruises from his tussle with Carl were fading. He'd shaved his beard and moustache, revealing the lines of his jaw and chin. Alice shut her eyes and heard the band playing Strauss again as she remembered dancing with Liam, longing to kiss the slight dent in the middle of his lower lip.

What's the harm, Alice? He'll never know. Before common sense could stop her she leaned down, braced herself with her hands on either side of Liam's head and brushed her lips over his. She meant for it to end there, but he made a deep, drowsy sound like a purr and opened his mouth against hers.

Her body simply mutinied. Alice's spine relaxed and her arms shook, threatening to collapse and drop her on Liam's chest. She felt his body heat through his hospital gown and thought it would melt her as their tongues met and moved in a slow, languorous dance. She'd been kissed with more fervor before, but never with more intimacy.

Reason returned gradually, between soft nips and nibbles. Someone could walk in at any moment – a doctor, a nurse, Liam's family. Breathless, Alice pulled away and looked into gold-flecked hazel eyes full of mingled desire and confusion.

Oh, Lord. What have I done?

"Alice, what the… What are you doing here?"

She caught her breath, fought to find her voice. "Carl's been hurt in a fight. They put him in this room." Frowning, Liam ran a hand through his tousled hair. Alice tilted her chin, held his gaze and waited. After all, he appreciated honest, straightforward girls, and he *had* kissed her back.

"They must have brought him in while I was asleep." He raised himself on his elbows and locked his gaze on hers. "Alice, did you… did we just…?"

Alice stiffened her spine and refused to look away. *In for a penny, in for a pound.* If only her lips didn't still tingle and her fingers didn't itch to touch him. "Yes. You seemed to enjoy it."

His frown deepened. "What kind of game are you playing?"

Alice threw a challenge into her voice. "I'm not playing games. I've wanted to kiss you since the social, so I thought I'd get it out of my system. You're leaving, and what Georgie doesn't know will never hurt her. So why not?"

Liam sat up. He looked sleepy and annoyed and oh, how she wanted to kiss him again.

"What about Stephen?"

"I'm not seeing Stephen anymore, and I've told him so. It wasn't fair to him. All I could give him was friendship, and he wanted more."

Liam spoke with a cold contempt that stung like a slap, taking her completely by surprise. "You mean you didn't want a man who was going to ship out and perhaps not come home. Well, better that than a letter. I saw a few men get those. So what do you expect me to do now?"

Somehow, Alice held back her hurt. She'd taken her chances, and she didn't regret it. "Nothing. I don't expect anything from you." A sly demon prompted her, or perhaps it was just self-preservation. "Did you think I was Georgie?"

"No… No!" His gaze locked with hers again. "Alice, you haven't just grown up. You've changed."

She faced him with her chin up. There would be time enough to nurse her feelings and her pride later. "You've changed, too, Liam. I'm sorry I offended you."

His anger faded, gave way to something raw that made Alice's heart ache. "You're right that I've changed. Don't forget it. You'd better go."

Once she was gone, Liam reached for his crutches. He

needed to move, to shake off the feel of Alice's soft, warm mouth fused to his. To be wakened from an after-dinner nap by the sweetest kiss he'd ever known, given by the last woman on earth he'd expect to do such a thing… Maybe he'd dreamed it after all.

To have the boldness to kiss him like that, and then coolly tell him she'd wanted to 'get it out of her system' – but there'd been nothing cool about her kiss. There was a lot more to Alice O'Neill than met the eye, and who had taught her to kiss like that?

He tried to hold on to his anger, but it deserted him just when he needed it most. 'You seemed to enjoy it.' What could he say to that, with her flavour and scent burned into his mind?

Balancing on his good leg, he got into his robe and tied the belt. He looked out the window with a frustrated sigh. He needed fresh air, and he wanted a drink. Well, he could forget about that until he got home. He'd had a few poor nights, lying awake with his leg aching and nothing to ease it, but his pain was diminishing now. As for fresh air, dressed in this damned rig the only choice was the hospital lawn.

He swung across the room and stood looking down at Carl for a moment. Christ, he'd certainly taken a beating, by more than one person if Liam didn't miss his guess. Maybe this would be enough to make Carl stop and think before raising his hand to Alice again.

Liam turned away. He knew well enough that Carl hadn't been thinking at all when he hit her. He'd been blind, lost in some private hell. Liam picked up the copy of *The Virginian* that Nolan had brought him and started down the corridor, swinging along on his crutches so quickly that nurses and other patients turned their heads. It eased his frustration somewhat to be able to move faster than he had with his cane. Out in the yard, he settled on a bench in the shade of an orange-leafed young maple and laid his book beside him.

Alice. As much as he wanted to, he didn't believe she'd dropped Stephen because he was going overseas. At the social, she hadn't looked like a girl dancing with the man she loved, and now she'd been honest enough to tell Stephen so. But if she wasn't playing games, that meant – Liam didn't want to think about what that meant.

It didn't matter. He was starting over, leaving Halifax, its memories and its complications behind, and if he couldn't forget the taste of Alice's sweet mouth, there were worse things to remember.

"Oh, God. It didn't take him long, did it?"

"That's exactly what I said." Standing in the hall, Alice peered past Georgie into the front room. "Are Mother and Dad home yet?"

"No, not yet." Georgie slammed the front door as hard as she could. "Damn, damn, damn Carl!"

"Georgie!"

"I may as well say it as think it, Alice. Well, it's an ill wind that blows no good. At least he'll be out of our way for awhile and he'll be kept out of more trouble."

With Georgie's heels clicking savagely on the hall floor behind her, Alice walked through to the kitchen. She propped the back door open to let in the breeze. "The doctor said he could have visitors again this evening, but only for a few minutes. He probably won't be awake. They've got him heavily drugged."

Flushed with temper and shock, Georgie poured herself a glass of water, drained it in two gulps and banged the glass down on the table. "I don't plan to waste my time on him. He brought this on himself."

Glad of the excuse to hide her face, Alice pulled a frying pan from the cupboard. Yes, Carl had brought his troubles on himself, just as she had. Liam might be free as far as Georgie was concerned, but he'd made himself clear enough with his 'What kind of game are you playing?'

But he kissed you back.

Chapter 8

Carl woke just after dusk, muttering in pain. The sound grated on Liam after his long, uncomfortable day. It was worth the discomfort it cost him to get up and cross the room to gloat.

"Evening. You're a sight for sore eyes, Carl. I guess you'd better stick to beating on your sister."

"Go to hell." Carl tried to lift himself onto his elbows, but couldn't manage it. His voice was thick and slurred, but the rage still came through. Liam quirked an eyebrow.

"Temper, temper. If you try to get out of that bed, I expect they'll strap you in." He settled in Carl's chair, making sure to shift it out of reach. "I don't imagine you feel much like conversation, or anything else. Almost makes me wish I were going to be here longer than I am. I'm going to enjoy seeing you go through hell, for Alice's sake."

Carl's eyes looked positively murderous now, in spite of his pain. Liam couldn't help giving the man some grudging respect. "You've got guts. I'll give you that. Too bad you haven't put them to some use other than tearing yourself and your family apart. But I guess you're going to have plenty of time to think about that, here – and probably in jail. And remember this – if you ever hurt Alice again, or any other woman I hear of, I'll see you in worse shape than you are now."

He heard Dr. Gregg's familiar footsteps coming down the corridor, threw Carl a lethal look and returned to his own bed. The doctor came in with a nurse and checked Liam's sutures, then closed the curtains around his bed for the night. He lay listening to the wind rattling the window, the beginning of a nor'easter. Nolan was out in it, on a ship, waiting to guide her out of port in the morning, as he'd mentioned last night. Afterward, he'd go home to Ruth.

Jealous? Of your own brother? Yes, a little, less of Nolan's marriage than of his solid sense of belonging. Something Nolan had earned.

Liam recalled the fear he'd seen in Alice's eyes the other day at her house. She didn't belong in her own family. Remembering bits and pieces of schoolyard gossip, the way she'd always seemed to blend into the background, he didn't think she ever had belonged. Perhaps that was what drew them to each other. A pair of misfits.

He pushed Alice from his mind and focused on getting comfortable enough to fall asleep. Later, well after midnight, a scream woke him. For a confused instant Liam wondered if he'd made that horribly familiar sound, but then it came again from across the room, a gurgling scream forced between clenched teeth. He grabbed his crutches and hopped over to Carl's bed.

"Carl, wake up." Liam shook Carl's shoulder and jerked back, close to falling, when he lashed out with a fist. Carl coughed and took a heaving breath that must be agony for his ribs.

"Slow breaths. That's it." Liam waited beside him while Carl fought to pull himself out of the nightmare. Finally he got control of his breathing and swallowed.

"Go back to bed, damn it."

Liam swung around on his crutches, but his nagging conscience stopped him. If he could get through to Carl it might lift a huge burden from his family's shoulders. "No. You woke me up, and you'll probably do it again, so I might as well keep you awake, too. You don't sleep much these days anyway, do you?"

Carl ignored him. Liam decided he'd be damned if he was

going to stand there on one leg and waste his time. He sat in the bedside chair and waited until a passing night nurse's footsteps faded away. If Carl didn't want to talk, he'd have to be goaded into it.

"Neither do I. The nightmares are getting fewer, though. If I can't sleep, it's usually because of my leg. So how did you get into this mess, Carl? Did you pick on someone your own size for a change?"

Carl shifted to face him. "You think one man did this to me?"

Liam restrained an urge to shake the man. Carl must be twenty-three or twenty-four by now, and he was still as easy a target as a sixteen-year-old.

"Actually, no. I've tussled with you, remember? I'd guess some of your friends left you in a tight spot. Didn't your mother warn you about keeping bad company?"

"It's none of your business."

The dark hid Carl's face, but Liam sensed him wearing down. His family had worn him down the same way. Not that he'd told them very much, but they'd made him admit to himself that he needed them. He leaned forward into the faint glow from the window.

"You're right, it isn't, but you'll have to tell the police. Anyway, fighting or selling liquor won't be enough to keep you from being sent back overseas. It wouldn't surprise me if they sent you back all the sooner to keep you out of trouble."

Carl snatched the water glass from his table and raised his arm to throw it, but Liam anticipated him, grabbed his hand and pried the glass from his fingers. Carl hurled curses at him, but he wasn't strong enough to do much else. Coughing again, he sank back on his pillow.

"I don't give a damn what they do."

Liam set the glass on the floor and watched Carl try to hide his pain. A real hardhead, one who likely held his own in the trenches – and more. No doubt his service record would make interesting reading, for insubordination if nothing else.

"I think you do. I think you'd rather die than go back, and that's what you're trying to do."

"Go to hell."

Liam grinned at him. "I just might, but not until you tell me what happened to you. If you don't, I'll sit here and keep you awake all night."

After a moment of silence, Carl swore under his breath. "I went downtown to help a friend out a scrape."

"Bootlegging?"

"Yeah."

"What was it? Did he owe the wrong people money?"

"Yeah. I went with him to help straighten it all out, and it turned sour. He got away. I didn't."

Liam could have written the script for that affair. He could have acted in it, too, if not for his leg. One or two of his sources of liquor weren't very careful.

"Do you remember hitting Alice?"

"No."

Liam saw real regret stamped on Carl's face. "I didn't think so. That might even work in your favour. You blacked out. I know it, and so does she."

Carl raised himself on his elbows. His voice cracked with anger and exhaustion. "It's none of your business, Liam. Go back to bed before I get a nurse in here."

Liam reached for his crutches and got to his feet. He'd done what he could. Now his eyes were gritty with lack of sleep, and Carl must be at the end of his rope.

"Carl, we've both survived things a man isn't built to survive. You can let it pull you under – you can even help it along – or you can fight it any way you can. For me, the only thing that's kept me going is my family."

Carl lay back with a short, bitter chuckle. "Family. Yeah,

right."

"Yeah. Like Alice."

The muted hiss of rain against the front room window blended with the sound of the piano. In the armchair, Alice closed her eyes to listen. The Chopin nocturne was another of Mother`s favourites. Today she gave the piece a meditative feel that fit well with the weather.

Alice put the nocturne on her mental list of pieces to learn. The list grew every day. She could read the treble clef and base clef parts of a simple tune now, though she still couldn't play them at tempo. That would come. She'd depended on her memory all her life, and it wasn't failing her now. She'd already come further with reading music than she'd thought possible in such a short time.

She glanced out the window. A car splashed along the street, sending jewelled droplets flying in the headlights' glow. Was Liam watching the storm, too, or was he already asleep? Warmth spread through her at the memory of his mouth caressing hers. She'd only made it harder to let him go, but she couldn't regret kissing him. She'd remember it when she was old.

It couldn't happen again. He'd never allow it.

Coward. Alice silenced the accusing whisper from her heart. Common sense wasn't cowardice, but the light she'd seen in Liam's eyes for that fleeting moment made common sense seem a shoddy virtue.

When her mother finished playing and headed upstairs to bed, Alice took her place at the piano and ran through the Schubert piece she`d been practicing. She knew it from memory now. She let the music flow through her while her mind took her to Liam's room. She came back to reality with the last chord to find her father and Georgie both watching her from the sofa.

"You've been playing a lot lately. It shows," Georgie said.

Dad nodded. "Yes, it does. If you'd practiced as much, years ago, you might have been able to do something in music. Alice, what's going on with Stephen? He hasn't been here since the social. I wouldn't have thought him the type to let Carl put him off."

Alice hadn't said anything to anyone about Stephen's last visit. Now seemed as good a time as any. She turned on the piano bench to face her father.

"Carl didn't put him off. I did. He dropped by the other night after dinner, and we had a talk. I don't care for Stephen the way he says he cares for me, and it's time he knew it. He's got too much starch in place of sand, I think."

Her father's temper flared as she expected. "Alice, it's time you grew up and got practical. You aren't cut out for a career—"

For the first time, Alice cut him off. The words just seemed to say themselves. "Oh? As far as I know I've been a career housekeeper for the last four years."

He looked as astonished as she felt. Dad and Georgie had squared off more than once over the years – they shared the same temper – but Alice had always responded with silence. Now, he didn't seem to know what to make of her. Instead of shouting as he usually did when challenged, he only grumbled.

"If you're not satisfied, go out and work like your sister and see what the real world is like."

Alice answered back, cool and crisp, wondering at the same time what had changed, why she simply didn't care anymore. "I'm thinking of it. If I can cook and clean in this house, I can cook and clean in another and be paid. I'd rather do that than marry Stephen. I'm going to bed. Good night, Georgie."

Looks of amused surprise from Georgie and shock from her father followed Alice as she left the room. What had come over her? Had discovering that she could learn to read music changed her so much?

Alice, it's about time you stopped believing that wanting something means you can never have it.

Chapter 9

Liam woke early, the ache in his leg less severe than at any time since his surgery. He'd grown so used to pain the lack of it felt strange. Across the room, Carl lay still. Would he even remember their talk? Liam hoped so, for Alice's sake.

After breakfast he settled back in bed and tried to read, but he couldn't keep his mind on his book. He'd wakened thinking about his cousin's boat shop, and the memory was still with him – the smell of wood shavings, the scent of the coffee Jess's wife Fanny used to bring out to them, Jess teasing him as he took the first steps toward learning to use a plane and chisel. Liam hadn't gotten much further than that before leaving the shop, and since coming home from overseas he'd dismissed the past along with the future – but now it wouldn't let him be.

Was he starting to want something again? Something, perhaps, that he could actually have?

Halfway through the morning, Nolan arrived for a visit on his way home from the Harbour. He walked by Carl's bed, then backtracked and took a long look at his face.

"Is that who I think it is?"

"Yeah. He was brought in yesterday. He got mixed up in some trouble downtown." Liam wished he could take more satisfaction in Carl's pain. "I might even feel sorry for him if he hadn't put a bruise on Alice's face."

"Yeah. Looks like he took a real shellacking. Couldn't happen to a nicer guy." Nolan settled in Liam's chair, leaned back and stretched his long legs out in front of him. "Why did they put him in here?"

"Because they knew how much I liked him, I guess."

Nolan flashed a grin. "I'm sure. So how much longer do you think you'll be here to enjoy his misery... er, company?"

The tired lines around Nolan's eyes were more pronounced than usual, making him look older than his thirty-two years. When had time started to spin so fast? The three years Liam had been away loomed large. "A few more days, until they decide I'm safe from infection. Which reminds me, will you tell Mum to bring me in some paper and a pen? I need to write to Celia."

A thoughtful crease appeared in Nolan's brow. "I wrote to her the day you had your operation. I told her you'd need some time to heal."

"Yeah. It'll be a while before I'll be able to stand all day."

"Having second thoughts?"

"Yeah, I guess I am. I want to talk to Jess. I haven't for ages. I think I might like working with him better than storekeeping, if I can handle it. I hate to let Celia down—"

"You wouldn't be, Liam. She said she didn't want you to feel obliged, remember? She'll find someone else to help her. Maybe you would like working with Jess better." A sly gleam lit Nolan's eyes. "I think Georgie would like that, too."

Liam shrugged off a pang of regret. He already missed Georgie, her fun and frankness. "I don't know. I told her the other day that I was planning on leaving, and she took it well. In fact, we more or less parted ways."

"You don't say." Nolan only shrugged. Had he known how Liam felt about Georgie better than Liam knew himself? "She's a sweet little package, but there are other fish in the sea and you've never had any trouble finding them."

The memory of Alice's kiss sparked Liam's temper. "You sound like Mum. If the two of you start on me, I swear I'll get on the first train out of town as soon as I can walk."

Nolan snorted. "You, swearing off women. Right." He

sobered. "You know what I think? I think things were starting to get just a little bit too serious with Georgie already, and that scared the hell out of you."

Liam refused to take the bait. He and Georgie had understood each other. "You're entitled to your opinion."

The crease in Nolan's forehead deepened, a sure sign he was about to put on his big brother hat. "Fine, I'll give it to you. Liam, at the memorial service, Father MacManus said Michael-John gave up his life so we could live ours to the fullest, and that we owed it to him to do just that. I agree."

"I sure as hell don't. Michael-John didn't give up his life. It was taken from him."

Liam regretted the words as soon as he'd spoken, they sounded so churlish, but Nolan let them roll off him. "And yours wasn't. I don't know how I would have handled that, but I think you've handled it well. Georgie O'Neill may not be the girl for you, but in my book she's no fool."

"No, she's not. She'll find someone who can offer her a lot more than I'll be able to for a few years."

Nolan leaned forward and gave Liam one of his summing looks. "Depends on what she's looking for."

Liam had no answer to that. What had Georgie seen in him – what would anyone see in him now? Any sane woman would shy away from the face he saw in the mirror each morning. A face almost as hard as Carl O' Neill's.

Liam hadn't hurt Georgie, because she had the sense not to let him. Alice, on the other hand, seemed to lead with her heart. With that thought in mind, after Nolan left Liam took his book to the patients' lounge down the hall. He had no intention of being in his room if Alice came in to see her brother. With the feelings she sparked in him, he had no business anywhere near her.

Alice stood in the doorway of Carl's room, her pulse

tripping as it should on the threshold of forbidden territory. Dad would be furious if he found out she'd been here again, but the thought of Liam's anger frightened her far more.

I've changed. Don't forget it.

He thought she'd used Stephen, and now she was trying to use him. Her sister's beau. Now he'd go away thinking the worst of her.

Her relief at seeing his bed empty shamed her. Father MacManus always said the troubles people brought on themselves were the hardest to bear. Alice understood that now as never before.

She tiptoed over to Carl's bed and touched his shoulder. He stirred and peered up at her between swollen eyelids.

"Alice… what are you doing here? Looking for Liam?"

Cheeks heating, Alice sat on the foot of his bed. "If that's what you want to think."

"You've got more nerve than I thought. Georgie had better watch out."

Carl's old mocking tone carried through, but somehow the sting was gone. He was too vulnerable now. Alice laid her hand over his.

"Before you left, Georgie and I were both sick of you chasing away any man who took an interest in us. I used to think you did it to be mean, but I don't think so anymore."

He pulled his hand away. "Why not? You were right."

Alice caught herself before she rolled her eyes. "I stand corrected. Carl, why did you come home?"

"Because I was sent. In case you've forgotten, I'm still in the Army."

Alice thought back to the day he'd arrived, the letter he'd said he'd written from England. She didn't doubt that he'd lied, but why? To spare Mother's feelings? "I don't believe you. You could have disappeared, gone West, gone North. The Army wouldn't have bothered to look very far. You let us think you were dead, then for some reason you changed your mind."

"It's obvious enough, Alice. I wanted a free roof over my head."

"And for that, you were willing to stay here, knowing you'd be shipped overseas again when your leave was up?"

Carl shrugged, then paled with pain as the movement jarred his ribs. He took a careful breath and relaxed onto his pillow again. "I wasn't thinking that far ahead. War teaches you pretty fast not to think beyond today."

"I suppose so. I also suppose the thought of being a deserter wasn't all that appealing." Alice looked into his eyes, trying to make a connection. "Carl, as much as you try to hide it, you have a sense of honour."

The contempt she'd seen so often flared. "Oh, please. I never knew you had such an imagination."

"I beg to differ. Growing up, none of us liked your friends, but you always stuck by them, even when you suffered for it. That's what happened to you this time, isn't it? The problem is you've never been able to tell who was worth sticking by and who wasn't."

Carl snorted. "Grandma O'Neill will never be dead while you're alive."

Alice couldn't help smiling as she remembered their grandmother's stiff ways and habit of preaching. "Maybe, but as I recall, she was usually right. That was the most annoying thing about her."

"Yeah, it was."

Alice settled back in her chair, seeing Carl at fifteen or sixteen, coming home half-drunk and quarrelsome. Carl at nine or ten, knocking down the playhouse she and Georgie had built in the yard. Carl at twenty, telling ne'er-do-well Cam Murphy he'd put his lights out if he spoke to Alice again. Cam had been killed overseas last year, and not even his own family regretted him. Why couldn't Carl believe anything good of himself?

"Carl, I want to understand what's happening to you, but you have to let me."

Just for an instant his tough front softened, exposing the vulnerability underneath. "You can't understand, Alice, and that's the way it should be."

Alice swallowed a scalding lump in her throat, remembering the chilling stories her mother read in the paper. 'Not a child under the age of eight is left alive in Poland. They have all died of starvation and neglect.' How many names of ruined foreign cities and villages were burned into her memory, along with images of Liam and Carl lying broken amid the destruction?

"Should be? For the whole time you were away, Mother read the papers and we imagined you in every battle. Every story we heard about terrible things happening to prisoners could have been about you. We couldn't help it, because we didn't know the truth."

But Carl had closed himself off again. "I just told you the truth. I came home because I needed a place to stay. Don't waste your time on me, Alice. You never did before I left, and there's no reason for you to start now."

The frustrated reply on the tip of Alice's tongue died there as Dr. Gregg came in. "Good morning, Miss O'Neill. Nice to see you again. Carl, it's good to see you awake. I'm sure you're sore enough, but are you having any trouble breathing?"

"No."

"Good. Miss O'Neill, there's a sitting room down the hall to your right where you can wait while I see your brother."

"Thank you. Doctor, I'd like to speak with you afterwards, if you've a moment."

"Of course. I'll find you there."

Carl's eyes shot daggers at her, but Alice ignored him. She wandered down the hall, found a door ajar and peered in. This must be the sitting room. When she pushed the door open and saw who was inside, a scorching blush rose from the tips of her toes.

Liam sat by the window, a book on his lap. At the sound of the door creaking he looked up, reached for his crutches and stood.

"Alice."

He looked different. It wasn't just that his bruises had faded. His eyes were less shadowed, his face less tense. Younger. He must have been in a lot more pain than he let on before his surgery.

He seemed more surprised than angry to see her again. Alice swallowed and took a moment to steady her voice. "Morning, Liam. Dr. Gregg's with Carl. He sent me here to wait for him."

He pointed a crutch at a chair. "Come in."

She half-expected him to leave, but he watched her as she crossed the room, a steady gaze she couldn't read. Alice stopped an arm's length away, close enough to feel the tension in him.

"How are you feeling?"

"I'm all right. How was your visit with Carl?"

She retreated to the nearest chair. Liam sat in the next one, close enough for the clean, warm scent of his skin to reach her.

"It was frustrating. I just wish he'd let me in, even a little bit. You've had your family to lean on, but he's so alone."

Liam's gaze met hers, searching, searing. "When you've gone through what Carl's gone through, you don't want to look at your family and see your memories on their faces. You want to see joy and..." Liam's voice trailed off as he looked away. "Innocence."

Alice's breath caught in her throat. There it was again, that raw longing in his eyes. As for innocence, was Liam thinking about the war, or using the word as it was used in the magazine articles Georgie read and scorned? The ones decrying the forward, reckless modern woman? But he'd gone out with Georgie. Alice couldn't see him as that much of a hypocrite.

"Do you still think I broke up with Stephen because he's

going overseas?"

Liam glanced down, shook his head. "No. I never really did."

It mattered more, much more than she'd thought. "Then you won't leave thinking badly of me."

"No, but I still don't understand you."

Thank Heaven for that. She'd shrivel with shame if he knew how she'd felt about him all these years. "Liam, I kissed you because I wanted to and it would hurt no one. It's that simple. I didn't mean to wake you, but then you kissed me back."

Liam's face flushed. Alice closed her eyes as he lifted his hand. His fingertips brushed her cheek, traced the cord at the side of her neck, sent waves of ice and flame over her skin.

"I thought I was dreaming, but I'm awake now. Very much awake."

She felt him lean forward. His breath feathered over her mouth, giving her a foretaste of him as her lips parted. Softly, so softly, he took her lower lip between his.

Awash in tingling pleasure, she curled her fingers into the front of his robe and felt him shiver. She heard a sigh, but didn't know if it came from her or Liam. Then he abruptly pulled away.

"Someone's coming."

The thundering of her pulse receded enough for Alice to hear footsteps in the hall. She opened her eyes and saw smouldering heat in Liam's before he turned away. She smoothed her skirt and ran a hand over her hair to tidy it, as if that could settle her rioting feelings. Somehow, she managed to greet Dr. Gregg calmly.

"I'll leave you alone." With a look that sent her heart racing again, Liam got to his feet. Afraid Doctor Gregg would see her legs shaking, Alice crossed them as he took Liam's chair.

"Doctor, I'm really concerned about Carl. He's been behaving erratically ever since he got home. We don't know much about what happened to him overseas, but I think he's badly shell-shocked."

"There hasn't been much opportunity to talk to him, but it wouldn't surprise me. I don't know the details of how he got hurt – that'll be for the military police to sort out – but it looks as if he's been running with a rough crowd." Dr. Gregg fitted his fingertips together and gave Alice a curious look over them. Her stomach fluttered. Would he notice the remnant of her bruise and put two and two together? If he did, he gave no sign. "What do your parents make of Carl?"

"My mother suffers from a chronic heart condition. This has all been very hard on her, but there isn't a lot she can do, and my father and Carl have never been close. I just wanted to tell you what I think and ask you to consider it."

Dr. Gregg nodded and stood, smiling. "I will. I'm glad your brother has one friend at court, at least."

"Yes. Thank you, Doctor Gregg. I'm sure I'll see you again."

As he closed the door behind him, Alice tilted her head back against her chair and let herself go limp. Her neck tingled with the memory of Liam's touch, and her lips ached for his. How could she let him go out of her life now?

But this time, *he'd* kissed *her*.

Chapter 10

The sour look Carl gave him when he returned to their room just wasn't what Liam needed, on top of his disgust with himself. What the hell was he thinking when he touched Alice? Attraction was no excuse to make the same mistake he'd made with Bea, doing his thinking below the belt. He stopped by Carl's bed to vent his frustration.

"Have a nice visit with Alice? Did she tell you she was the one who came running yesterday when she heard you'd been hurt? The devil knows why, but she's a soft-hearted girl. She'd feel sorry for a lame dog in the street."

Carl glared at him again. "How did you know she was here?"

"We bumped into each other."

Carl's hands curled into fists. His temper would be more volatile than ever now that he was off morphine, and Liam was only too willing to provoke it. The thought of Alice carrying bruises revolted him more than ever now that he knew the feel of her soft skin.

Carl's eyes shot sparks. It must be killing him to be too weak to vent his anger with punches. "It's Georgie you're after, isn't it? Leave Alice the hell alone. She's Stephen's."

That flicked on the raw. It wasn't his place to set Carl straight, but Liam snapped without thinking. "Alice is through with Stephen."

Carl sat up, suspicion edging out his anger. "She told you that?"

Great. Why couldn't you keep your mouth shut? Nothing to do now but bluff it out. "Yeah. I wasn't surprised. At the social, they didn't exactly look like a happy couple."

"Dad isn't going to be pleased with her."

The casual contempt in Carl's tone goaded Liam into snapping again. "I think it's time Alice got a little appreciation at home, before she finds a job and tells your father to get himself another housekeeper. Georgie sure won't take her place."

Carl lay back and shook his head. His mouth was stiff, but a smirk came through in his voice. "Alice, find a job? That's not likely to happen. My little sister is a looker, I guess, but she isn't very bright. She never even learned to read."

"What?" Liam caught himself gaping like an idiot.

Obviously pleased to see him at a loss, Carl nodded.

"She had a bad case of measles when she was seven or eight and missed almost a year of school. She never caught up."

It was on the tip of Liam's tongue to call the man a liar. If he'd ever seen intelligence in anyone's eyes, he saw it in Alice's. She spoke as well as Georgie, and Liam still remembered her rich, pure soprano ringing out from the choir at church. She had real talent, and her mother, of all people, ought to have seen it.

"That makes her unlucky, not stupid."

Carl dismissed his sister with a shrug. "Maybe, but she hasn't managed to learn since. Mother gave up trying to teach her. Not that it matters. Her looks will get her a husband, if she has the sense to use them."

So that was why Alice had never belonged. A shame, but all Liam could think of was her subtle glow, her voice, her kisses. He leaned over Carl's bed, close enough to see fear flicker in the man's eyes.

"When she marries, I hope she tells the lot of you to go to hell. When I have my appointment with Dr. Gregg this afternoon, I'm going to tell him to move me to another room. I'm likely to strangle you in the night if he doesn't."

Alice halted in confusion just inside Carl's room. His bed

and Liam's stood empty and stripped. She checked the patients' lounge, found it empty as well and stopped a passing nurse.

"Private Cochrane's been moved down the hall to room 206, miss. Lieutenant O'Neill…" The woman's face coloured. "Are you family?"

"Yes, I'm Lieutenant O'Neill's sister."

"I see. Well, you'd best speak to Dr. Gregg about him. I'm afraid I'm not free to give you any information."

Skin prickling with dread, Alice searched out Dr. Gregg. Grave faced, he drew her aside into an empty consulting room.

"I'm glad you're here, Miss O'Neill. I would have called your home earlier this morning, but I remembered what you told me about your mother and I didn't want to shock her. I'm afraid your brother walked out of here in the night."

Alice's breath left her. Carl wasn't fit to be out of bed. As far as she knew, the only money and the only clothes he had were what she'd brought him from home. His ribs were strapped and he'd hurt his head. He might be lying in the streets somewhere right now.

"What? How could he?"

Dr. Gregg smiled with as much resignation as sadness. Carl's must be only one of many hard stories he could tell. "He's a tough young man, one of the toughest I've seen, and I've seen a few. His injuries are painful, but they wouldn't keep him from walking. Do you have any idea where he might have gone?"

"If he left here, he doesn't want to be found. He wouldn't go home. I know that." Alice wiped away tears with her sleeve. Where did Carl have to go? Dr. Gregg put a hand on her shoulder.

"I'm sorry, Miss O'Neill. We've already informed the police. There isn't much more I can do."

Alice walked blindly down the hall to the sitting room and slumped into a chair. She'd better pull herself together and decide how she was going to tell Mother about this, if the police hadn't already shown up at the house and told her. Alice's stomach knotted at the thought. When had Carl ever thought of anyone but himself?

Perhaps he'd said something to Liam that might be a clue. Alice found his room and lifted her hand to knock on the closed door, then slowly lowered it again. Maybe he didn't want to be disturbed. As one of the last people to speak to Carl, the police would probably talk to him anyway. There was no other way Liam could help, and – the thought settled on her like iron – what if he'd changed rooms to avoid her? Perhaps he regretted kissing her. Why make him think her more forward than he already did?

She ached for the reassurance of seeing him, but he might have no desire to see her. Alice did an about-face and hurried to the stairwell. Right now, she was needed at home as soon as she could get there.

Liam put his book down as the orderly came in with his lunch tray. The morning had flown. He eyed his meal with a distaste that had nothing to do with the food.

Either Alice hadn't wanted to see him, or she hadn't come in to visit Carl this morning. If not, was it because her father had found out about her visits? Thoughts of her being browbeaten by Frank O'Neill did nothing for Liam's appetite. He wouldn't even consider the possibility that Alice's father might strike her as Carl had.

Damn, he was sick of this. Confinement and boredom were bad enough without this restless ache in his chest. He needed to be home, where he could start working on his future.

And where he could make sure Alice was all right.

He shouldn't have kissed her, and he wouldn't let it happen again, but no one was going to abuse her as long as he lived and breathed. Liam closed his eyes and tasted her again, felt her small shiver of pleasure as he teased her mouth. A soft-hearted girl, as he'd told Carl, with a wealth of warmth and passion to offer a man, but she'd want the permanent kind of relationship – if Liam knew anything about women.

Right. You thought you knew Bea.

If Alice had decided to avoid him, that only meant she deserved a lot more credit for good sense than Carl gave her. Maybe someday there'd be a place in Liam's heart for a wife and family, but the road from now to then had a lot of bends he couldn't see around.

When he'd worried down some of his soup and rolls, Dr. Gregg came in on his rounds. He checked Liam's hip and gave him a satisfied nod. "We won't need to keep you much longer. It's been a week and a half since your surgery, and you're healing well. I think we'll be able to send you home on Friday, if you give me your word you'll follow instructions and not overdo."

The tension in Liam's chest eased a little. He'd promise his soul if it would get him out of here. "That I will. No offense, but I'm going stir-crazy. Doc, do you know if Miss O'Neill was in this morning?"

Dr. Gregg's grey eyes turned serious. "Yes, she was. I want to talk to you about her and her brother. Yesterday when you asked me to move you, you told me that you got injured fighting with Lieutenant O'Neill. Why did you wait that long to tell me?"

Liam snorted. "Because I enjoyed seeing him in pain. Besides, I thought I'd try to get through to him for his sister's sake. The fight happened at their home, because Carl slapped her. He blacked out and went into a rage. I'm sure you've decided by now that he's suffering from severe shell-shock."

"Yes. Tell me, did he talk to you at all? Say anything about how he got hurt this time? He wouldn't say anything to me."

Liam hesitated. He might despise Carl for hitting Alice, but soldier-to-soldier he also respected the man's nerve, and there was a code of honour. "I thought the military police would deal with all that later."

Dr. Gregg sat in the bedside chair and sighed. "Liam, Lieutenant O'Neill walked out of here last night. He's missing, and he's in no condition to be on his feet, let alone on the streets. I expect the police will want to talk to you, too."

Liam gave in. The military police probably knew the circumstances of Carl's fight anyway, and the man needed to be found. He'd caused his family enough heartache already.

"He told me he tried to help a friend straighten out a bootleg deal gone bad, and it backfired. That's all. He'll be hiding out with some of his crowd downtown, if he hasn't left the city completely. I'm sure he could manage that, with some help from his friends. This will be hard on his mother and Alice."

Dr. Gregg's brows lifted. "Alice?"

Liam's face heated. "Miss O'Neill. Doc, I promise I'll use my head and be careful, but I need to get out of here as soon as I can."

"Mother, you know Carl. He'll survive." Standing in the kitchen, Alice hugged her mother close. "I'd rather think of him starting over somewhere than going back overseas."

Mother stepped back, her eyes full of deep sadness. When she found her voice, it was only a whisper. "He never knew how much I loved him. Not when he was growing up. Not before he left, and not when he came home. How can that be, Alice? I tried."

Alice tried to sound matter-of-fact. "Carl has never been able to see things like that. He doesn't read people any better than I read print, and that isn't your fault."

Mother glanced down at her hands and ran a finger over her wedding ring. The gold band had become loose in the last year, because of weight lost due to illness and worry. The small diamond winked in the light from the window. Dad's ambition had been a lot bigger than his pocketbook when he married.

"Your father and I went through a rough time while I was expecting Carl. I was young, just your age – and I was spoiled. I had to learn to be a wife. When Carl was born, he was… such a gift." She caressed the ring again. "I loved him so much I think your father felt left out. Perhaps that's why he and Carl have never been close. Alice, I can't tell your father this."

"I'll tell him." Alice struggled to keep her voice from trembling. Mothers and sons. She remembered how her heart had ached for Meg Cochrane at Michael-John's memorial service. Was it possible for a mother to love a child too much?

If so, I'm not going to let it happen to me.

Later, after the city police had come and asked a few cursory questions, Alice retreated upstairs. She needed to gather her strength to face Georgie and her father when they came home. She stepped into Carl's room and stood quietly, letting the familiar ache settle on her as it had all last winter, when they'd thought him dead.

When she was very small she and Georgie and Carl had played here, building blanket tents, turning the closet into a secret cave. Later, when they'd grown apart, Alice had only entered this room to sweep or dust. Carl had never put much of himself in it, nothing in the way of pictures or books or the usual things boys hoarded. When he left, it was as if he'd never lived there.

Alice opened the closet door and breathed in a whiff of stale liquor. Nothing here except a half-empty bottle tucked back in a corner and Carl's kit bag, still packed, on the shelf.

On an impulse, Alice lifted the bag onto the bed and began pulling out the worn khaki shirts and pants. Carl hadn't taken anything personal with him overseas, no reminders of home. It seemed he'd brought nothing personal back.

She stacked the folded clothes in a dresser drawer, closed it and turned the bag upside down to make sure it was empty. A small, partially-squashed cardboard box tumbled out and fell open on the bed. Alice let out a yelp of surprise.

The Military Cross. Carl had been decorated.

She picked up the strip of blue-edged ribbon with the silver Maltese Cross suspended at the end, ran a finger over the engraved crown on one of the cross's arms. Why hadn't they heard? The papers published the names of local men who'd been awarded battlefield honours. Alice remembered how her heart had leapt when Mother read Liam's name on a list of men mentioned in field dispatches. If the family had somehow missed Carl's name, surely a neighbour would have seen it and brought it to their attention. Perhaps Carl had received his medal after his escape, and the news hadn't filtered through military channels yet.

Alice descended the stairs slowly, the medal warm in her hand. She found her mother at the piano, leafing through a music book, her eyes still dark with sadness. Eyes that were meant to sparkle like her older daughter's. Georgie had inherited Mother's looks, Alice her temperament. The least likely temperament to match a hard-nosed, driven man like Dad.

Mother had married at eighteen. Alice didn't remember much about her mother's parents, but her aunt Sarah lived in the old family home in Bedford, a house no larger than this one but with a lot more elegance – a home where daughters grew up cultured and artistic.

No two people could be more different, but Mother and Dad had met and married within six months. A mistake? Alice couldn't call it that, not if her mother had felt the way she felt when Liam kissed her. An ordinary, everyday tragedy?

Definitely.

"Mother, look at this. I found it in Carl's room." Alice held out the medal. Her mother's breath caught.

"I don't understand. He never said—"

"I know." Alice laid the medal on the edge of the keyboard,

where it shone against the gleaming mahogany. "I dare anyone to say a word against Carl now. Dad, Georgie, I don't care who. I just dare them."

Misty-eyed, Mother rose from the piano bench, slipped the medal into her sweater pocket and disappeared upstairs. She didn't come down until suppertime. She waited until the meal was nearly over before pulling the medal from her pocket and laying it on the table.

"Frank, Georgie, Alice found this in Carl's room today."

Georgie let out a low whistle. "What do you know? Big brother is just full of surprises, isn't he?"

Mother's gaze connected with Dad's. "I'm afraid this isn't the only surprise we've had today. The police have been here. Carl walked out of the hospital last night. He's missing."

Dad picked the medal up by its ribbon, held it for a moment, then sighed heavily and laid it down again. His face showed more disgust than regret. "Who'd have thought it? Too bad he couldn't have shown himself a man here as well. Luck to him, wherever he's gone."

Mother's hand smacked the table. Everyone jumped. She faced Dad with blazing eyes, her voice ringing with anger. "He's going to come home one day, Frank, and I'm going to welcome him when he does. He's my first-born and I'm proud of him."

With the new strength she still didn't understand, Alice added "So am I." Dad looked from her to Mother, snatched his napkin from his lap and threw it down.

Proud of a brawling drunk." He stalked from the room, leaving silence in his wake. Mother didn't wilt. While a tight-lipped Georgie cleared the table, Alice got up and hugged her mother.

"You're right. He will come home some day, when he's ready. And Dad won't have a choice but to be proud of him, too."

Sunday morning, Alice woke with no desire to get out of

bed. Her head ached after a poor night's sleep. The excitement of finding Carl's medal had faded, leaving only gnawing worry. There'd been no word of him, and no one was looking very hard. The overflow of soldiers and sailors in the city kept the military and civilian police too stretched to have time to search for a man who didn't want to be found.

Dressed for church, Alice stood at her bureau, frowning at her reflection in the mirror. In spite of her smart wine-coloured suit and stylish black cloche with matching burgundy trim she felt drab and colourless, and she knew why.

It had only been three days since she'd seen Liam, but already the kiss they'd shared seemed more like a dream than a memory. Amazing how doubt could creep in so quickly. Within a few days he'd be home, and then as soon as he healed, he'd be gone.

St. Joseph's was about half-full when the O'Neills arrived – the Cochranes' pew still empty. A few minutes later, when her parents and Georgie were looking elsewhere, Alice craned her head. They were coming in now, Jack and Meg followed by Nolan and Ruth and the children, and behind them, on his crutches, Liam.

She snapped her gaze to the front before he saw her, but not before his mother did. Alice fought off a blush. When had he been released from the hospital? Would he stop to speak to her after the service?

He will if he wants to. Alice didn't look back again, but Mass was wasted on her. When it ended she took her time getting to the door, to make sure Liam got out ahead of her. Lagging behind Georgie and her parents, she emerged from the church and paused while her eyes adjusted to the bright sunlight. When the family in front of her descended the steps, leaving her a clear view, there Liam was on the sidewalk talking to a friend of his father's. His family must have gone on without him.

The older man moved away but Liam stayed there, waiting.

Mother, Dad and Georgie were already halfway down the hill. Alice reached the bottom of the steps with her heart thundering so she thought Liam must hear it. She could have been fifteen again.

When their gazes met, her excitement died. She saw no glow in Liam's eyes this time. He looked distinctly uncomfortable as he moved toward her.

"Alice, Dr. Gregg told me about Carl. Has he been found?"

From his cool tone, it seemed Liam did regret kissing her. Alice moistened her dry mouth and stood a little taller. She wouldn't let him see that it hurt.

"No. When did you get home?"

He swung a step closer. "Friday. I had to swear to Dr. Gregg on my grandfather's grave that I wouldn't move without my crutches and that I'd follow his instructions to the letter, but he agreed to release me a little early. I wanted to make sure you were all right, that you weren't in trouble at home."

That would be like him. At heart, he hadn't changed since that day he'd touched her years ago. Simple acts of kindness, nothing more. Alice smiled for him. "Dad still doesn't know I visited Carl in the hospital, but even if he did, you wouldn't have to worry about me, Liam. Dad's never laid a hand on me or Georgie, and not on Carl very often."

She saw his relief. Wondered at it. Had he really thought Dad would beat her?

"Good. How's your mother handling the news about Carl?"

"Not too badly, all things considered. Something's happened that made it a bit easier."

"What's that?"

"We found out that Carl brought home a Military Cross. We've got no idea how he earned it, but I suppose we'll find out soon enough. So, Mother has something to be proud of. It helps."

Liam whistled, reminding her of Georgie. "You don't say. I

didn't know he was an officer until Dr. Gregg told me."

"Neither did we, until he got home and we saw his uniforms. He never told us." The truth was, Carl had only written home once, before he was sent into action for the first time, a letter full of bravado. Apparently it hadn't failed him.

"I told him he had guts." Liam came another step closer. "Alice, I want you to promise me something. If Carl comes back, or if things get bad at home for any reason, I want you to come to me."

The sudden intensity of his gaze, the emotion behind the words, threw her off balance. How could she go to him when he was a thousand miles away? "But you'll be leaving soon."

He flushed as if he'd spoken without thinking. "While I'm here, then."

With every second she spent looking into his eyes, Alice's confusion grew. What was he thinking? If he regretted kissing her, why was he doing this?

"Liam, I –"

"Promise."

Alice took a deep breath. This might be the last time she spoke to him. She didn't want him to remember her voice trembling.

"All right, I promise."

Liam nodded. "Good. I should be going, or Mum will send Nolan after me. She's tougher than Doctor Gregg. Goodbye, Alice." He swung by her. Before rounding the corner, he stopped and looked over his shoulder.

"Remember, you promised."

Chapter 11

She'd promised. Until – unless – she needed him, the best thing he could do for her was leave her alone.

Nolan was at work, Drew at school and Ruth had taken Emily downtown to run some errands. The quiet of the dull grey afternoon settled heavily on Liam, laden with memories of chilly autumn days in Bea's flat, with a coal fire on the hearth and cock-a-leekie soup for supper. Days so full of life and laughter they seemed unreal when he returned to the grim reality of the trenches. Days of dreaming about bringing Bea home, introducing her to his parents. Nights when they'd made love until they fell asleep, sated and spent. All a lie.

He'd seen the hurt on Alice's face yesterday after church. The permanent kind. She'd never know what a favour he'd done her by backing off. She'd likely be engaged by spring. He'd better spend his pity on Carl. A man didn't come home with a Military Cross unless he'd earned it. Sure, he'd turned his back on help, but only because he was too raw to accept it.

The thought of Carl gave Liam an idea. Perhaps he could do Alice a favour. A former Army comrade of his lived down on Granville Street. Barney didn't have much to fill his days. He liked company, and not much that went on downtown escaped him. He might have heard something. Liam put on a jacket, turned his back on the empty house and caught a tram downtown.

Saturday shoppers added colour to the dark storefronts of brick and stone. Below Barrington, closer to the Harbour, the shopping district gave way to warehouses, ship's chandleries and, here and there, a small shop with its windows artfully covered with posters advertising 'bon tabac.' The young ladies from Montreal who ran these shops did sell tobacco, but their real business went on in back rooms, each furnished with its couch, red lamp and bowl of disinfectant. Liam had tried them once or twice when he was newly home and still aching for Bea's touch, but not since he'd moved in with Nolan and Ruth. They'd never tolerate him buying women, and that kind of escape was more costly and even more fleeting than what he could find in a bottle.

He climbed a set of stairs to a flat over one of the tobacco shops on Granville and rapped on the door with a crutch. He heard slow, halting footsteps, then a familiar voice, harsh with sleep.

"Where do little boys go who tell lies?"

"To the front, sir." The joke came from a cartoon Liam had seen in *Punch* overseas, early on when a lot of youngsters lied about their age to get a taste of the adventure of war. The guard chain on the door rattled as it slid back.

"Tenth?"

"Fifteenth."

"Stand to!"

The door opened. Barney Race, once Liam's comrade in the Twenty-Fifth Battalion, Canadian Expeditionary Force – tenth plus fifteenth – leaned against the door frame. Thinning sandy hair on end, shirtless, wearing a rumpled pair of old khakis, Barney put on a shaky grin.

"Liam, what have you done to yourself?"

"Doctor got hold of me again, trying to give me a new leg."

Barney held the door open. "Just this morning I said to myself, 'I haven't seen hide nor hair of Liam for three weeks. He must have found himself a girl, and she must be good.' Come in."

The flat smelled of cigarettes, stale rum and despair. A cot in one corner, a scarred, wobbly drop-leaf table with two chairs and a couple of packing crates made up the furnishings in this room. Barney shuffled over and dropped onto the cot.

Wounded in the back at the Somme, the same day Liam had been hit and Michael-John killed, Barney walked painfully on good days. He had no family, so he spent his days drinking away his pension and most of what he made bootlegging. He could have afforded better lodgings, but he just didn't give a damn.

Liam returned the grin. "I should be that lucky. How've you been, Barney?"

"Can't complain." Barney took in the remains of Liam's bruises and shook his head. "You've been in some kind of a brawl, I'd say."

"Yeah, that's what landed me in the hospital. I need something for the pain."

Barney answered with a bark of laughter. "And I thought this was a social call."

"It is. Have I come at a good time?"

"Yeah, sure. I got a shipment in last night, from my Boston cousin. Tennessee whiskey."

"That's music to my ears. A couple of bottles for now."

"In the other room, in the blanket box."

The small back room held nothing but a heavy, battered wooden chest. Barney only kept a few bottles stowed away here. Friends stored the rest for him. Liam didn't know where and didn't want to know. He stuffed two newspaper-wrapped bottles in the small satchel he'd brought along. In the other room, he passed his money to Barney.

"Tell your cousin thanks."

"Sure, next time I see him. He was leaving port for home this morning. Now sit down and pass the time of day, Liam."

Grateful to rest, Liam lowered himself onto a chair and leaned his crutches against the wall. "I'm wondering if you've heard anything of an old neighbour of mine, Carl O'Neill. He got home since I saw you last, and he's got the shakes pretty bad. He was in one hell of a scrap last week and ended up in Camp Hill, in my room. He walked out in the night a few days ago, and it wouldn't surprise me if he's lying low somewhere down here."

Barney shook his head. "I heard about that little party, but nothing since. I'll keep my ears open."

"Thanks."

They chatted for twenty minutes or so, rehashing stories of their first days in Europe, when they'd both been full of fear but also full of purpose. Now, for Barney, the purpose was gone. It chilled Liam to think that he'd started walking down the same path when he arrived home. If not for his family, he figured he'd be standing in Barney's shoes now.

Out on the street again, Liam stood, uncertain. Home, or down to Hollis Street, where chances were he'd find more familiar faces? Home, where Nolan and Ruth and the children would banish the thought of what his life would have become without them. Home.

That evening after supper, he took Nolan aside. "Could I drive you to work tomorrow and borrow the car? I want to drive out to Prospect and have a talk with Jess."

Nolan glanced out the sitting room window at his second-hand Model T. "Are you sure you're up to it? The road out there can be rough."

Liam rolled his eyes. "You sound like Mum again. If the doctors couldn't kill me, Liza Jane won't."

Nolan studied Liam's face for a moment, as if he saw something new and different. His worried frown lifted to a smile. "You're welcome, then, if you think the old jade will get you there." He clapped Liam on the shoulder. "Don't worry about me getting to work. I'll manage. You can get an early start. Say hello to Jess for us."

Ruth saw him off in the morning, after an early breakfast. With her hands on Emily's shoulders, she watched as Liam cranked Liza Jane until her motor came to life, coughing. Bought last year after Dad's elderly mare died of colic, the car had plenty of quirks – a personality of her own.

Ruth's brow furrowed with concern. "Liam, I'm not sure this is a good idea. Why not wait a couple of weeks?"

"Because a couple of weeks from now it will be a lot colder." He hoisted himself to the seat. Dr. Gregg would scream bloody murder to see him, but with his visit with Barney fresh in his mind, Liam didn't feel like waiting. He needed to start taking steps toward his future. "Don't worry, Ruth. I'll be home by suppertime."

At first he had to give all his attention to the car. Liam had only driven once or twice since coming home and not often before going overseas, as the family hadn't owned a car. Working Liza Jane's three pedals with one foot took some concentration. Fortunately, once he left the city for the winding wagon track that followed the coastline southwest from Halifax, he could cruise.

Travel over the dry summer had left the track hard and relatively smooth. The day was fine and breezy and the road worth the journey, taking Liam through small fishing villages fronting on sparkling water. He couldn't remember when he'd last been out for a drive like this. The simple freedom of it quickened his pulse.

As the feel of the clutch and gears came back to him he let his mind wander, until he caught himself imagining Alice beside him, brook-brown eyes sparkling, hair whipping around her face. Liam put her firmly from his thoughts. He was making this trip for a reason.

He wished he could have called first, but Jess didn't have a phone. Liam had only spoken to his cousin once since coming home. The twenty-odd miles between Prospect and Halifax loomed large in the winter, and summer was too busy for Jess, between fishing and the boat shop. He might not need any help, but the only way to find out was to ask.

When Liam came to the top of the hill above Prospect, he idled the car and let his gaze sweep the cluster of weathered buildings and church spires reaching for the sky, backed by the foam-topped Atlantic. The deep, rhythmic crashing of the surf carried up to him on the wind, freighted with memories of the summer he'd spent here, a lifetime ago. Why hadn't he felt the pull of it then?

You were a kid. Seventeen, looking no further ahead than Saturday night. There'd been more money to be made and more girls to chase in Richmond.

He let Liza Jane coast down the hill to Jess's grey-shingled house, perched on the edge of the bay with the shop beside it and a strip of rocky beach behind. A little girl in pigtails and a red calico dress opened the door and poked her head out. That would be Maud, Jess's youngest. Liam remembered her as a baby not yet walking. She must be close to five now.

"Mum, there's a man here."

Fanny's head appeared above her daughter's. Surprise swiftly changed to shock. Jess's wife hadn't seen Liam since before he left for Europe. This was the hard part about reconnecting with people. They couldn't help reminding him how much he'd changed.

"Good Lord, Liam, is that you?"

"In the flesh." He eased himself from the car, balanced on his good leg and reached for his crutches. His hip felt the journey, but not too badly. "How are you, Fanny?"

With her black hair and eyes, rosy complexion and ample figure, Fanny always reminded Liam of a plump, glossy robin. She almost hopped as she hurried across the lawn to hug him.

"I wouldn't have known you." She stepped back and looked him up and down. Liam headed off her questions.

"You haven't changed at all. Is Jess around?"

"Yes, he's in the shop. Maud, run and get your father. He'll be wanting a cup of tea about now anyway."

The little girl scampered to the shop and came out with her father in tow. Jess's round face split in a wide grin. Broad, burly and as dark as his wife, he crossed the yard with his hand extended, welcome in his deep blue eyes. "Good to see you, Liam."

"You too, Jess."

His cousin's grip nearly made Liam wince. Few who hadn't seen it would believe that Jess's big, rough hands could work artistry on wood. Inside, seated at the table with tea and hot baking-powder biscuits, he looked Liam over.

"You weren't on crutches the last time I saw you."

"I won't be in another week or so. Just had some more work on the leg. How about you, Jess? Are you busy these days?"

"Busy?" Fanny snorted as she buttered a biscuit for Maud. "Sometimes I think I'm a widow, and all the time I worry about him making me one by working himself into his grave."

Jess smiled and pinched her arm. "It isn't that bad, Fanny-girl, but I had enough to do and then some over the summer, too much to do much fishing. I expect I'll be kept out of trouble through the winter, too. I've a few mackerel boats lined up for repairs, and one that needs a new deck and planking from stem to stern."

The morning took on an added glow, brighter than any morning since Liam had come home. He heard it in his voice, wondered at it. How long had it been since he'd felt like this?

"Could you use some help? I wouldn't expect you to pay me until I can be of some real use, of course. I'm hoping that won't be long."

Jess held his gaze. Liam's didn't waver. Finally his cousin sat back and sipped his tea. "You're serious about this, aren't you?"

Jess didn't waste time making up his mind about people, and not everyone passed muster with him, but Liam knew he had. He drew a relieved breath.

"Yeah. I don't think the rail yard will be the place for me now, and I don't want to end up stuck in an office."

"No, I can't see that either. When you were here before and left at the end of the summer, I wondered why. You have a knack."

Liam refilled his cup and smiled, a smile he felt deep inside. "I was seventeen, Jess. I had other things on my mind."

Jess shook his head and chuckled. "I don't think it had much to do with your mind. Come out whenever you care to, Liam, and welcome. We've got a spare room upstairs for you. It's good to see you getting back on your feet again."

They finished their tea and headed back out to the shop. Sitting on a sawhorse, Liam breathed in the scents of sawdust and salt water and glanced around at the tools hanging on nails on the walls, at the wooden jigs Jess had made to help him cut curves, at the steam box at the end of the shed. Liam would be starting at the beginning, as much an apprentice as Jess's thirteen-year-old son, but it didn't matter. This was where he wanted to be.

"Jess, when will you be coming into the city again?"

Jess looked up from the dovetail joint he was making and put down his coping saw. "Saturday. Fanny wants to do some shopping."

"Tell me where to meet you, and I'll come back with you then."

Chapter 12

"Try it again, Alice. You've got the notes, but your phrasing is a little rough."

Alice started over, trying to shape the musical phrases of *Beautiful Dreamer* more carefully. This time when she finished, her mother nodded satisfaction. "Much better. Now the Chopin."

The Chopin nocturne was much more challenging. Alice played it slowly, not worrying about tempo. It sounded stiff, but she didn't hit a wrong note.

"Alice, are you reading as you play?" Her mother joined her on the piano bench.

"No. I can't keep up."

"With your memory, I don't know that it matters."

"Maybe not." Alice rose and closed the piano. "We'd better start supper. Dad and Georgie will be home soon."

In the kitchen, she watched her mother out of the corner of her eye as she pared potatoes. The new medication the doctor had prescribed at Mother's last appointment seemed to be working well. Her colour was better and she hadn't had a bad day in over a week.

The remains of a sunset lit the brooding clouds in the western sky and the reflected light made the kitchen seem golden. The days were growing short as the year grew old. It didn't seem possible that three weeks had passed since she'd spoken to Liam outside church that Sunday.

His plans must have been made then, but he hadn't seen fit to tell her. He'd been absent from church the next week, and that

Tuesday Georgie had come home from a Red Cross meeting with the news.

"It seems Liam isn't going to his sister's after all. His mother told Mrs. Henneberry tonight that he's gone out to Prospect to spend the winter working in his cousin's boat shop."

So he was twenty-five miles away instead of a thousand, but it made no difference. Even if she hadn't heard the undercurrent of hope in Georgie's voice, actions said it all. He didn't consider his plans any of Alice's business. Liam's impulsive demand that she go to him if Carl returned had been just that, impulsive.

It had hurt so much to see Liam when he first came home, changed in every way. Alice couldn't help but be glad that he'd found something he wanted – even though it wasn't her – but the thought of the coming winter chilled her to the bone.

At the sound of a car slowing and idling out front, Mother dropped her paring knife. "That's not your father's cab." Alice stomach fluttered as it always did now when anyone called unexpectedly.

Carl.

"I'll see who it is."

She opened the door to a young city policeman with a canvas satchel in his hand. Red-faced from the cold and from obvious nerves, he stepped inside at her invitation. Alice guessed he hadn't been on the job very long. Her mouth went dry with dread.

"What is it, officer?"

He cleared his throat. "I should speak to your parents, miss."

"My father isn't home. You'd better speak to me."

The young man swallowed, looking more uncomfortable by the second. "Very well. Is Lieutenant Carl O'Neill your brother?"

"Yes, he is."

He held up the satchel. "Do you recognize these things?"

Alice's stomach turned over when she peered inside and saw

the clothes she'd taken to Carl when he was in the hospital. "Yes, they're my brother's."

His flush deepened. "I'm sorry, miss. One of our patrolmen found these things down on the waterfront, along with these." He drew a small brown envelope from his coat pocket and pulled out a thin cord.

It held Carl's identification tags.

"I'm afraid it looks as if your brother may have drowned."

When Alice spoke, her voice sounded strange and distant to her ears. "*Drowned*? Are you saying there's been an accident?"

Looking even more distressed, the young man shook his head. "No, miss."

His meaning slowly seeped into Alice's numb mind. She pressed a hand to her stomach, afraid she'd be sick right there in front of him. "You think he – Oh, dear Lord."

She took the cord from his hand. The tags dangled at the end, two small discs made of some kind of cardboard-like fibre with a galvanized coating, one a red circle, the other a green octagon. Stephen had told her once that the red tag was to be removed for administrative purposes when a soldier was killed, while the green tag was to be buried with the body.

They were crude things compared to the beautiful medal Carl had earned, but the tags had actually *been* there, around his neck, when he earned his medal. They bore mute witness to everything he'd endured, everything that had driven him to—

No. Carl was nothing if not a fighter. She couldn't believe he'd commit suicide. Either he'd run into foul play, or he'd chosen this way to simply disappear. A cruel way, but he'd let the family believe him dead before. Why not again?

Pull yourself together, Alice. Mother is going to need you.

She tucked the tags in the pocket of her skirt and steadied her voice. "Was – was there a note?"

"No. Only what I've shown you."

Her mother's footsteps sounded in the hall behind her,

followed by a shocked gasp. "Alice, has Carl been found?"

"No, Mother. Just some of his things." She took the canvas bag from the policeman. "Thank you, officer. What's your name?"

"Conroy, miss. If there's anything else you can tell us about your brother—"

"I'm sorry. We've heard nothing since he was reported missing from the hospital. If we think of anything, we'll let you know. Thank you, Officer Conroy. Good night."

Clearly aware that he was being hustled away, he left. When Alice turned from the door her mother stood waiting, braced for what was to come.

"Tell me."

They'd both learned over the past year that imagination was worse than the truth, so Alice told her, avoiding any hint of what the police had already assumed. "The clothes I took to Carl in the hospital were found in this bag down on the waterfront, along with his dog tags. I – I think he's left us again."

Tears came to her mother's eyes. "Alice, he never really came back. Now he never will."

"You're getting it, Liam. Try again, and take your time."

Liam took the scrap of oak planking Jess handed him and made a few passes with the plane to take off most of the roughness along one edge. Then he switched to a finer plane and ran it over the same surface until it shone like silk. Jess looked over his shoulder.

"Check the thickness. It looks a bit uneven to me."

Liam held the thin board up, scanned its length and swore under his breath. Jess was right. Grinning, he gathered an armful of scraps from the shop floor and dumped them in a pile by Liam's chair. "Practice."

Liam rose, stretched and took a few steps. His leg would

bear his weight now. He still needed his cane to walk any distance, but he vowed that by Christmas, he would walk with ease – without it. Another couple of months. The way the weeks were flying by, the time would pass before he knew it.

It seemed he'd come to Prospect yesterday, and it seemed like he'd been here forever. He spent his days in the shop and his evenings with the family. Liam didn't get a whiff of pity from any of them. Jess expected him to work as hard as he was able. The children, Everett and Clara and little Maud, accepted him as an uncle, while Fanny ruled them all with an iron hand so well hidden in a velvet glove that Jess rarely noticed.

Liam moved to the window to watch the sun sink into the bay. It cast shifting ribbons of scarlet and orange on the smooth waves that creamed and broke on the shore. This was the time of day when he missed Nolan and Ruth and the children the most. Odd for Liam to be homesick when he'd left Richmond because he no longer felt at home there. Or was he just tired of living in other people's houses?

Jess lit the lantern and hung it from its hook in the rafters of the shop. They worked for another hour, until the stars pricked the black velvet of the moonless sky and scattered gems of light on the bay. After supper, Liam stayed at the kitchen table with a cup of tea and the Halifax paper a neighbour had brought over at lunchtime. He scanned a page of local news and burned his mouth with hot tea when a picture of Carl O'Neill, in uniform, caught his eye.

Decorated Soldier Missing, Feared Dead

Personal belongings found last night on the Halifax waterfront have been confirmed as belonging to Lieutenant Carl O'Neill of Russell Street, who recently returned home from the front. Lieutenant O'Neill went missing a month ago from Camp Hill hospital, where he was recovering from

> *injuries sustained in an altercation with men city police say are known to them.*
>
> *This paper has also learned that shortly before returning home, Lieutenant O'Neill was awarded the Military Cross for gallantry in the field. In September of 1916, at the battle of Guillemont, he and his men found themselves trapped and thrown into confusion by enemy fire. The Lieutenant devised an escape route, rallied his men and led them out of danger, his bravery resulting in him receiving a wound in the shoulder and being captured by the enemy. He later escaped, and had returned to Halifax on recuperative leave...*

Liam stared at the picture. It must have been taken before Carl shipped out. Unsmiling – eyes shadowed by the brim of his cap – he faced the camera like he might face an enemy.

Liam had heard of Guillemont, a nasty affair fought over miserable terrain. Carl had come out of that hell shining, but his medal hadn't kept hell from catching up to him.

When they pulled what was left of Carl's body from the Harbour, who would have to identify him? Alice?

What a waste. What a goddamn waste!

Bile rose in Liam's throat. He threw down the newspaper, climbed the stairs to his room and rummaged in his duffle bag for one of the bottles of whiskey he'd bought from Barney. Liam hadn't felt the need for it since coming out here. Until tonight. He sat on the bed, poured a couple of inches of amber liquor into his water glass and tossed it down. It burned its way to his stomach and nearly came right back up. Gagging, he clenched his fists and held on until he could breathe again, then sank back on the bed and closed his eyes.

As the whiskey seeped into his blood, Liam broke into a sweat. His heart thundered, and his breathing quickened to panicked gasps when he heard them.

Barney. Michael-John. A chorus of shouts and whispers ringing up and down the line.

"Here we go!"

"Our Father who art in Heaven –"

"Join the party, boys!"

"Thy kingdom come –"

He saw as well as heard them, all the men he remembered. In desperation he squeezed his eyelids tighter, but he couldn't shut out the visions any more than he could the voices.

Blue sky ranged above him, sliced by the dark edge of the trench. Unbelievably, a bird's trill rose above the din of artillery fire. Liam choked on the reek of fetid mud, putrefying corpses and primal terror. His own shout rang out with the others.

"Michael-John!"

"Here, Liam. See you at suppertime!"

Drenched with sweat, Liam lunged upright and opened his eyes. The disembodied voices – most of which would never be heard again outside of a nightmare – faded into the darkness.

He pulled a match from the box on the nightstand and fumbled with the match-safe on the coal-oil lamp. The match went out before his shaking fingers could get it to the wick. He tried again and managed to get the lamp lit. As its welcome glow filled the room, he curled himself up tight and laid his head on his knees.

"Son of a bitch!" Liam pounded his fists on his mattress. "Not now!" He had too much at stake here. He scrambled to his feet and started pacing while his mind whirled, desperate to grasp something… anything… to anchor it in the here and now.

Alice. He pictured her, tall and slender as a reed, her voice as soft as her lips, soft and sweet. She could never be his – maybe no woman ever could be for more than a few hours here and there – but Liam's whole mind, body and spirit called her to him as a talisman against his memories. He felt her in his arms, tasted her on his tongue, until he was lost in a haze of longing that pushed everything else aside.

At last, knowing sleep wouldn't come any other way, he undressed, grabbed a washcloth and used his hand to ease his body's need. Soul-deep loneliness took its place. He tipped some water into the wash-basin, washed and crawled back under Fanny's quilts, suddenly exhausted.

After extracting that promise from Alice – an impulse he should have let die at birth – he was more or less duty bound to see her, to find out how she was coping with the news about Carl. Nothing was certain, of course, but Liam wouldn't give good odds that she'd see her brother alive again. He remembered the look in Carl's eyes when he hit her.

So you'll see her once more. Liam owed her that much. He also owed it to her to make sure that was all the involvement he had with her, but that didn't keep him from falling asleep with his thoughts wrapped around her.

Alice huddled deeper into her blankets, clinging to her dream. She lay in Liam's arms, his body warm and solid beneath hers, his scent surrounding her. The feel of his chest hair against her cheek, the rhythmic rise and fall of his breathing – though she'd never experienced this kind of intimacy with anyone, it felt so real. If only it didn't have to end.

On the edge of sleep, she brushed her fingers across her pillow case and felt the texture of his hair, soft and coarse at the same time. She kept her eyes closed until the sensation faded, then opened them to the sober light of a grey autumn Saturday morning.

Was dreaming of him worth the disappointment of waking? If Alice could have answered that question, perhaps Liam would haunt her sleep less often. Since she'd seen him last, she'd dreamed of him almost every night and wakened with the same leaden sense of emptiness.

He and Carl were both gone. The promise Liam had drawn

from her meant nothing now. She couldn't go to him with her grief, because that would be to admit what she wouldn't admit until she saw her brother's dead body with her own eyes. That thought tore her heart in two. Liam had spoken on an impulse born of the passing attraction between them, nothing more. He hadn't shared his future plans with her because she had no part in them.

Alice rose and tiptoed to the bathroom. No one else was up yet. She had time for a bath before starting breakfast. Steam clouded the bathroom mirror as the tub filled. The furnace fire in the cellar had gone out, but the water in the tank of the coal-fired heater was still hot. Dad would stoke it again when he got up to make sure there was enough hot water for the morning.

She lifted her nightgown over her head, pinned up her braid and tipped some lemon verbena-scented bath salts into the tub. The fragrance rose to greet her as she stepped in. She sank down, leaned back and closed her eyes.

Instead of soothing the ache deep inside her, the gentle lapping of the water on her body only made it worse. Biting back a sigh of frustration, she washed quickly and reached for her towel. The rough scraping of the cotton brought the blood to her skin. The memory of her dream made it run faster.

Back in her room, Alice took off her robe and confronted her fresh-scrubbed, nude reflection in the mirror. She saw a graceful young woman's body with creamy skin, long, shapely legs, and small, elegant breasts, a body she had no need to be ashamed of. The same was true of her face, except for the sadness in her eyes. Ten years from now would she be standing in the same place, a brittle, dried-up woman with only a drab middle age to look forward to?

She squared her shoulders and shook her hair back. No. She'd keep her banner of youth flying in the face of whatever came. She'd never believe that Carl had taken his own life, and she'd always believe that her love for Liam went with him every day, colouring his life with her caring even though it wasn't returned. If that and her music had to be enough, it would be.

She planned to take a trip down to the city market this morning. She used the tortoiseshell combs Aunt Sarah had given her for her birthday to fasten her hair in shining swirls, put on her prettiest lace-edged corset and thought about silk stockings, but settled for lisle – more practical. By the time she'd dressed in her ivory middy blouse and royal blue serge skirt, her self-respect had crept back. She gave her waistband a final tug to straighten it and headed downstairs.

After breakfast Alice put on her scarlet wool jacket, grabbed her umbrella and caught the tram downtown. The market set up every week at the junction where Brunswick Street branched to follow the curve of Citadel Hill. Vendors overflowed the large warehouse and set up their stalls outdoors, hawking meat and farm produce, dried and fresh fish from the villages down the shore, baskets and crafts of all kinds from the Indian and black communities outside the city. Old met new here, with wagons and carts interspersed among trucks, all crowded onto narrow streets never intended for so much traffic.

The sky threatened, but the rain held off. Alice tucked her umbrella into the basket on her arm and eased into the press of shoppers. A gust of wind swirled uphill from the Harbour, carrying a complex mixture of odours: horses, humans and everything they were selling, along with a good measure of dust from the street. Alice got grit in her eyes, pulled out her handkerchief and wiped it away, then stopped and wiped her eyes again. Could it be?

Yes. Climbing down from the seat of a cart full of dried cod, carrying his cane but not using it, was Liam.

Her heart gave one great bound, then skipped ahead. He limped, but not very badly. Hatless, his gold-bronze hair glowed in contrast against the black of his pea-jacket. She'd know him at a glance anywhere – and would for the rest of her life.

Duffle bag over his shoulder, Liam took a couple of steps before he saw her. When he did, Alice saw his shoulders stiffen and his stomach draw in with a swift breath. He quickened his pace. With her pulse beating a rapid tattoo, she stepped into a space between two vendors and waited for him.

Her heart stuttered again when he got closer. Liam had put on some muscle and his face had filled out a bit, but more than anything Alice sensed a new energy coming from him, a sense of purpose. His work must agree with him, but he looked a little tired.

He stopped a pace away. Tension hummed in the air between them, so thick Alice thought everyone nearby must feel it. Their gazes met and locked. Her knees trembled. If only he weren't so dear to her. She swallowed and moistened her mouth.

"Liam, I... It's good to see you."

"Alice. A neighbour of Jess's was bringing a load of fish up the shore, so I got a chance to come home on his boat." He fussed with the strap on his duffle bag, looked down briefly. "I read about Carl in the paper. I'm so sorry. Have you heard anything?"

"No." At a loss for words, Alice stood staring into his eyes, entranced as always by the pattern of brown and green and gold. Liam shifted his weight and broke eye contact. He certainly didn't seem pleased to see her.

"Don't give up hope."

"We aren't."

"How's your mother handling it?"

"As well as can be expected."

After another awkward pause, Liam reached out as if he meant to take her hand. Instead, he pulled his hand back again and sighed. "Are you on your way home?"

Alice glanced down at the empty shopping basket on her arm. Hadn't he noticed it? "Are you?"

"Yeah."

She'd raise eyebrows at home returning empty-handed, but it was all the invitation Alice needed. She stepped out from between the stalls and started north along Brunswick. Without comment, Liam walked beside her.

She watched him out of the corner of her eye. Silent, he seemed locked in a struggle with emotions she couldn't guess. *Does he care? Like I do?* Alice fought to contain the hope that bubbled from some secret spring deep within her. Meanwhile, some primal part of her rejoiced at his nearness, at the strong lines of his profile. So close she could reach over and touch him. This was the Liam she'd held in her heart all these years, the Liam who loved her – in her dreams. He used his cane, but he walked so quickly she had to work to keep up.

But he'd had surgery six weeks ago. He shouldn't be walking across town like this. When they came to a tram stop, she touched his hand.

"Liam, slow down and let me catch my breath."

He stopped beside an old elm. Alice looked up at the waving lace the leafless branches formed against the grey sky. "Winter will be here before we know it. So... how've you been?"

Liam shrugged. "I've been well. I like working with Jess. I'll like it more when I know what I'm doing." He laughed.

Alice studied his face and restrained another urge to touch him, to smooth away the fatigue she saw there. "I think maybe you're working too hard."

"I need to start making up for lost time." He hesitated, obviously struggling for words. "So you know now how Carl earned his medal. Alice, whatever happens, try not to judge him too harshly. I can't."

Something in Liam's tone wrung her heart. It implied something so bleak. Before she could stop herself, she took his hand. "Yes, we saw the piece in the paper. Mother read it to me. As for judging him, neither can I. I only wish he'd found his strength, like you."

He pulled his hand away, incredulous. "Me?"

He meant it. He really didn't see how far he'd come. Aching for him, Alice nodded. "Liam, haven't you looked at yourself lately? You're healing and you've found something worthwhile to do. I remember what you looked like when you got home—"

"I haven't changed that much."

His shoulders were high and tight, his jaw set. Alice would have let things lie, but behind Liam's stubborn front Alice saw the same raw longing she'd seen before. It gave her the boldness to lay her hand against his chest. Through the wool of his jacket, she felt his heart racing. Hers began to beat like the wings of a captive bird against its cage.

"If you say so." She slid her hand up to his shoulder. He flinched at her touch. "Liam, what are you afraid of?"

His hand covered hers. "Hurting you."

That just wouldn't do. As a child, Alice had lost her father's respect because he had to protect her. She wouldn't take that risk with Liam. She touched a finger to the corner of his mouth.

"That's my risk. I'm willing to take it."

Heat flared in Liam's eyes before he closed them and bent his head. His breath was warm, his lips cool as they brushed hers once, then again. Alice's hands curled into fists as she waited for more, aching to reach for him, afraid he'd pull away. He did, with a sigh that voiced her frustration.

"Alice, this makes no sense. I don't have a home of my own. I don't have a paying job. My pension will be ending soon, now that I'm fit to work, and when it does, Jess won't be able to give me much more than room and board."

"That doesn't worry me." And that kind of practicality didn't explain his wariness. Liam was his father's son. To both, obstacles existed only to be overcome. "Is that really what's bothering you?"

He turned away with a shrug. "Isn't it enough?"

Alice touched his hand to make him face her. "That isn't

answering my question." Liam's brows drew together in a frown.

"You don't know me."

True enough. Or was it? They'd rarely spoken, but she'd watched Liam for years. She knew how he worked, how he played, how he behaved with his family. Had she known any more about any man she'd gone out with?

"So tell me what I should know."

His eyes searched hers, like they had at the hospital when he talked about innocence. He shook his head. "Ask Ruth what I'm like to live with."

Alice tilted her chin and grinned. "I don't need to. I'm sure you're impossible. You were born with a temper, and it grew with you." She sobered and held his gaze. "Liam, the last time I saw you, why did you ask me to come to you for help if I needed it?"

He frowned again. "Because I won't let Carl or anyone else abuse you."

"Because you care about me."

A flush crept up Liam's neck. "In a way."

In a way. Alice took a deep breath and took the risk. "You told me I was strong, remember? Were you lying?"

Liam glared at her. "Of course not."

"Prove it."

With her next breath Alice found herself in his arms. She got one glimpse of hazel eyes that had darkened to smoke before he fisted a hand in her hair and covered her mouth with his.

He kissed her. Oh, how he kissed her. All Alice could do was cling to him while the force of his need – and her own – overwhelmed her. Then, in a heartbeat, everything changed. The hand in her hair gentled. The kiss turned slow and sensual. As Liam relaxed, Alice melted against him, her arms around his neck. He held her close and pressed his lips to her hair.

"Did I prove it?" He spoke on a shaky exhale.

Alice's voice was no steadier. "I'd say so." Strong? She must be, or she wouldn't be standing right now. No one had ever kissed her with such fierce, possessive intensity.

When she looked up, Liam's eyes held a new softness. "Alice, you've been on my mind since the day you kissed me in the hospital. If you won't run away like you should, I guess there's not much I can do about it."

"No, there isn't." Heart singing, she reached up to kiss him again.

Welcome home, Liam.

Chapter 13

Liam blinked in disbelief when he realized they were passing the North Street train station. He didn't recall getting there. He might have been seventeen again, walking home with Barbara Purcell after his first passionate kiss.

Passionate? Jesus, Mary and Joseph!

He'd come home to see Alice, but he hadn't expected her to knock him over. He hadn't been prepared to lose his breath when he saw her at the market. He hadn't imagined she'd respond to his kisses like that.

Maybe she was a lot more like Georgie than he thought, but Georgie had never looked at him like Alice did, with a glow in her eyes that made his stomach knot with fear.

Lost in thought, she kept pace with him, her hand soft and warm in his. Liam watched her out of the corner of his eye while conflicting emotions pulled him in every direction, and a part of his heart he'd thought dead and buried woke to raw, aching life.

He promised himself that if he hurt her, it would be honestly.

"Alice, I want to take you home and talk to your parents. I don't want anyone to think we've been hiding anything."

She looked up at him, her eyes serious. "I don't want that either. Especially with Georgie."

Liam thought over the time he'd spent with Georgie, what he'd done and said. He had no regrets, unless it made trouble for Alice. "Do you think she'll be hurt?"

"Yes, but I don't think she'll show it."

"Did she tell you that she and I talked?"

"Yes."

"Good. Georgie and I never lied to each other. If anyone gives you trouble over this, they're going to have to answer to me." Liam intended to make that clear to her father, especially. He hadn't forgotten what Carl had told him in the hospital. It was time Alice received some respect.

Both nervous, they talked little on the rest of the journey. They could have cut the waiting short by taking a tram, but Liam needed the time. He'd forgotten how frightening hope could be. Maybe Alice felt the same way, as she raised no objection to the walk.

When they got to her house, he took her in his arms. He'd overtaxed his leg a bit, but adrenalin kept pain at bay.

"Ready?"

Alice smiled and touched her lips to his. "Ready."

They walked around to the kitchen door. As luck would have it, the family was there, with the table set for an afternoon snack. Liam and Alice stepped inside hand in hand.

A fierce blush swept over Georgie's face. Her father's eyes flashed, then turned cold. Her mother's widened with shock. Liam took a deep breath.

"Hello, everyone. Alice and I need to talk to you."

No one answered. He swallowed and went on. "First, I was really sorry to hear about Carl. There's nothing more I can say, except I know that whatever happened, he couldn't help himself. As for why I'm here... While I was laid up, I did a lot of thinking. A lot of that thinking was about Alice." He stopped to choose his words. He didn't want to give away that fact that he and Alice had talked in the hospital, because she wasn't supposed to have been there. "Since I've been out at my cousin's, I've kept thinking about her. I got a chance home this morning. We ran into each other at the market and it turns out that she's been thinking of me, too. So, we're going to be seeing each other."

Still nothing but shocked silence from everyone. He took

another calming breath. "Neither of us wants to hurt anyone, but we aren't going to go behind your backs. Georgie, I never meant to hurt you, and I've never lied to you. Not once. I hope you believe me, because I want us to be friends."

Before Georgie could answer her father spoke, his voice cutting. "Liam, you aren't the man I thought you were. How long is it going to be before you can support yourself, let alone a wife? Long enough for another girl to take your fancy, probably. And Alice – you should be ashamed of yourself."

Anger boiled up inside Liam. He would have said something harsh, but Alice squeezed his hand and spoke up.

"That isn't fair, Dad. I stayed away from Liam and kept my feelings to myself, because he was going with Georgie. If he hadn't broken off with her, I'd still be keeping my feelings to myself. But he did break off with her, and she told me she accepted that. If I'd thought she'd be hurt, we'd have moved a lot more slowly."

Her mother shook her head, disappointment on her face. "Alice, I want you to be happy, but—"

Frank's fist hit the table, making his wife jump and Liam wonder if the man had used that fist on her. "Don't try to excuse her, Helen. She had a perfectly good man in Stephen, but she couldn't be content with that. She had to have her sister's beau. What kind of a girl does that make her?"

With an effort of will, Liam bit back the scathing words on the tip of his tongue. If he voiced them he'd be likely to follow up with a blow, and he didn't want that between him and Alice's father. He glanced at her and was glad to see anger instead of hurt on her face.

"Alice, I've heard enough and I think you have, too. Celia's room at Mum and Dad's is empty. You'll be more than welcome there until everyone's had a chance to think. Get what you need and come with me."

Her father stood. "No daughter of mine is going to disgrace

herself like that while I'm alive."

Fists clenched, Liam took a step forward. *Keep your temper, for her sake.* "Don't say another word. I'm staying at my brother's tonight, I'm going back to Prospect tomorrow, and you know my parents. There'll be nothing disgraceful about it."

Frank glared at him, then backed down. "She's needed at home."

Alice looked her father in the eye. "Maybe you should have thought of that before now."

Frank's gaze turned as cold as his voice. "If you go with him now, don't plan on coming back here."

Helen's face turned white. "Frank—"

"I mean it, Helen."

Alice still faced her father, slender shoulders straight, gaze steady. "Liam, I'll go get my things." On her way out of the room she paused to lay a hand on her mother's shoulder, then Liam heard her feet on the stairs.

Her voice had only wavered a little, but that was enough to send anger surging through him again. She didn't deserve this. It took all his self-control to keep his fists and his voice down.

"You're a real piece of work, Frank, but you're her father, so I'll only say this. It would serve you right if you never saw Alice again, but if you do and you lay so much as a finger on her, I'll beat you to within an inch of your life."

Georgie still hadn't said a word. She rose from her chair with a strained look on her face. "He told the truth, Dad. He never lied to me. Guess Alice is as full of surprises as Carl. Don't worry over it on my account. Liam, I'll be seeing you around."

She left the kitchen. The front room door closed a couple of seconds later. With a last glare at Liam, her father got up and marched after her, leaving Liam facing Helen. Even in her shock, she looked healthier than she had the last time he'd seen her. Perhaps that was why he wanted to blame her for not having the spine to stand up for her daughter.

Liam took Frank's seat and let his anger go. Alice's mother had every right to distrust him right now.

"Mrs. O'Neill, if he doesn't come to his senses, does Alice have anywhere else to go?"

She nodded. "Yes, she'll be welcome at my sister's in Bedford."

"Good. I want her to have choices. Look, I know this is all really sudden, but I care about Alice. I never wanted to put her in this position. I promise to be as honest with her as I was with Georgie. I'm going to be in Prospect all winter and I'll only be home the occasional weekend, so we'll be taking our time. I hope you'll give me a chance."

Helen's features were a lot like Georgie's, but they'd lost their animation. Liam guessed that had happened years ago. He hoped Georgie would never have reason to look this sad and defeated. Helen held his gaze briefly, then shook her head.

"I want to, Liam. We've already lost Carl. I don't want to lose Alice, too, but I also don't want to see her hurt, and I'm not sure you know what you want."

"I don't blame you. Things have changed a lot for me in the past few weeks. I'm doing work I didn't think I'd be able to do again. For the first time since coming home, I feel like I have a future. Alice and I are going to take one step at a time."

Alice reappeared with a pair of small suitcases in hand. "I'm ready. Liam, are you sure about this?"

He gave her what he hoped was a reassuring smile. They'd said what needed to be said. Now, he just wanted to get her out of here.

"Yeah, I'm sure. Mum and Dad will be pleased to have you."

Alice put her suitcases down and wrapped her arms around her mother. "Please trust me on this, Mother. We'll talk soon. I love you."

Her mother hugged her back. "I love you, too. Take care of

her, Liam."

Liam breathed a sigh of relief when he closed the kitchen door behind them. The temperature had dropped sharply in the last hour or so, and a few snowflakes sifted down to melt on the brown grass. Not a cheerful day, but he hardly noticed. He couldn't remember when he'd felt this alive. Or this vulnerable.

When they reached St. Joseph's at the top of the street, Liam drew Alice into the protection of the ell and gathered her close. She felt good, so good in his arms, but the hurt of her father's words showed on her face now.

"Are you all right, Alice?"

She smiled, a smile tinged with sadness. "I will be. I knew Dad wouldn't be pleased. I don't let him get to me."

He touched her cheek. "Yes, you do. There's no way you can help it." He drew her closer and spoke without thinking. "Carl told me in the hospital that you never learned to read. That's a shame, but it doesn't give your father the right to insult you. A beautiful, talented lady like you doesn't have to take that from anyone."

Alice stiffened in his arms. Liam wished he could call back his words. They smacked of pity. He tucked a finger under her chin, covered her mouth with his and kissed her until she relaxed against him with another sigh. When she met his gaze afterward, her sadness was gone, replaced by a sly twinkle.

"We'd better get out of here, Liam, before someone sees us and tells Father McManus."

They walked on. As far as Liam was concerned, nothing more needed to be said. He cared a hell of a lot more about who Alice was than about who she wasn't.

The family was in for a surprise. They hadn't seen him in a month, he hadn't told them he was coming, and now he was bringing Alice home with him. Picturing Nolan's grin, he turned the corner of Kaye Street with Alice's hand in his.

He knew she couldn't read. He knew, and he didn't care. Alice still hadn't taken it in when they reached Liam's parents' house. Her stomach started to flutter. What kind of a reception could she expect? She barely knew his family, except by sight. They might share her father's opinion of a girl who'd go with her sister's beau.

Liam threw her a mischievous glance as they climbed the porch stairs. He knocked on the front door instead of just walking in. When his mother answered it, her dark eyes opened wide in astonishment and pleasure.

"Liam! Why didn't you call?"

"You know Jess doesn't have a phone, and besides, I wanted to surprise you. Is dinner ready?"

She laughed and hugged him. "Come in. Look at you! I'd say Fanny's treating you pretty well. You look like you've gained ten pounds."

Alice took the joy on Meg's face as a warning. She was possessive of the son who'd come home to her from overseas, perhaps all the more so because of the one who hadn't. It took a moment for her to notice that Liam had a companion. Her joy changed to puzzlement, then to shock when she saw the small valises Alice carried.

"Do you have something to tell us, Liam?"

Liam hurried to explain. "Yeah, I do. Alice and I have decided to start keeping company. When we told her father, he didn't take it very well, so I invited her to stay here for a few days."

Obviously relieved, Meg offered Alice a reserved smile. "I see. Come in out of the cold, dear."

Holding Liam's hand, Alice did.

She'd never been inside the Cochranes' home before. It was a little smaller than hers and the furniture she saw in the front room as they passed was simpler, but the biggest difference was one Alice couldn't define at first. It came to her as she and Liam stopped in the doorway of the smaller sitting room off the kitchen, where the whole family was gathered.

She felt no tension in the air, no simmering anger.

Nolan's children sprawled on the floor with paper and crayons scattered around them. Dainty little nose in the air, Emily drew wobbly red circles on her sheet, stalling while her brother waited impatiently for the red crayon to finish the Union Jack on his drawing of a battleship. Nolan and his father sat on the sofa playing cribbage, laying their cards on the coffee table. Jack pegged out and sniffed loudly.

"Does anyone smell skunk?"

Nolan threw down his cards in disgust and muttered something under his breath that made Ruth, in the armchair across from her husband, raise her eyebrows. They lifted higher when she noticed Liam and Alice.

"Look who's home."

The men looked up from their game. Nolan took in Liam and Alice with a swift, surprised glance, then a wicked grin spread across his face.

"Liam! Coming through the front door like that, we thought you were a salesman."

Liam imitated his father's sniff. "Smells a little off in here, doesn't it? Dad, why don't you do the world a favour one of these days and let him win a game? I came to the front door because I brought company."

Jack spoke up. "So I see. Hello, Alice."

All eyes were on her, curious and expectant. Liam drew her into the room and gave the rest of the family the same explanation he'd given his mother. Alice watched their faces and hoped they couldn't hear her heart pounding.

In Jack, she saw the man Liam would be in thirty years, with strong features still sharply defined, close-cropped blond hair turned to silver and fine lines around his shrewd hazel eyes.

Jack's gaze didn't waver from Liam's while he spoke. When he finished, his father gave Alice a cool, appraising look. She didn't falter. He nodded.

"You're welcome. We know your father. He's always been a good provider, but not the easiest man to live with."

Ruth said nothing. Of course, it wasn't her house, but her expression said she was reserving judgment. Nolan's dark eyes gleamed as if he found the whole situation amusing. Alice could only imagine what he'd say to Liam when they were alone. She found it easier to face his father.

"Thank you, Mr. Cochrane. You're right about Dad, he has always been a good provider, but right now, this will make things a lot less awkward for me."

Liam's jaw tightened. Alice knew he was remembering the scene at her house. Jack picked up on his son's anger. His expression softened.

"It's no trouble. Celia's room is yours for as long as you need it."

Liam squeezed Alice's hand. "Thanks, Dad. Alice, I'll show you your room."

The nervous pressure on her chest eased as they climbed the stairs. At least Liam's family wasn't condemning her out of hand. Her cheeks warmed at the memory of Nolan's grin. She believed the stories she'd heard about him sowing his wild oats in his sailing days.

Liam led her into his sister's room and switched on the ceiling light. Alice set her suitcases in the closet, shrugged out of her winter coat and laid it on the bed's pale green knitted spread. The room suited the clever, outgoing girl she remembered from her school days, pretty and feminine but without a lot of frills. The walls were hung with a small floral print paper in shades of yellow and green, the iron bedstead enamelled in brown, the nightstand and dresser painted white in contrast. Though the Cochranes had electricity, an oil lamp with a bowl of white porcelain and a hand-painted shade still stood on the nightstand. Liam picked up the framed wedding photo on the dresser.

"It's hard to believe Celia's married. She didn't meet Matthew 'til after Michael-John and I left for Europe. He came here from Ontario to visit a college friend, and the rest is history."

A lighter blonde than Liam, with a feminine version of his square chin, Celia radiated happiness. Her husband stood smiling beside her. Alice looked up from the photo and saw a frown on Liam's face.

"It must have been hard to miss her wedding. So you've never met Matthew?"

"No. He shipped out just after they were married." Liam shrugged and set the photo back in its place. "I'm not big on weddings. I don't mind missing Celia's, as long as she doesn't become a widow before I get to meet her husband."

His expression contradicted his words. The regret made sense, but the anger surprised her. Alice put her hands on his shoulders.

"You missed three years of your family's life. I can't imagine how that feels. Liam, I like your parents."

He smiled. "So do I. I didn't know how much until I left."

"Nolan, on the other hand... He scares me a little."

That made Liam laugh. "Give Nolan as good as he sends and you'll get along fine." His hands settled at her waist. "I know you can. Don't worry, they're all going to like you, too."

Until they found out what Liam already knew about her. Alice still couldn't comprehend that he didn't seem to care.

"How can you be so sure?"

He pulled her against his chest and gave her a slow, sultry grin that made her tingle to her toes. "What's not to like? Alice, I have to go back to Prospect tomorrow. Let's make the most of tonight." He shook his head. "Seems like it's been a long time since this morning."

He bent to kiss her. Alice kissed him back, felt and shared the hope and excitement and confusion running through him. Counting by heartbeats, it seemed a lifetime since morning.

"We'd better go downstairs or Nolan will guess exactly what we've been doing."

Liam nipped at her bottom lip. "I'm sure he already has." He switched off the light and took her back to his family.

After a supper of fish chowder with molasses brown bread and a generous serving of good-natured teasing from Jack – with a couple of significant looks from Nolan thrown in – they all gathered in the front room. Alice stepped in and almost squealed like a happy child.

"You have a piano. Do you play, Mrs. Cochrane?"

"No. We inherited it from my oldest sister when she passed away. Liam's cousin Jess's mother. Celia used to play a bit, just for her own amusement, but none of the rest of us does. Maybe Emily will when she's older. Heaven knows if it's in tune, but try it if you like, dear."

Alice slid onto the bench and played a couple of soft chords. The piano was only slightly out of tune and its tone was warm and mellow. She closed her eyes and played the Chopin piece she'd been practicing, letting all the emotion of the day find a voice through the instrument. When she finished, she faced a row of surprised faces, Liam's most of all. He smiled with pure delight.

"I had no idea you could play like that, Alice."

"Of course she can," his mother retorted. "She's Helen O'Neill's daughter. You don't remember hearing Helen play when she was younger, but I do. Play something else."

Alice ran through a Scott Joplin rag, feeling as free as the music. She wouldn't have to set her practicing aside while she was here. She followed the rag with *Shenandoah*, singing as she played. Meg's eyes shone with appreciation.

"I've always liked that tune. Your mother was never a singer,

Alice, but you certainly are. I miss hearing you in the choir."

"I'm thinking about joining again in the New Year." By then, she should be able to read well enough to get by – with a lot of work. She'd always loved blending her voice with others, but when the new choir director insisted on giving sight-reading tests, Alice had known she didn't stand a chance. By January, if she kept working hard, she would.

She played *Beautiful Dreamer* and two or three other tunes they all knew. Liam's gaze never left her. When she stopped playing, he seemed to shake himself out of a trance.

"You're right, Mum. I shouldn't have expected anything else. Alice, you should be playing in a concert hall." He threw a teasing glance Nolan's way. "Have you recovered enough to take a beating at poker?"

"Put your money where your mouth is, Liam. Dad, you in?"

Jack was. They set up in the dining room. Ruth took the children home to bed, while Meg and Alice did the supper dishes and listened to the poker game's progress. Nolan won the first pot and gloated over his father until Liam roared with laughter. Meg's eyes took on a soft glow.

"This has been a quiet house for the last three years, even more so since Celia married. It's good to see Liam acting more like his old self."

For Alice, Liam's laughter brought a pang of mixed emotions. It was very good to hear, but her family had never laughed together like that. She set the bowl she'd just dried on the counter and glanced over her shoulder into the dining room.

"I think so, too. Of course, I was only sixteen when he left, but..." Her voice trailed away as her face heated with a blush. She hadn't meant to say that. Meg paused, dishcloth in hand.

"Had you noticed him then?"

It was too late to deny it. "Yes."

Meg dropped her dishcloth in the sink and leaned against the counter. A slender woman and short by contrast with her tall husband and sons, she tilted her head to hold Alice's gaze.

"What does Georgie make of you and Liam?"

Alice looked into uncompromising dark eyes. "I think she's disappointed, but he'd already broken off with her. Nothing happened between us before that. She knows he didn't tell her any lies."

Meg appeared to think about that for a moment, but she wouldn't yield yet. "Now that Liam's getting back on his feet, I don't want to see him knocked down again."

Alice couldn't help liking Liam's mother for her protectiveness. They loved him together. She only hesitated a moment before telling Meg what Liam wasn't ready to hear.

"Of course you don't. Mrs. Cochrane, I'm going to tell you the truth. I trust you to keep it to yourself. I've cared for Liam for a very long time. Hurting him is the last thing I want to do."

After a long moment, Meg smiled. "I believe you."

They finished the dishes in companionable silence while Alice savoured her relief. Now she had to live up to her words. Liam was still finding his way. What if his path took him in another direction, away from her?

She'd wait for him if he asked her to. She'd let him go without blame if she had to, because somehow the years had turned her girlish dreams into something real. Because she loved him.

When the card game ended, Liam's father called out from the dining room. "I'm going upstairs, Meg."

Nolan chimed in. "Night, everyone. Better expect Liam for breakfast. Get your beauty sleep, Alice, you'll have to look good enough for both of you."

"I should be able to manage that," she called back. "If not, I'll ask Ruth for some pointers. She's had plenty of practice."

Liam's laughter joined with Nolan's. He walked into the kitchen grinning. "Well said, Miss O'Neill. Nolan took two dollars from Dad, so he's feeling full of himself."

Meg dried her hands on her apron, took it off and hung it up beside the stove. "Of course. Some things never change. It's bedtime. Good night, you two."

She disappeared down the hall. Alice felt another blush coming on. It wasn't much past ten o'clock.

"Do your parents always go to bed this early?"

"Not always." Liam walked her into the small sitting room and drew her down on the sofa beside him. "They don't need to be hit over the head."

Alice leaned against him and closed her eyes, enjoying his nearness. It didn't seem possible that this morning she'd felt as grey as the sky. "You're very lucky, Liam, but I think you know that."

"I do." His fingers traced the curve of her cheek. "Now come here. I've been waiting all night for this."

Eyes still closed, Alice felt Liam's arms wrap around her, warm and strong, pulling her tight against his chest. As she breathed in his scent, her last coherent thought was that if this were another of her dreams, she never wanted to wake. Then, she could only feel as Liam's lips traced a tingling path along her jaw line to her mouth. She turned her head to meet him halfway. As his mouth sealed over hers, she heard the same low, purring sound of pleasure he'd made in the hospital when she kissed him awake. Her bones melted at the memory and the reality. She felt Liam's breath catch as her body yielded to his, heard wonder in his voice.

"God, Alice, what have you done to me?" He gripped her shoulders and tipped her onto her back. Heavy and solid, his body pressed her into the sofa as he stretched out above her. "I'm shaking. You'd think I was an eighteen-year-old kid."

Alice opened her eyes and caught a glimpse of the passion in Liam's before he kissed her again. She ran her hands over his shoulders, felt them tremble – or was that her?

"I'm shaking, too." She tilted her head back to give him

access to her throat. He nuzzled her, traced the cord at the side with his tongue before coming back to her mouth again. She slid her hands down his back and pressed him closer while she welcomed his hungry kiss. As his tongue grew more insistent their bodies began moving together, causing the sweetest sensation Alice had ever known. They were on the edge of losing control when Liam broke the kiss and raised himself on his elbows. He took a couple of ragged breaths, looked down at her and shook his head.

"We need to slow down."

He sat up and ran a hand through his hair. Alice lay with her head against the arm of the sofa, muscles clogged, body craving his weight. She caught her breath, took Liam's hand and pulled herself up beside him.

"Yes, we do. I've never done that before."

She'd never heard her voice sound like that before, husky with desire. Liam leaned back and looked at her as if he were seeing her for the first time. "I couldn't tell. I shouldn't have been surprised, though, after hearing you play earlier."

Alice reached up and found her combs hopelessly askew. She took them out and let her hair fall free. Heat raced over her skin again at the feel of her soft curls brushing her neck as Liam's fingers had done.

"What do you mean?" But he was just staring at her. Mesmerized.

He played with one long lock, rubbing it between his thumb and forefinger. "Beautiful… And don't you know? When you play, you change. You let yourself go. It's sexy as hell."

Alice didn't know. Music had always been her way of escaping the world, of leaving her limitations behind. She'd had no idea that feeling came through to others. The thought made her a little uncomfortable. Was it only Liam's biased opinion?

"It's the only thing I do well."

Liam chuckled. The heat in his gaze made her crave his

weight again. "Not by half, lady. Oh, not by half." He stood, lifted her hand to his cheek, kissed her palm. "I'd better get over to Nolan's, or I'll end up having you for breakfast instead of having breakfast with you. Good night, Alice. Sleep well."

Slowly, he let her hand go and left the room. Alice heard the kitchen door close behind him. When she could trust her legs to carry her, she crept upstairs.

Could this be real? Could life be more like a passionate symphony by Tchaikovsky than a quiet Schubert melody? If so, she couldn't quite believe it yet.

Chapter 14

Liam woke at sunrise and lay still, enjoying the quiet of the house, anticipating the day ahead. He'd have to be at the wharf to meet Jess's neighbour's boat by three in the afternoon so they could make Prospect by dark, but he had the best part of the day to spend with Alice. The glow that spread in his chest was brighter than the watery sunlight streaming in his window.

You're in deep trouble, Cochrane.

He couldn't wait to see Alice's sweet face at the breakfast table. How would she look? Dewy and fresh. Kissable. Appetizing. Yeah, that was a good word. Appetizing enough to get him in way over his head.

Just like Bea. She'd made him tremble, too. But now he was home and he could take his time with Alice – a luxury he'd never had with Bea. Perhaps it would make all the difference.

He got up, pulled on his robe and glanced out the window. Yesterday's snow had amounted to nothing, but a heavy frost had tipped the grass and leafless branches with silver. He headed for the bathroom, the floor stinging-cold beneath his bare feet. A finer day than November usually offered.

After bathing and shaving, Liam stood in front of the full-length mirror. At Jess's, he'd been too busy to notice the changes in his body. He gazed in surprise at the new muscles in his arms and chest, but the biggest difference was in his face. He looked a lot more like he had before going overseas.

He removed the towel around his waist and looked down at his injured leg. A snarled network of reddish, thickened scars ran over his left hip and down his thigh, which was smaller than the other due to the muscle they'd had to remove in England – but not as small as it had been, not by a long shot.

He remembered wrestling playfully with Bea, her lithe body struggling under his, enjoying his strength. He'd never again be the man she knew. What would she think of him now? What would Alice think if she—

He imagined Alice's long fingers gliding over his skin, and all thought of his scars vanished. He watched his arousal grow before he turned from the mirror, grinning.

If last night is any indication, she thinks you're man enough for her.

He returned to his room, pulled on a pair of black twill pants and a green flannel shirt and descended to the kitchen. After a trip to the cellar to get the coal-fired furnace going, he kindled a wood fire in the range for Ruth. Nolan wanted to get an oil stove because it would be easier for her to manage with him away so much, but Ruth was used to cooking with wood and liked it, so the old range remained. Once the fire caught hold, Liam shrugged into his jacket and crossed the street to his parents'.

When he opened the kitchen door Alice glanced up from setting the table. A smile spread across her face and dimpled her cheeks – dimples like dents in cream.

Appetizing. Oh, yeah.

She came toward him. Liam met her halfway and gathered her in his arms. "Morning. Did you sleep well?"

"Very well." The memory of last night's kisses shone in Alice's eyes as she looked up at him from beneath her lashes. Her height brought her lips tantalizingly close to his, an invitation Liam couldn't resist.

She tasted of minty toothpaste, mixed with her own unique flavour. It taxed his self-control to keep the kiss within respectable limits in front of his mother, who stood at the stove frying sausages.

Their savoury aroma made Liam's stomach rumble. He stole up behind his mum, filched a triangle of buttered toast from the plate on the counter and dodged when she swatted at him.

"For heaven's sake, Liam, breakfast will be ready in five minutes. Get some coffee and sit down."

Alice's cheeks dimpled again, as he'd hoped. He wanted to make her smile, wanted to make up for the ugly scene at her house yesterday, to distract her from the worry she must be feeling over Carl – though she didn't show it. Every day that went by made it less likely that he'd be found. That could mean Carl hadn't died, or it could mean that before he'd gone into the water, he'd weighted himself so he wouldn't surface quickly. The detritus of two centuries of shipping was strewn on the bottom of the Harbour and some of that could easily catch and hold a body pulled by the tide.

Liam poured two cups of coffee from the enamel pot on the stove and handed one to Alice. They sat at the table, she sipping, he washing down his stolen toast and trying to make sense of what had happened to him. He'd known Alice all his life and never noticed her, until that night at the social. Now, he couldn't take his eyes off of her.

Forget understanding it. Just enjoy it while it lasts.

He got so caught up in watching her out of the corner of his eye that he started at the sound of his father's voice. "Morning, Liam. You must have brought the sun home with you."

His gaze strayed to Alice again. "I did."

Mum set a plate of sausages and toast on the table, with a bottle of maple syrup and a jar of raspberry jelly. While they ate, Liam told them about the boat shop.

"Jess has me learning how to shape wood, how to steam it and bend it, and how to use his tools. I remember some of what he taught me before, but it's been so long I might as well be starting from scratch."

Dad nodded as he spread jelly on a slice of toast. "Jess is a craftsman, all right, but I can't think he'll have full time work for you, Liam. He doesn't get enough repair work to make ends meet without fishing, and young Everett's getting old enough to help him now."

Liam swallowed a savoury bite of sausage dipped in maple syrup. He'd never take good food for granted again after his years of living on field rations. "Yeah, I know, but if I can learn enough, there'll be work in some of the bigger yards down the shore. Lunenburg, maybe."

Dad lifted a shoulder. "Maybe."

Liam knew what his father was thinking. Merchant shipping was turning to steel more and more every year, but there were still schooners being built to fish the Grand Banks and there would always be smaller boats like the ones Jess built and repaired. Liam liked the idea of building something that could travel the world, of knowing that doing his work well could mean life or death to a ship's crew in a storm, but he'd build houses or furniture if he had to. There would always be work of some kind if he learned and practiced his craft well enough.

If he'd thought a little more as a kid and stayed with Jess instead of going into the rail yard, he'd be that much further ahead now. He chided himself for his impatience. The future wasn't going to land in his lap just because he'd started caring again.

After breakfast he and Alice did the dishes while his parents dressed for church. Liam noticed again how beautiful her hands were, remembered the music they'd coaxed from the piano last night, how it had affected him – or was it just her that had affected him?

No. He'd noticed her talent years ago, long before he'd noticed *her*.

"Alice, I'm thinking about last night."

Her fingers brushed his as she handed him a glass. Her eyes took on a sensual glow. "So am I."

"I mean when you were playing piano. Have you ever thought about performing?"

"No. I've thought about giving lessons to children, but..." Alice shook her head. "There's no way I could get the formal training I'd need. There are theory exams and—"

"No one who heard you would care what exams you'd passed. I'm no expert, but surely your mother's told you how talented you are?"

Alice looked away as she reached into the sink for another glass. "She always encouraged me to play for my own enjoyment, but she gave up teaching me theory when I was seven or eight. I've only started working at it again over the past couple of months." She met his gaze again and straightened her shoulders. "I can read music now – slowly."

Liam couldn't hide his surprise. "You can read music, but not words?"

"Yes. I have no idea why. It just makes sense to me, but words on paper don't. Anyway, I'm not sure I'd want to play on a stage."

He saw the doubt in her eyes, hated her family for putting it there. "All I'm saying is, don't sell yourself short. Too many people have been doing that to you for too many years. Don't do it to yourself."

Her smile flashed again. "You make me feel like anything is possible."

"You do the same to me." Liam kissed her lightly, then hung his dish towel over the back of a chair. "I need to go change for church."

Liam returned from Nolan's just as Alice came downstairs dressed for Mass. She'd put on a deep burgundy suit that hugged her curves and heightened the colour in her cheeks, swept her hair back into a sleek knot and pinned a matching burgundy hat over it – a soft-brimmed affair as silly as all women's hats were, but somehow it accentuated her delicate profile.

Her face lit up at his smile of approval, but she was nervous. Her family would be at Mass, and there would be gossip if she didn't take her usual place with them. He slipped his arm around her.

"You're beautiful. I'll be proud as punch walking in with you, but if you don't feel comfortable sitting with us, I understand."

She leaned into him and held his gaze. "I'll sit with you. Mother will understand, and that's all I care about."

When they reached St. Joseph's, Liam stepped aside to let Alice walk into the church ahead of him. She smiled at him before going in, showing no trace of nerves. He was the one with a knot in his stomach. Engaged couples sat together in church, not couples who'd started their relationship yesterday.

It seemed Alice had thought of that. She slid into the Cochranes' pew before Nolan's family, so they would be between her and Liam. He'd watched her family out of the corner of his eye as she passed them. Her mother smiled. Her father and Georgie showed no reaction at all. Alice might have simply stayed with friends overnight and decided to sit with them at Mass on a whim, except for the fact the O'Neills and Cochranes had barely been acquaintances before Liam had started seeing Georgie. He took his seat beside Ruth and resigned himself to being a topic of conversation over a few dinner tables later.

Mass began. Since coming home, Liam had only gone to church for his parents' sakes. He'd seen too much of humanity at its worst to believe any longer in a compassionate God, but today, as he made the responses he'd known by heart since childhood, a strange thing happened. Kneeling there with his family beside him and the familiar faces of neighbours around him, in the church where he'd been baptized and confirmed, an emotion sprang from an unknown well deep within him.

Gratitude. Plain and simple gratitude for being alive.

He glanced at Alice and caught her watching him. Maybe there was a place in the world for miracles after all.

The day passed all too quickly. Once dinner was over and cleared away, Nolan and his family went home and his parents paid a call on friends down the street. Liam and Alice settled on the sofa in the small sitting room again. She tucked her feet underneath her and cuddled into the crook of his arm, her head on his shoulder.

"I wish you didn't have to go back so soon."

"So do I, but I'll be home next weekend." Liam kissed the top of her head. Hell, he missed her already. "I'll come home every weekend I can. Jess will understand."

Alice looked up with regret. "I wish I could write to you."

Liam took her face between his hands. Would she ever believe how little he cared that she couldn't write to him? "All week I'll be looking forward to coming home on Saturday, telling you about my week and hearing about yours. That'll be better than a letter."

Alice laid a hand over his against her cheek. "But letters you can keep. Something to keep would make this seem more real." Her dimples showed again. "I'm being silly, I know. I'm glad you like your work, and I'm proud of you."

"And I'm proud of you." Liam touched a finger to one of those sweet little dents in her creamy skin. "Play as much as you like while you're here. Mum and Dad will enjoy it."

Her happiness dimmed. "I can't impose on your parents forever, Liam. I can go to Aunt Sarah in Bedford—"

Liam brought her closer, held her gaze. "Alice, listen to me. You're not imposing. You're welcome here."

"I know, and I'm thankful."

"If you go out to Bedford, I'll have to take the train or borrow Nolan's car to see you. We're going to have little enough time together as it is." He ran a thumb over her lips. "I don't have to leave for another hour. Let's not waste it talking."

He lifted Alice onto his lap. Her arms twined around his neck as his mouth captured hers. They spent the rest of their time making memories, giving each other something to hold on to through the week ahead. When Liam had to go, he found it even more difficult than leaving Bea when his furlough was up. On the front porch, he kissed Alice one more time before walking away. Halfway down the street he turned for one last glimpse of her standing there, waving. He already missed her so much he laughed at himself.

Man up, Cochrane, you aren't going to war this time. You're only going to work. You'll see her next Saturday.

Chapter 15

Silly girl. He hasn't gone to war this time. He'll be back on Saturday.

Alice scolded herself as she unpinned one of Jack's shirts from the clothesline. Liam hadn't been gone twenty-four hours, and she missed him as if he'd been gone a month.

She'd never forget the day his battalion sailed for Europe. She'd felt too foolish to go down to the pier and join the crowd there to see the ship off, so she'd spent most of the day up on Needham Hill, nursing her broken sixteen-year-old heart. It had broken again the next year when Carl shipped out. It saddened her to know she might never see her brother again… but Liam was coming home in a few days.

To her.

She'd spent the morning helping Meg with the laundry, working the wringer while Liam's mother stirred the washing in the tub. Everything had dried quickly in the sun and frosty air, and now the clothes and linens were ready to put away. Alice finished unloading the clothesline and hurried inside with the full basket, shivering. She hadn't bothered with her coat.

"Where do you want this?"

A fragrant blend of raisins, spices and molasses perfumed the kitchen. Meg stood at the counter, mixing cake batter in an enamel bowl. She scraped the batter into a pan and wiped her hands on her apron.

"Thanks, Alice. Would you mind taking it up to Liam's room? It's the one next to yours. Just empty it on the bed. I'll be up in a minute."

Alice carried the laundry basket upstairs to the small, plain bedroom beside Celia's, tipped the contents onto the bed and began folding. Meg soon joined her. As they worked, Alice's gaze strayed to the picture hanging on the opposite wall, of Liam and his brothers. Liam sat on the kitchen step next to Michael-John, who held a football. Liam might have been sixteen. He grinned at the camera, his lighter hair and heavier build in contrast with his two lean, dark brothers. A handsome young man of twenty-one or twenty-two, Nolan stood on the top step behind him. Meg's expression softened as she followed Alice's gaze.

"That was taken ten years ago. It's my favourite picture of the boys."

Alice could see why. Their personalities showed clearly across the years. She picked up the flannel shirt Liam had worn Saturday, folded it and set it aside. "Liam's always been close to his brothers, hasn't he?"

Meg stood holding one of Jack's sweaters, her eyes still on the picture. "Yes, especially Michael-John. He was only twenty-one months younger than Liam. Nolan's six years older. He signed on his first ship at seventeen, so the younger two didn't have the chance to get to know him as well growing up." She shook the sweater briskly and picked a piece of lint from the shoulder. "Michael-John and Liam both loved sports. They both played football and hockey in school, and Michael-John was on the Dalhousie track and field team. He was a distance runner."

A lump formed in Alice's throat. Liam hadn't only lost a brother, he'd lost a friend, and he'd lost the ability to do things he'd loved. "When Carl was reported missing last year, it hurt, and now, knowing he's lost again, it hurts… so much… but I can't imagine losing a child."

Meg's crisp voice turned gentle. "I think having one missing would be worse. Those letters, holding out hope – that's cruel. At least we knew." She glanced around the room that must hold so many memories for her. "We were lucky we didn't lose Liam, too. He was in the hospital for four months, and he spent another two in a convalescent home before he was well enough to ship home."

Alice's heart lurched. The neighbour who'd first mentioned to her that Liam had been wounded had also said that he was recovering. In her relief that he was out of the fighting, she'd taken that report at face value. As for the wait, it wasn't unusual for transport home to take months. "I didn't know that."

Meg spoke as if there was no one else in the room. Alice wondered if Liam's mother had ever talked to anyone about those painful weeks. "He got a serious infection in his wound. He almost didn't make it. I couldn't get passage on a ship to go to him. Then the doctor's letter came, saying he was out of danger."

Alice shivered. What had it been like for Meg to be so far away when Liam needed her? "No wonder he was so long getting home."

"He was shell-shocked, too, and they wanted to watch him." A fleeting frown crossed Meg's face. "I don't think it helped that..."

"What didn't help, Mrs. Cochrane?" As soon as the words were out of her mouth, Alice felt a blush rising. *Don't ask so many questions.* She braced herself for a cool answer, but Meg smiled as she handed her another folded shirt.

"Liam doesn't like talking about his time overseas, and I think he'd rather I didn't talk about it either. This is his. Will you put it in the dresser? Top drawer."

Alice turned to the dresser behind her, opened the top drawer and tucked the shirt inside. She ran her fingers over the crisp cotton as she imagined Liam desperately ill, and among strangers. What he'd said the night of the social came back to her.

I'm asking about Carl because I'm more like him than you might think.

It had taken six months for Liam to recover enough in mind and body to be sent home. He'd come even farther than Alice had thought. She closed the dresser drawer and faced his mother across the empty laundry basket.

"Mrs. Cochrane—"

A quick smile from dark eyes. "Please call me Meg."

Alice returned the smile. "Meg, if you're really all right with my staying here, I should go home and get some more things. I also need to talk to Mother. She left church before I got a chance to speak to her yesterday."

In the space of a second's silence, some distance dissolved between them. Alice had never felt more accepted in her own home.

"You do that, Alice."

She heard the opening bars of *Moonlight Sonata* from the street, quietly let herself into the house and stood in the front room doorway, listening. Her mother saw her reflection in the piano's polished wood and looked over her shoulder. The knot of tension in Alice's stomach began to ease. Mother looked thoughtful, but not troubled. Dad couldn't have vented his anger on her too strongly.

"Alice! Come in, dear."

Alice covered the distance between them in a couple of strides and pulled her mother into a hug. "Hello. You look fine."

Mother held her close, then drew back to look at her. "So do you. Are the Cochranes treating you well? "

"Yes." Alice sat on the piano bench beside her mother and put an arm around her. "How's Georgie?"

Mother looked down at the keyboard and played a soft chord. "You know Georgie. She doesn't show her feelings."

No, she doesn't. That's one thing we have in common. Alice smothered a pang of guilt mixed with doubt. She'd always played second fiddle to Georgie. Why should she feel guilty over getting what she wanted for a change, and getting it honestly? "I know. I never meant to hurt her, Mother."

Her mother faced her again. "I'm sure you didn't, and I'm sure you think this – attraction – between you and Liam is real, but Alice, I think he might be the kind of man who can't stay with one woman."

Alice held back a sigh. Georgie could stand on her own feet and nobody had ever messed with Carl, but slow Alice needed to be watched and warned. "Mother, maybe you're right. Maybe he'll hurt me, but I have to take my chances. Is Dad still in a temper?"

"You know your father." Her mother laid a hand on her knee. "Give him a week or two."

On a sudden spurt of anger, Alice rose. "Why is Dad the only person who's ever been allowed to get angry in this house? If anyone else does, it's an insult. Georgie and Carl never cared, but I did. That's my problem with him."

Her mother looked up at her with a resigned smile. "Alice, I don't suppose I can make you understand, but your father loves you in his own way."

Yes. Dad had seen to it that his daughters had the best he could give them, but his best had never included warmth or affection, at least not for Alice. It irked her to think she still hoped for it.

"Maybe. I just wish I could feel that he cared when I'm with him."

When Jess's neighbour decided to take his fish to town on Friday afternoon instead of waiting until morning, Liam jumped at the chance to go along. It had been a long week, waiting to see Alice again. She was right – it would have been nice to be able to write, but then not hearing from her heightened the anticipation.

Headed up from the Harbour, he paused on the corner of Granville. He hadn't seen Barney Race since going out to Prospect. Better pay a quick call before heading home. Now more than ever, Liam wondered how Barney survived from day to day, with nothing to look forward to.

When he knocked on the door of Barney's upstairs flat, no one answered. Odd. Barney rarely left his place this early. On his way out, Liam stepped into the tobacco shop downstairs. The pretty brunette behind the counter looked up with a smile when the bell over the door chimed. Her artfully made-up brown eyes had seen too much, but the smile was genuine.

"Liam, it's been a long time. You look well." With her French accent, his name came out 'leem.' She couldn't be more than twenty-two or twenty-three, but he suspected she'd been on her own for a long time. He snapped off a casual salute.

"Merci, Guylaine, toi aussi. Comment ça va?"

Guylaine let out a silvery laugh. "Speak English so I can understand you."

He pretended to be miffed. "Is it my fault that my French comes from Paris, not Montreal?"

She rolled her eyes. "You know as much French as all the other soldiers who come in here."

Liam took a breath scented with fruity tobacco and shifted his duffle bag to his other shoulder, chafing to be gone. "Yeah. Guylaine, do you know when Barney went out? I want to see him, but I don't have time to wait around."

She leaned on the counter and shook her head, setting her bobbed curls swinging. The sparkle in her eyes dimmed along with her voice. "You didn't hear? I'm sorry, Liam. Two weeks ago, Suzanne and I found Barney in his flat, very sick, very hot. We called a doctor. He told us Barney had bad lungs. I don't know the English word—"

A deadly chill ran through Liam. Since Barney had been shipped home he'd never looked healthy, but Liam had always put that down to drink and pain. Now that he thought about it, Barney had always seemed to have a cough. Liam supplied the ugly word Guylaine wanted.

"Tuberculosis?"

"Oui."

"So he's in the hospital? Where?" If it meant Barney would get the care he needed, this might even be a blessing in disguise – if his illness hadn't progressed too far. Surely he couldn't be that sick. Liam would have noticed.

"Non. Il est mort. He passed away last Wednesday." Guylaine reached out to lay a hand over Liam's on the counter. "I am sorry," she repeated, her voice soft. "I know you served together. He called you his friend."

A weight of grief descended on him. How close had he been to not coming here tonight, to not bothering? He pulled his hand from Guylaine's.

"Did he? I sure as hell don't know why."

He turned on his heel and stumbled out onto the street, stomach churning. *Shit, Liam, pull yourself together. It isn't like you were close.*

No, he and Barney hadn't been close. As far as Liam knew, Barney hadn't been close to anyone. In the trenches he'd always been ready with a joke, but he never had much to say otherwise. He came and went on his own and kept to himself on his furloughs, but when the fighting started you didn't have to look over your shoulder to see if Barney was with you, because you knew damn well he was. He'd deserved better than to be sent home and forgotten. A hell of a lot better.

Liam found his way to the nearest speakeasy, already full of soldiers, sailors and stevedores looking to get an early start on the weekend. He ordered a double Scotch, found an unoccupied corner and took a bracing swallow.

Here's to the last man to fall, Barney.

He tossed back the rest of his drink. It wasn't enough to

banish his grief. He returned to the bar for another.

After Meg and Jack turned in for the night Alice sat up in the kitchen, copying some music she'd brought with her from home on Monday. She still couldn't call her transcriptions beautiful, but they'd come a long way since she started. She heard the melodies in her mind as she carefully drew the notes on her staff paper. The pen didn't feel foreign in her hand anymore.

She looked up at a sound and saw Liam at the back door, his face blurred by the frost on the window. On a rush of gladness, she hurried to meet him. The gladness evaporated when she opened the door.

Whiskey fumes hit her in waves. Liam leaned heavily against the door jamb, taking all his weight on his good leg. He didn't have his cane. His face was bruised again, but what truly frightened her was the haunted look in his eyes.

The same look she'd seen in Carl's.

She took Liam's duffle bag, dropped it on the floor and stepped back. The way he stiffened told her he didn't want to be touched.

"What happened to you?"

He pushed past her to the stove and lifted the coffee pot. It held what was left of the after-supper brew. He fumbled a cup from the cupboard, filled it and drank. Dry-mouthed, Alice took a step toward him.

"I asked you a question."

Liam kept his back to her as he answered. He didn't slur his words, but she'd never heard his voice sound so flat and cold, not like himself at all.

"Nothing's happened. I got an early chance in and decided to have a drink downtown before coming home."

"A drink? You can hardly stand. What happened to your face?"

"I ran into something."

"Someone is more like it." Alice took another step toward him. He flinched when he heard her.

"I'm all right, Alice. Go to bed."

"You aren't all right, Liam."

"Go the hell to bed!" He spun around and threw his hands out wide with such force that he knocked her backwards. She lost her balance and fell. He stared down at her in horror, the same expression she'd seen on Carl's face the day he'd disappeared.

"Christ, Alice, I'm sorry."

Alice scrambled to her feet, torn between anger and fear – fear for Liam, fear for herself. She didn't want to watch him go down the same road as Carl.

"Don't apologize to me. You're the one who's going to suffer. What are you going to tell Jess if you aren't fit to work on Monday? You'd better go to bed in the sitting room. You aren't going to make it to Nolan's."

She'd been through too many scenes like this at home. Alice steeled herself against an overwhelming urge to comfort him, gathered up her staff paper and turned in the kitchen doorway. He stood with his back to her again, stiff and unyielding.

She left him there.

Liam took another mouthful of stale coffee. It made his stomach roll. He set the cup in the sink and took slow breaths until the nausea faded.

You're pathetic, Cochrane. Pitied Barney, did you? Look at yourself.

He stared at his reflection in the kitchen window. Eyes red-rimmed, a bruise on his jaw, he looked like hell. He'd lost track of how much whiskey he'd consumed, couldn't recall the face of the man he'd bumped into at the bar, didn't remember what either of them had said, but fists had flown and they'd both been tossed out on their arses. They'd neglected to throw his cane after him.

He'd landed on his bad hip, but there couldn't be much damage or he wouldn't have been able to stagger home and behave like an ass to Alice. Why the hell hadn't he just gone to Nolan's?

He turned away from the window with loathing, made it to the sofa in the sitting room, stretched out and closed his eyes. The clock in the front room chimed eleven. Sometime before it chimed again, he fell asleep.

A brush against his shoulder woke him. Something soft tickled his neck – the familiar texture of the knitted afghan from the armchair across the room. Liam opened his eyes, saw Alice leaning over him, her face barely visible in the darkness.

"Go back to sleep, Liam. I didn't mean to wake you."

He sat up, wincing. His head throbbed and his mouth tasted disgusting. What a sight he must be.

"What are you doing up? It's still the middle of the night."

"I woke up, so I thought I'd check on you."

He switched on the floor lamp next to the sofa. Alice stood at the edge of its circle of light, wearing a blue flannel nightgown, her long braid hanging over her shoulder. Liam died a little inside when he noticed smudges left by tears on her cheeks. He should have known something like this would happen.

"I should never have brought you here, Alice. I knew I'd hurt you."

She stood back with her arms crossed and her shoulders high. "I'm not hurt, I'm angry. I grew up seeing my father come home drunk, and when he stopped, Carl started. I won't live that way again."

Did she have any idea how sexy she looked with flushed cheeks and an angry sparkle in her eyes? Sexy and vulnerable. "That's exactly why I should have left you alone."

Her stance softened just a touch. "Liam, I know you don't

do this often, or I wouldn't be here. Why tonight?"

"Why not?"

Liam hoped to make her angry enough to leave him alone, but she only rolled her eyes. He resigned himself to the inevitable. Frank O'Neill's daughter wasn't going to go away unless he gave her something.

"I stopped to visit someone downtown before coming home. Barney Race. We served together overseas. I found out he died of tuberculosis last week. Only that's not really true. The real truth is Barney gave up on life because nobody gave a damn."

He'd given her more than he intended. Alice held his gaze until Liam had to look away.

"I'd say you did."

"Then I did a damn poor job of showing it." Liam blew out a breath, trying to lift the painful weight of grief from his chest. It didn't shift. "We fought together, but we never knew each other well. We were wounded on the same day. Barney didn't heal well. He couldn't do much in the way of work, and he had no close family that he ever mentioned. He took up bootlegging. I saw him when I wanted a bottle. That was all."

To his utter surprise, Alice knelt in front of him and took his face in her hands. "No, that wasn't all, but you couldn't give him his health back."

Her tone stripped the skin from Liam's soul. He closed his eyes so he couldn't see the compassion on her face. "I didn't even know he was really sick, but I should have. The signs were there. I just didn't see them. I didn't bother."

"You were fighting your own battles."

"That's no excuse."

Alice rose from her knees and sat beside him. Her touch on his hair drew his gaze to her again. She shook her head. "Then you must think I'm responsible for whatever's happened to Carl."

That made no sense. Couldn't she see the difference? "Carl was your brother. You went to him in the hospital when no one else would. He knew you cared."

She moved a little closer. The scent of her skin cut through the smell of stale whiskey. "And I'm sure Barney knew you cared, too."

He called you his friend. Guylaine's words in the tobacco shop took on a new meaning. "You don't know that."

"I know you."

Alice slipped her arm around him. Part of him wanted to shout at her to leave him alone, that he didn't deserve or want her comfort, but Liam couldn't find the will. He lowered his head to her shoulder, buried his mouth against the soft skin of her throat and let the taste of her soothe him.

Alice wrapped her arms around him and cradled him against her. Liam nuzzled deeper into her neck and gave himself up to her warmth. Pathetic as it made him, he didn't have the strength to do anything else.

"Alice, how can you give a damn about me?"

He felt her smile against his hair. "I give a damn because you have the backbone to start your life over instead of sitting at home feeling sorry for yourself. Because you're a son and brother your family can be proud of."

He pulled out of her embrace. She was romanticizing, just like he'd feared – but he didn't see it in her eyes. "For what? If it weren't for them, I'd be in Barney's shoes. Or Carl's."

Alice took his hands in hers and looked him over, a gaze that showed no recognition of all the changes in him, all the damage. That saw a man who no longer existed.

"Liam, you almost died serving your country. There's no shame in needing your family to help you get back on your feet."

Was that it, then? Did she not see him any more clearly than strangers on the street? If so, he needed to set her straight now. "I punched Nolan once, not long after I got home. Nearly knocked him out. I could've really hurt you tonight."

Those amber eyes still looked steadily into his. "I'm not afraid of you."

Her gaze was way too soft, as was her voice. She didn't understand. So, Liam would have to show her.

"You should be."

Chapter 16

Nothing he could say would shatter her rose-coloured glasses, so he'd have to let actions convince her. Better he frighten Alice now than hurt her more deeply later. Liam pushed her back onto the sofa cushions and crushed her mouth under his in a brutal kiss that should have made her scramble to get away, but after one moment of shock her body turned liquid under his. Instead of trying to escape, she dug her fingers into his shoulders, anchored herself to him and kissed him back. The ground shifted, leaving Liam struggling for balance like a novice boxer sparring with a champion. Without a target, his anger simply turned to lust.

As Alice's flavour and scent enveloped him, his mind shut down. Liquor still simmering in his blood, blind, deaf to everything but his pulse hammering in his ears, he gathered Alice's nightgown in his fists and pulled it up to her waist. Without tenderness or finesse, he slid his hands beneath the fabric and ran them over her. Her body tensed. "Liam..."

He silenced her with another rough kiss as he filled his hands with her breasts, then he shifted to bury his mouth against Alice's neck again, suckling and nipping her soft skin, lost in the taste and feel of her until she twisted beneath him and pulled his hair. Hard.

"Liam, please. We can't. Not now."

The fear in her voice cut through the haze of whiskey and need. Liam lifted his head. He lay between Alice's thighs, his hips grinding against her. He didn't recall undoing the buttons on his trousers, but they were undone and he was hard and aching, ready to drive into her.

To rape her.

He'd almost raped Alice.

He pulled away from her so quickly he fell off the sofa. On his knees, heart galloping, breath coming fast, he looked up at her. Her eyes were wide with shock and glistening with tears. One slipped down her cheek. When he felt tears in his own eyes, Liam hid his face against the sofa cushions.

"God, Alice... I... Oh, God."

He started shaking, couldn't stop. His body seemed to have a will of its own. When he opened his eyes, he thought he'd see Alice but instead of Alice's feet and ankles extending below her nightgown, he saw something else.

A slender foot protruded from the darkness of the doorway of an abandoned cottage outside St. Eloi. The foot had belonged to a young girl, fifteen or sixteen, her dead body naked, the mark of a man's hands on her throat, her long, coltish legs stained with blood from between her thighs.

The tears came, bitter and scalding, choking him, tearing him apart as he fought to control them. Then he felt Alice's fingers in his hair.

"Liam, it's all right. I'm all right."

She slid closer and lifted his head. Liam's cheek settled on warm flannel. Alice cradled his head in her lap and ran her hand over his shoulders. "Sssh. It's all right."

She kept whispering to him as her fingers slid through his hair and over his back. Her voice and touch gradually stilled his shaking and stopped his tears. He swallowed, took a ragged breath.

"Alice – I never—"

"Sssh. I know."

Another breath and he got to his feet. Alice held out her hand to him, but Liam didn't take it. He sat on the sofa, as far from her as he could get, and wiped his face with his sleeve.

"Now you know what a pathetic excuse for a man I am. Go upstairs, and catch the train to your aunt's in the morning."

He wasn't looking at her, but he felt her get up. "All right, if that's what you want, but right now I'm going to make a pot of coffee."

Alice half-expected Liam to leave the room after her and go upstairs, or to his brother's…to go somewhere to get away from her, but he stayed on the sofa. She filled the coffee pot and set it on the stove, returned to the sink and splashed cold water on her face. Liam's scent rose from her nightgown, and she felt the beginnings of a bruise on her neck where he'd bitten her.

For shame, Alice. It would have served you right if he hadn't stopped.

She hadn't wanted her first time to be like this. Not when Liam had been drinking, not when he was full of grief and bitterness. She should have made him stop right away, but what he was doing had felt so good, until it got out of control. And seeing him so shaken afterwards, despising himself when she was just as much to blame, chipped a piece off Alice's heart. If he packed her off to Bedford in the morning, it would be just what she deserved.

She left the coffee to perk and returned to the sitting room. Liam had settled into the corner of the sofa and closed his eyes. He must be exhausted after working a full day and going through such an emotional storm afterward. Alice thought he was asleep, but when she sat beside him he moved to make more room for her.

"Is that coffee ready yet? I need it."

"No, not yet."

The lamplight brought out the planes and angles of his face, emphasized the misery there. Alice rested her hand on his knee. "Liam, you didn't take anything from me that I didn't want to give. And when I asked you to stop, you stopped. It wasn't easy to get through to you, but you stopped."

He touched her cheek lightly, the way he had all those years ago, and gave her a bleak smile. "That isn't good enough, Alice. Not for you… Not for me."

She saw the fear in his eyes. Scared and stubborn. Perhaps Liam was a little bit like her brother after all, though she'd never tell him so. Arguing had never worked with Carl, either.

"All right, we'll leave it at that."

She curled up in the other corner of the sofa, giving Liam space. "You know, I've never said how sorry I am about Michael-John. Your mother told me the two of you were close."

Liam shifted a little to face her. She thought he might resent her bringing up the subject of his brother, but he looked relieved to talk about something other than what had happened between them.

"Yeah, we were. I never got to know Nolan as well, not until this summer. He was away so much from the time I was eleven or twelve."

"I saw the picture of the three of you in your room. Maybe if Carl had grown up with a brother, things would have been different for him."

"Maybe." Liam rolled his shoulders and tilted his head back against the sofa. "Maybe he would have been more of a brother than I was to Michael-John – when it mattered."

"Liam, stop it right now!" Alice winced as her voice rang off the ceiling. She went on in an angry whisper. "There was nothing you could have done to save your brother, any more than you could have saved Barney."

Liam straightened up, his eyes clouded with grief. "You weren't there. We should have gone over the top together that day, but I let Michael-John go on his own. Yeah, he was kind of touchy about standing on his own feet and not looking like he was depending on me, but I should have insisted. I promised myself when we enlisted that I'd make sure he came home in one piece. Did a good job of keeping that promise, didn't I?"

"Oh, Liam –"

"Strange thing is, he turned out to be stronger than me. He handled it all better than I did. He was more afraid of talking to girls than he was of fighting." A fleeting, bitter smile crossed Liam's face. "He wanted to be a doctor, to spend his life helping people. That's a kicker, isn't it?"

He'd reject sympathy, so Alice didn't offer it. "What would have happened if you'd gone over the top together?"

"If we'd both started from my position, maybe neither of us would have been hurt. We wouldn't have been in line with the machine gun battery that killed him."

Alice drew her knees up and curled her arms around them, hugging herself against her own regrets. "So you might not have been hurt and he might not have died that day, but both of you might have been killed the next. You can't think like that, Liam. I wonder all the time if I could have said or done anything differently for Carl, but he made his own choices. So did Michael-John."

"That makes no sense, Alice. Nothing you could do would have made a difference to Carl. He has to help himself first, but Michael-John wasn't sick. I could have reasoned with him. I should have reasoned with him."

Did Liam really believe that? Yes. He'd gotten so lost in his own guilt that he couldn't see the parallels between her situation and his. Alice reached out to trace the line of his bruised jaw with a finger. Liam had the face and body of a fighter, with the temper to match. She wouldn't stand by while he lost his battle with himself.

"That coffee should be ready."

She brought them each a steaming cup with cream. She'd found out last weekend that he liked it that way. As they drank in silence, Alice's eyelids grew heavy. Liam's kept closing of their own accord. When he'd emptied his mug, she held out her arms to him. "Now come here and rest."

He peered out the window. "The sun's coming up."

"I know, but your parents won't be up for another hour. It's Saturday. Come here."

It seemed Liam was too tired to argue. He settled into her arms. "Don't… let me sleep… too long. I'm going to need the rest… of that coffee…"

He was asleep. Alice picked up the afghan from the floor, spread it over them and leaned back, trying to get comfortable. Morning would come soon enough, but for a few more hours, she was still here.

Sunlight streamed through the window and knifed into Liam's eyes. When he turned his head away, the muscles in his neck knotted in protest. He lay with his head pillowed on Alice's breast, her arms around him. It took him a moment to remember how they'd ended up this way.

Barney was dead, and Liam was going to put Alice on the train to Bedford in a few hours.

He propped himself on his elbow and looked at her. Still asleep, her soft lips still a little swollen from his kisses, she was one sweet sight. He swore when he saw the bruise he'd put on her throat.

Christ, you're an ass, Cochrane.

What was done was done, and he wouldn't make things better by lying here until his parents came down and found them. They might tolerate an occasional fight – after all, hadn't Dad had his share? – but poor conduct with women was a different story. Liam gently brushed Alice's hair back from her face and shook her shoulder.

"Wake up, Alice. It's time we were moving."

"Mmmm." She opened her eyes, smiled sleepily. The smile vanished as she remembered. "How are you feeling?"

"All right. I'm going over to Nolan's to clean up. You'd better get dressed, and put on something with a collar."

After she left the room, Liam stood and tested his weight on his bad leg. It held him. It seemed it could take a little punishment now.

At the kitchen sink, he splashed his face and combed some water through his hair before heading across the street. A bath and a shave helped, but he still looked and felt seedy enough when he returned. Lucky he'd managed to slip in and out of Nolan's without waking the house. Meeting him with this face and an empty stomach wasn't high on Liam's list of ways to start the day.

Alice and his parents were in the kitchen. She'd put on a grey skirt and a blue blouse with a lace-edged collar that hid the bruise on her neck. She looked pretty as always, but her eyes showed traces of her sleepless night. Was that what she'd look like every morning if she saddled herself with him?

His parents showed no surprise when he walked in. Either they'd heard him last night, or Alice had told them he'd come home early. Dad's mouth set in a stern line Liam knew all too well.

"Liam. What time did you get in?"

"Late last night."

"You look it."

"Yeah."

His mother looked over her shoulder, then dropped her wooden spoon in her pan of hash browns and turned around.

"You've washed, but I can still smell whiskey on you from here, and look at your face. Liam, you know we don't mind having Alice here, but if you're going to come home and spend your time in those places downtown—"

"I know. Mum, I found out last night that a friend of mine died. Barney Race. You've heard me mention him. I decided to have a drink in his memory. I ended up having a few too many.

You're right. Those places aren't for me, not anymore. As for Alice, if she weren't here, I'd probably still be downtown."

His father shook his head. "Jess will have you out on your arse if you aren't careful, son."

"Yeah. So, am I welcome for breakfast?"

Mum rolled her eyes. "Of course you're welcome. Alice, pray that if you ever have children, they'll be girls."

Through the meal, Alice chatted easily with Mum and Dad. They obviously liked her. It really was too bad Liam couldn't let her stay. Being welcome must be a nice change for her, but at least she didn't have to go home to her father. That might have made him think twice, but after last night it was clear she'd be better off almost anywhere out of his reach. Until he got himself together – if that ever happened – they didn't belong under the same roof.

After breakfast, Dad took his coffee to the sitting room and motioned for Liam to follow. The room still smelled of liquor and Alice. Dad settled in the armchair and sipped, looking at Liam over the rim of his cup.

"Liam, that girl thinks a lot of you."

"Yeah. More than she should."

"Why do you say that?"

Liam didn't answer. What he'd said to his mother was true – he'd come home last night because even while he was wallowing in grief and self-loathing, he'd known he needed Alice. He couldn't put that into words, and he sure as hell couldn't tell his father how he'd treated her.

Dad took another sip of coffee. "Alice grew up in Frank O'Neill's house, with Carl for a brother. She isn't looking for perfection in a man, and if she was, she wouldn't know it if she fell over it. Your mother and I have been waiting for someone like her to come along for you. Don't miss your chance."

His chance. With most women, last night would have ruined everything, but Alice was still here. Maybe Dad was right – she'd never been treated the way she deserved to be treated by a man, so she expected too little of him. All the more reason to put some distance between them.

"Dad, I think it will be better if Alice goes to her aunt's. It won't look very good if she stays here much longer, and maybe if she goes, it will make her father wake up and start treating her like a human being."

"Maybe. We've met her aunt, and she seems all right." Dad frowned. "Why do you think Frank is so hard on Alice, anyway?"

Liam hesitated. Maybe it wasn't his place to tell them, but his family would have to know sooner or later. "When I was in the hospital with Carl, he told me Alice never learned to read. He said she was sick when she was small and missed a lot of school. She says she's tried to learn, but it didn't work."

His father's frown deepened. "Liam, that girl is sharp as a tack."

"I know. I don't understand it either, but she's admitted it to me. I think that's mainly why she has problems with Frank. The whole family seems to think she's slow."

"Then they're the slow ones." Dad drained his mug, rose and put a hand on Liam's shoulder. Take your time, Liam, but don't sell her short."

"Yeah." As if he hadn't done that in the worst possible way last night.

His father held his gaze. "Don't sell yourself short either."

The sound of cupboard doors closing told Liam the women had finished the breakfast dishes. If Alice were to make the morning train, she needed to get packed and down to the station. He returned to the kitchen as his mother was leaving. Alice dried her hands and faced him. Liam saw in her eyes that she knew what was coming, but he wasn't going to brook any arguments.

All right, Cochrane, tell her it's time to go.

"I just thought of something, Alice. It's such a mild day. We might not have another like this until spring. If Nolan will lend me his car, I'd like to take you out to meet Jess and Fanny. I can drive you to Bedford afterwards."

A flash of happiness lit her eyes and just as quickly passed. "That sounds like a wonderful idea, Liam. It's warm as September today." Liam's hands balled into fists. *What the hell are you playing at, mister?* But at least he had today to try to make up for last night.

Nolan agreed to lend him the car, in exchange for half a lifetime's worth of chores. Alice packed a picnic lunch and within half an hour, they were off. Liam took a sideways glance at her as they turned onto the shore road. Her face glowed with pleasure, just as he'd imagined it would the last time he drove out here. Her family had never owned a car. An outing like this was as much of a treat for her as for him.

The day and the way were beautiful. After almost a week of cold, dour days November had decided to mimic spring, with a mild breeze and sunshine. The bright red leaves of the cranberry bushes that grew in low spots contrasted with the stunted black spruce and exposed granite of the rugged shoreline, where the constant sea winds scoured away the soil, and the ocean shimmered in the distance. They didn't talk much. Alice seemed content to enjoy the scenery, and Liam was more than happy to watch her.

As he had before, he stopped the car on the crest of the hill overlooking Prospect. Alice tucked her wind-whipped hair back under her black knitted tam and took in the view.

"I've never been out here before. I can see why you like living here."

The voice of the slow surf carried up to them, little more than a whisper, a sound forgotten by Liam for years – but not really. It had been there somewhere, buried in his memory, waiting for him to find his way here again. "Yeah. As a kid, I resented Nolan sometimes for going to sea and being away so much, but I understand him better now."

Alice shaded her eyes and scanned the shoreline. "Which house is your cousin's?"

Liam pointed. "The grey one right on the shore, down there."

He doubted if Alice had ever been inside a fisherman's house. She'd grown up in the city, with a city girl's interests, but he saw only appreciation on her face as she looked down at the village.

"Let's go. I want to meet Jess and Fanny."

"They want to meet you, too."

When they pulled into the yard, Jess came out of the shop to greet them. "Now I know why you were so hot to get out of here yesterday, Liam, but what happened to your face?" When Liam just shrugged, Jess rolled his eyes and grinned. "The more things change, the more they stay the same." Fanny bustled out of the house, eyes wide with curiosity.

"Alice, Liam's told us about you. You're staying for dinner, of course."

Liam shook his head. "You weren't expecting us, so we brought a picnic." Fanny would never forgive him if he didn't give her a chance to chat with Alice, but he planned to keep it short. He wanted her to himself.

After tea and a piece of Fanny's gingerbread, Liam and Alice set off walking along the road out of the village. Halfway up the steep hill, a side path led away from the houses onto an expanse of rough land that Liam had come to love since he'd moved here. It reminded him of the Yorkshire moors in England. Flaming red cranberry and dark creeping spruce clung to the stony soil where they could, in hollows and sheltered places, until they gave way to the bare rock where scouring winds swept up from the bay. Then the land ended abruptly in a tumble of rocks where cormorants and gulls stalked and squabbled.

Liam led Alice to a small hollow where a pair of boulders stored the sun's heat and provided shelter from the wind. He set down the picnic basket and spread the car blanket over the dry, springy brown grass. Alice sat and held out her hand to him.

"This is perfect."

Liam eased himself down beside her. "Like it? I found this spot one day last week and promised myself I'd bring you here." He hesitated, the words he'd chosen so carefully on their drive forgotten. "Alice, I don't know why you didn't walk out on me last night, but since you didn't, I want to make it up to you."

"Liam, I understand. You don't have to—"

"Yes, I have to." He interlaced his fingers with hers and held on tight. Did Alice really need to hear this? "Last spring when we were fighting our way through St. Eloi, Barney and I pulled the body of a young girl out of a cottage. Pretty French girl, dark hair, dark eyes, maybe sixteen. She'd been raped and strangled."

It hurt to see the horror in Alice's eyes, but he needed her to understand why he'd become such a wreck last night. Needed her to believe he would never treat her like that again. She shivered, but she didn't look away.

"The terrible stories the recruiters tell – I've always tried to believe most of them aren't true."

He took a few careful breaths and swallowed the bile that rose in his throat. "This one was, but it had a twist. A few days later, a man from our battalion confessed. He said he'd met her alone outside the village. He'd managed to get his hands on some liquor and he started talking to her, teasing her. He spoke pretty good French. He talked her into a couple of kisses, but it went too far. He panicked and killed her, then carried her back into the village and dumped her body. Figured if he was caught, he could say he'd just found her and blame it on the enemy."

Alice took in a swift breath. Her face had gone very pale. "What became of him?"

"He was court-martialled and executed." While the rest of the men watched – but Alice didn't need to know that. Liam looked out toward the bay, recalled her face after he'd mauled her, tears glistening on her cheeks in the light of the sitting-room lamp. Nothing was black and white anymore. "I thought he deserved it. I still do, but sometimes I wonder. Did the war make him lose his conscience, or did he never have one?"

Alice eased her hand from his, slipped her arm around him and laid her head on his shoulder. Even through their coats her warmth reached him, found its way to his heart. "Liam, I'll never believe you could rape a woman. What happened last night happened because I wanted you, too. I kissed you back, remember?" She lifted her head to look into his eyes, then leaned in and pressed a kiss to his mouth, soft and light. Then another. "Do you believe me?"

The delicate fire of her kisses stole his breath. He could only nod in answer. Alice smiled against his lips. "Good."

Then she placed her palms on his chest, pressed him onto his back and kissed him again.

How did she know? What instinct told her he was too raw to take control? Heart pounding with desire, Liam fisted his hands and lay still under her sweet onslaught. His nails dug into his palms as he fought to relax, to let Alice set the pace and take what she wanted from him. It was the hardest thing he'd ever done. Her tongue danced with his, teasing and retreating, daring him to follow. Meanwhile, she made short work of the buttons on his coat and shirt. One moment he felt the chill of the sea air on his chest, then the next her clever fingers were gliding over his skin, leaving trails of heat. And all the time her tongue kept working its magic.

Jesus, Mary and Joseph!

Finally she pulled away and sat up. Cool air rushed in to fill the void between them. Soft and thoughtful, her amber eyes searched his. A chill ran through Liam that had nothing to do with the fresh breeze playing across his bare chest. She seemed to see right through to his soul.

"Liam, I want you to touch me, too. I trust you."

All he could do was stare. "After last night, how can you say that?"

She smiled. "Because it's true."

Still holding his gaze, Alice worked the buttons on her coat and blouse. They fell back, revealing her bruised throat and slender, creamy shoulders above her lace-edged slip and corset. She shivered as the breeze hit her, then she leaned over Liam and covered his mouth with hers again.

He'd have to be more than human to resist her. He pulled his arms from the sleeves of his jacket, tossed the sides of the blanket over Alice's back and molded her to him.

Working blind, he undid the top hook and loosened the front lacing on her corset, then brushed the straps of her slip from her shoulders. Her breast settled into his palm as if it belonged there, a perfect handful, small and firm and tipped with velvet.

Easy. This is for her. He traced her curves, teased the tip, while he kissed her eager mouth with all the tenderness he could muster. He'd never been so aware of a woman – every breath, the smallest response to his caresses. And God, she was responsive. His touch seemed to set her on fire.

He played with her breasts until their kisses began to grow too hungry for safety, Alice's sighs of pleasure too seductive. Then Liam eased her down beside him and held her close, her head nestled in the hollow of his shoulder.

Maybe it was just because it had been so long since Bea, but his heart cracked wide open. Light poured into all the dark corners. Alice wasn't put off by the scars on his body or his soul. The way she'd looked at him last night wasn't blind romanticism. In her eyes, he was whole.

Cocooned in the thick blanket, they lay together for awhile, simply enjoying the contact. Last night's broken sleep had left both of them tired, so they napped a little, kissed a little, and talked a little. Then they dressed, had their picnic and roamed the shoreline, enjoying the rare gift of a day to spend. They'd both been so busy, Liam with his work and Alice with her music, that they'd forgotten the freedom of having nothing to do.

When the afternoon shadows grew long and the warmth of the sun faded, they started for home. Liza Jane was cranky about starting, so sunset overtook them on a lonely stretch of the shore road instead of close to the city as Liam had intended.

As they passed a small cove where the water reflected the red and orange of the western sky, he slowed the car so they could enjoy the view. Maybe this was better after all. Why end the day too early? Alice slipped her arm under his.

"I'll always remember this night and this spot. It's – Liam, look out!"

Liam barely managed to swerve in time to avoid the cat that dashed in front of them. If he'd seen it first they likely would have been fine, but Alice distracted him just long enough for one of the front tires to slip off the road. Liza Jane toppled into the ditch. Liam and Alice landed in a tangle of arms and legs against the passenger side door.

Chapter 17

"Damn!" He rolled off her, tried to sit up and banged his head against the car's roof. "Ouch! Are you all right?"

Alice raised herself on her elbows, shook her head to clear it and held a hand to her ribs. "I don't think anything's broken. How about you?"

"Same here". *Well done, Cochrane.* If he hadn't been so wrapped up in her, this wouldn't have happened, but why did she have to yell? "What a mess. If you hadn't distracted me—"

"I couldn't help it. That animal startled me. It's a good thing we weren't going any faster."

"You're right. Nolan is never going to let me hear the end of this." Liam crawled across the seat, pushed the driver's side door open and climbed gingerly out. Stars glittered overhead in the deep blue, moonless sky. In a few minutes it would be as dark as pitch, and the headlights were powered by the motor, which had cut out. He let himself slide over the back of the car, landed with his feet in six inches of frigid, muddy water, and cursed again. "Climb out, Alice, and be careful."

Her hatless, tousled head appeared above the side of the car. "Here I come."

"Slide over the back. I'll catch you. It's a mess underfoot."

Carrying the car blanket, Alice clambered out and slid off the car. Liam caught her, turned and set her down on the side of the road, but at the wrong moment the soft edge of the ditch gave way. Alice lost her footing and slid into Liam with enough force to make him lose his balance. He landed on his back in the mud, with Alice on top of him. With a muffled "Son of a bitch!" she squirmed off him and got to her feet. On his knees, Liam stared at her.

"What did you just say?"

"You heard me." In the last of the daylight, she stood in front of him, her coat wet and plastered with mud, her soaked skirt and stockings clinging to her legs. The angry set of her jaw made her look very much like her father.

"You're Frank O'Neill's daughter all right."

Liam couldn't be sure in this light, but he thought she was blushing. He climbed out of the ditch, extended a hand to help Alice, then looked up and down the road. Of course, this had to happen on the most deserted part of it.

"The last house we passed was a mile back, and the next one is just as far ahead. We'd better start walking."

Alice looked up at the clear sky. "I suppose so. We'll freeze if we don't. It's going to be a cold night."

With typical suddenness, the unseasonably mild day had already turned sharp. Soaked to the knees, his hair and jacket plastered with mud, Liam took her hand. They kept to the middle of the road to avoid the ruts at the sides and walked as fast as they dared, but that wasn't fast enough to keep warm. By the time they saw a light up ahead, Liam's feet were numb, his hip ached fiercely and Alice's teeth were chattering.

The house was little more than a fishing shed, but smoke curled from the chimney and lamplight glowed from the windows. Liam knocked and prayed that whoever came to the door wouldn't shut it in his filthy face.

Feet shuffled across creaking boards. The door opened a crack. An owlish dark eye peered out at about the level of Liam's shoulder.

"What d'ye want?"

The voice quavered with age. Liam couldn't tell if it belonged to a man or a woman. He tried to sound reassuring.

"We ditched our car a mile or so back toward Prospect. It's getting cold, and we need to find shelter 'til morning. We were hoping you could help us."

"Humph." The door opened a little wider and revealed a face as creased as well-worn shoe leather. The little old man's stove-black eyes darted from Liam to Alice and back. "I've no room for yez here."

Alice spoke through clenched teeth. "Can you tell us who might? I don't think I can walk much further."

He glanced down at her gloved left hand. "Are yez husband and wife?"

Liam restrained an urge to yank the door open and push his way inside. He put his arm around Alice. Her skirt was sopping, her coat was wet through in places, and her feet, like his, were soaked. He'd seen men die of hypothermia overseas. He wasn't going to waste much more time with this curmudgeon. The old man humphed again.

"Out joy-riding, were yez? What can yez expect?" His few tufts of yellowish-grey hair floated like cobwebs as he jerked his head. "That house across the road was my brother's. Now it's mine. He died back in the spring. Yez can stay there."

The door slammed in their faces. Alice and Liam exchanged glances. Her mouth twitched with laughter.

"Nice man."

"Very." Liam looked over his shoulder at the tiny, grey-shingled house across the road. The roof sagged and probably leaked like a sieve, but a stovepipe jutted from its middle. Right now, nothing else mattered. "Come on."

The back end of the house stood on stilts above a small inlet, the front was anchored on solid ground only a yard or so from the road. Liam swung the door open, pulled a box of matches from his coat pocket and lit one. The flare of light showed him a cramped, but reasonably clean space with a squat, cylindrical wood stove, a rusty iron bedstead with a mattress, a hand pump and sink with a small cupboard beside them, a chair and a tiny square table made from a packing crate. The place seemed dry and, blessing of blessings, a lantern stood on the table. He picked it up and felt liquid shift in the base. In an instant he had it lit. Alice closed the door and shut out the darkness.

"Home sweet home."

"Yeah. Get out of your wet things, Alice, and wrap up in the car blanket. You'll be better off in bare feet than wet shoes. I'll have a fire going in a minute."

A box in one corner held some kindling and a few pieces of cordwood. Liam knelt in front of the stove and hoped the pipe wasn't blocked. He kindled a fire and found that it drew reasonably well. When he got up stiffly and turned around, he found Alice huddled on the bed, wrapped in the car blanket, which she'd somehow managed to keep dry when they fell.

Judging by the pile of clothes on the chair, she'd stripped down to her skin. She'd found some dishtowels in the cupboard and used one to wipe the mud from her face and hair. She was shivering, a good sign. Her body was still working to keep her warm. Liam filled a dented enamel pot with water, put it on the stove to heat and held out a hand to her. "Come sit by the fire."

He pulled the mattress off the bed and laid it on the floor for her, then, sitting on the bed frame, he pulled off his boots and socks and undressed. He hadn't been this cold since his last winter in the trenches. He used another of the dishtowels to clean up as best he could, then, wrapped in the coarse grey blanket that had been on the bed, he joined Alice by the stove.

The shadowy lantern light emphasized her delicate profile and gilded her hair. Below her blanket, Alice's slender, shapely feet and calves gleamed white, drawing Liam's gaze. He brushed his fingers along her ankle. Her skin felt like chilled marble.

"Come here." He lifted her feet to his lap and began chafing them. He didn't notice that brisk rubbing had changed to caresses until Alice moaned softly.

"Mmmm. That feels good."

Desire coiled in Liam's belly again. They'd already flirted with danger today. He should stop this now, but—

"Does it?" He traced the curve of Alice's calf with his fingertips. She leaned back on her hands, let her head fall back and closed her eyes.

"I don't think our host would approve."

"Probably not." He let his blanket slip down to his waist to free his other hand. The fire's warmth was just starting to spread through the little shanty, but the heat in Liam's blood kept the chill at bay. He began stroking Alice's other foot, massaging the arch, until the skin was pink and warm and a flush bloomed on her cheeks. She let out a soft sigh.

"Liam, everyone at home will be worried about us."

"There's nothing we can do about it until morning. Right now, all I'm worried about is you."

That adorable, concerned frown was too much for Liam. He scooped Alice up and onto his lap – a sweet, slender armful. If he'd learned anything overseas, it was that life was made up of moments. He had no intention of wasting this one.

Her arms circled his neck as their lips met and melded. Her blanket slipped from her shoulders and bared her to the waist. He caught a whiff of the same perfume she'd worn at the church social, along with the clean, fresh scent of her skin and the musk of her desire for him, a combination that made his head spin.

Remember what she said earlier? She trusts you. Clinging to that thought, he tipped her back on the mattress.

The fire in Liam's eyes scorched Alice's skin. As it had last night, her body turned torpid with desire under his weight. After today's taste of the pleasure he could give her, she knew that if she didn't stop him now, she wouldn't stop him at all. Somehow she found her voice.

"Liam... if I get pregnant, you know Dad will turn me out for good. I love you – I have for years, but—"

Poised above her, leaning on his elbows, he froze. "What?"

So now he knew. Alice couldn't find it in her to regret it. She smiled and touched his cheek. "It's always been you for me, Liam. Ever since the day you found me crying and stopped to find out why. I've tried to forget it, I've gone out with other men… but there you have it. Some feelings just don't go away. What you did to me this afternoon felt so good, I'm afraid..." Words failed her when he brought his face close to hers.

"Alice, I give you my word I won't get you pregnant. You said you trusted me."

She nodded. "I do."

His mouth fused to hers with all the passion of last night, only this time he was with her completely, body and soul. Every kiss, every touch. When he tasted the hollow between her breasts, his low moan vibrated in her core.

"Mmm. Alice, you taste like heaven."

She held her breath, waiting for him to capture her nipple in his mouth, but instead he turned her over and began exploring her back with his lips, nibbling her shoulders, dropping hot kisses along her spine. Then his fingers slid between her thighs and stroked her where she ached for him the most. Alice closed her eyes, curled her fingers into the lumpy mattress and held on for dear life as waves of sensation broke over her. She thought her body would explode with need when he stopped.

"God, Liam, please—"

He turned her onto her back again and looked down at her, his face taut with passion. "I want to see your face when you go over the edge." Then his fingers were there again, teasing her, dipping inside her. The lantern's light dissolved in a starburst as the tension inside her shattered into shards of pleasure that pierced her heart as well as her body. Liam was right there with her, kissing her, whispering to her, until she came down from her peak and nestled in his arms.

This was why she'd waited for him all these years.

Neither of them spoke. Alice didn't have words for what she was feeling, and Liam seemed to know without being told. How? A fragment of memory flashed into her mind, something his mother had said – or refused to say.

'I don't think it helped that—"

"What didn't help, Mrs. Cochrane?"

'Liam doesn't like talking about his time overseas, and I think he'd rather I didn't about it, either.'

Now, lying in Liam's arms, she understood. He knew how she felt because he'd loved someone before. Only for some reason, that person hadn't been there when he needed her most. When he'd come so close to dying.

She knew, because neighbourhood gossip would have told her otherwise, that Liam hadn't been seeing anyone seriously before he enlisted. In fact, he'd been starting to get a bit of a reputation for following in Nolan's footsteps as a ladies' man. So, Liam must have had a girl overseas. Had she died? Left him? Had he left her?

It's none of your business, Alice. If he wants you to know, he'll tell you when he's ready. All that mattered was that he was here with her now, and that he'd just taken her to a peak of pleasure she could never have imagined. Now it was his turn.

She sat up. Liam watched her, his eyes – leonine eyes, she'd always thought, with their flecks of gold – smoky with passion. Alice let her gaze roam over him, from his face with the light from the open stove flickering across it, to his chest with its sprinkling of dark curls that dwindled to an intriguing trail down his lower torso. He'd put on muscle and could stand to put a bit more on his solid frame, but just as he was, he took her breath away.

Her heart squeezed painfully as she got her first sight of his scars. *Oh, love, if I could have been there for you when she wasn't – whoever she was.* For the last three years, Alice had lived with the shame of not doing any war work, while other girls went overseas as nurses or ambulance drivers, worked in factories at home or at the very least, joined the Red Cross like Georgie. Her mother's health had excused Alice to some extent in the neighbours' eyes, but not in her own. For an instant, she envied Liam's nurses almost to the point of hatred.

Knowing he was watching her, she didn't let her gaze linger on his scars. Instead, she shifted it to his arousal. She took his hard length in her hand and bent to brush her lips over his mouth.

"Does this feel good?" She stroked him lightly. She heard his breath catch in his throat.

"Yeah. Oh, yeah." His mouth opened under hers. She lingered for a slow, heated kiss, then turned her attention back to his sex. Slowly, stomach fluttering, she bent her head. What if he didn't like her mouth there? But instinct told her he would.

Her instincts were true. When her lips and tongue touched him, his body went rigid and his hips bucked.

"Oh, angel."

She kissed him, swirled her tongue against his taut, silky skin, then blew across the moisture she left behind. He trembled. As she ran her lips over him from base to tip the smell and taste of him became part of her, marking her as his. When she glanced up, Liam's face was a mask of pleasure so intense it looked like pain. He spoke through clenched teeth.

"Easy, sweetheart, or this is going to be over way too soon."

Alice shifted to kiss his mouth again. As her tongue danced with his, she trailed her fingertips across his chest and down to his scars. They represented months of pain. She wanted to give him an equal measure of pleasure.

"We couldn't have that." Slowly, lightly, she kissed her way back down his body and began caressing his sex again with her lips and fingertips, feeling his body react, keeping him on the edge. It gave her a heady sense of power to see how her touch affected him, and it tugged at her heart to see the raw emotion in his eyes. When his essence finally spilled from his body, he called her name.

Satisfied, Alice pressed a soft kiss to his mouth. Liam took a shaky breath, then threaded his fingers into her hair and gave her a slow, wicked grin.

"If I didn't know you'd never done that before..."

Blushing hotly, Alice propped herself on an elbow. "I haven't."

"I'm teasing you, Alice." His grin softened. "Love, you're a natural."

The shanty was warm now. Alice got up, rummaged in the cupboard for two more dishtowels and dipped them in the pot of water on the stove. She gently wiped Liam clean with one, used the other to wash herself and tossed them into the fire along with the ones they'd used earlier. She felt a bit rude destroying them when they belonged to someone else, but they were worn to rags anyway.

She shut the stove door, blew out the lantern and settled into Liam's arms. He pulled the car blanket up around them. The sounds of their breathing mingled with the murmur of the water outside and the crackle of the fire. Starlight glimmered faintly through the window.

After Liam's deep, even breathing told her he was asleep, Alice lay still, listening and thinking. He'd asked her today if she could live in a home like his cousin's. Jess and Fanny's house was a palace compared to this, but a far cry from her home.

She'd always taken her social position for granted – the pretty clothes, the ample food and comfortable surroundings. Someday, Liam would earn decent money as a craftsman, but he might never be able to provide her with all the things she was used to.

She smiled in the darkness. If a one-room shanty could become her world just because he was with her, she'd never need more than he was able to give. Listening to his heartbeat, she drifted off to sleep.

Chapter 18

Liam felt a twinge in his shoulder muscles as he shifted on the lumpy mattress. The feel of a warm weight beside him, a smooth leg tucked between his, made him think for a moment that he was back in Chelsea. Then he remembered and opened his eyes.

The first dim light filtered through the salt-speckled windows of the shanty. Alice's sweet face was close to his, partly curtained by her hair. Her right hand was splayed on his chest, fingers curled lightly. The memory of what those fingers and that mouth had done to him last night stirred his body, and the feelings she'd drawn from him stirred his heart. The kind of feelings he'd thought he'd never have and didn't want to have again. And more.

Too late. He'd have to deal with them.

He hated to wake her. With the blanket down around her shoulders, her hair in a tumble, long lashes touching her cheeks, Alice looked good enough to eat, but there was no time. Liam's stomach told him he'd missed supper last night, and they had to find someone with a team of horses to get Liza Jane out of the ditch. He gave himself five minutes to watch Alice sleep before he brushed her hair back from her face and kissed her.

"Rise and shine, sweetheart. We've got to get moving."

"Ugh." She sat up, grimacing. "I'm full of as many kinks as this mattress has lumps."

He grinned. "We may not have had the softest bed, but the company was good."

She smiled back, a knowing, sensual smile. "Yes, it was."

Their clothes were mud-stained and bedraggled, but dry. They washed and dressed, put the mattress back on the bed and stepped out into the frosty dawn. Alice cast a doubtful glance at the house across the road.

"The lamp's lit. He must be up. I suppose we should say thank you."

Liam's stomach growled again. "Yeah. You never know, he might offer us breakfast."

When they knocked, the old man opened the door a crack and peered at them suspiciously, just as he'd done before. "Ye're on yer way then?"

Alice nodded. "Yes. We wanted to thank you."

His scowl deepened as he stared up at Liam. "Thanks is all very well."

Liam fished a dollar out of his jacket pocket. "This is for you. Is there anyone close by who has horses? We need to get our car back on the road."

Their host reached for the money and quickly pulled his hand back inside. He jerked his head in the direction of the city. "Two houses that way." Then the door slammed shut.

Fortunately the middle-aged fisherman who lived two houses away had a more hospitable disposition. He hitched his shaggy dapple greys to his fish cart and made room for Alice on the seat. Liam stood in the back, breathing in the aroma of salt mackerel, as they drove back to the car. By the time the sun was fully up, they had Liza Jane back on the road. For a wonder, she started without complaint. They thanked the man with the team and climbed in.

"Alice, where's that picnic basket?"

They made breakfast out of the leftover ham sandwiches from yesterday. An hour later, they pulled into Nolan's yard. Their day out of time was over. They went to church with the family, laughed and joked over Sunday dinner about their night in the shanty and their none-too-genial host, and resigned themselves to Nolan's teasing. When it came time for Liam to leave, Alice stood on the porch in his arms and linked her fingers behind his neck.

"'Til Saturday."

"'Til Saturday. Friday, if I can manage it." Liam looked into her eyes and wished he could pick her up, carry her to his room and spend the rest of the day making love to her. "It's going to be a long week. Alice, thank you for helping me pick up the pieces Friday night. Thank you for giving me a second chance." He ran his fingertips over the curve of her cheek. "To think you were here for me all these years and I didn't know it."

She smiled. "I took care to make sure you didn't."

He wasn't ready to say 'I love you,' but he gave her a kiss that said it for him. Alice picked up his duffle bag and fitted the strap over his shoulder.

"Go."

She watched him out of sight from the porch, waved at the last moment before the hill came between them. It wasn't until late that evening Liam realized they'd both forgotten Alice was supposed to have gone to her aunt's yesterday.

Alice let her fingers drift over the piano's keys as lightly as snowflakes were landing on the Cochranes' front room window. Thursday afternoon already. Would Liam be able to get to Halifax on Friday night again? She ran through *Moonlight Sonata* with half her mind on him. She hadn't anticipated how difficult it would be, only seeing him on weekends.

She'd brought the music from home. When she turned the page, a note her mother had pencilled in the margin stood out. *Tempo.* A reminder to watch her pace. Alice recognized the form of the word the same way she recognized a series of sixteenth notes.

Regret nagged at her. She'd been home to see Mother on Monday and found that nothing had changed. Alice had developed a warm affection for Liam's parents, and she knew how much they missed their daughter, but in fairness, she couldn't stay with them much longer. She'd talk it over with Liam on the weekend. Perhaps going to her aunt's would be best, even though she'd lose some time with him.

She paused when someone knocked at the front door, then started playing again when she heard Meg's footsteps in the hall. The door opened and closed with only a brief exchange of words between Meg and a man. When she heard no footsteps returning to the kitchen, Alice left the piano and poked her head around the front room door.

Meg stood in the hall, reading a slip of paper. It looked like a telegram. She looked up with a start when Alice stepped out of the front room.

"Meg, what is it? I hope it's not bad news."

It certainly didn't seem like good news. Concern and a little anger showed in Meg's dark eyes. "No... at least, I don't think so." Frowning, she scanned the paper again. "This is for Liam. I think it's from someone he knew overseas. She sent this from Montreal. She's going to be arriving in Halifax on Saturday."

"*She?*"

"It's signed 'Bea.' Liam mentioned that name to me once, when he was waking up after his surgery. He told me they were involved, but it didn't work out."

A cold chill settled in the pit of Alice's stomach. "He must have been quite 'involved' with Bea if he gave her your address. Does she say why she's coming?"

Meg folded the telegram and slipped it in her apron pocket. "No, just that she's coming to Halifax and wants to see Liam – actually, she says she *needs* to see him."

The chill in Alice's stomach turned to nausea. She could think of only one reason why Bea would use the word 'need.'

A child.

Her temper rose as she recalled the sight of Liam's scars. "She's come a lot further than she would have had to go to be with him when he was wounded."

Meg put an arm around Alice's shoulders. Her voice was soft with sympathy. "Yes, she has. Liam won't forget that she wasn't there for him, whatever her reason for finding him now. She can't expect to just walk into his life again, especially now that he has you."

Alice shrugged her off. "I guess that's up to him."

She climbed the stairs to her room, sat on the bed and waited for her stomach to stop churning. Celia's smiling face confronted her from the wedding photo on the dresser.

I don't care much for weddings. The anger in Liam's words her first night here took on a different meaning now. So did the way he'd treated her the night he came home drunk. Maybe that hadn't all been about his brother and Barney.

Holding her stomach, Alice lay back on the bed. She didn't cry, but the burning ache behind her eyes hurt more than tears. She lay still and closed her eyes. It couldn't hurt this much for long.

A few minutes later, Meg stepped firmly into the room and sat on the edge of the bed. "Alice, this won't do. If you love Liam, you've got to be willing to fight for him."

Alice sat up and curled her arms around her knees. "Meg, he might not be mine to fight for. What if – what if he married her and never told anyone? You know Rob Murphy came home this spring with a French wife and told his family nothing beforehand. The only reason Liam would have told this Bea how to reach you is so she could write if something happened to him and she – she needed you."

After a moment's thought, Meg seemed to make up her mind about something. She leaned forward and held Alice's gaze.

"Liam told Jack something last weekend. I found it hard to

believe, but I've been watching you this week and I know it's true. You've never learned to read, have you?"

Alice flinched, then straightened her shoulders. She wouldn't let her shame show. "No, I haven't."

She saw the last thing she expected in Meg's eyes – admiration. "Alice, I would never have known. All I can say is, it doesn't matter to Jack and me, and I know it doesn't matter to Liam either. Maybe he did love Bea – or at least he thought so – but he's been a different man since he's gotten involved with you, and that's what matters to us. As for marriage, I don't think he'd keep that from us, not for this long, even if it didn't work." She pulled Alice into a hug. "Now, I can't picture any daughter of your father rolling over and playing dead for a rival. You didn't with your own sister, so why do it now?"

Alice saw herself standing in a ditch in the dark, swearing, while Liam grinned at her. She took a deep breath.

"You're right. I've got my wind back now, Meg. Thank you."

"You're welcome."

Meg left her alone. Unable to help it, Alice sat there on the bed, imagining what Bea looked like. Was she blonde or dark? Alice pictured her with blue eyes and a peaches-and-cream English complexion. She saw a child, too, with fine blond curls and the makings of Liam's strong features. A pang of longing tore through her.

Stop it. If she was meant for him, she would have been there when he needed her.

After a long evening and a restless night, she stole down to the kitchen early, made coffee and toast, then put on her coat and slipped out. She'd given Dad enough time. If she no longer had a home, she needed to know.

Georgie was clearing the breakfast table when Alice opened the kitchen door. Her sister set the dishes in the sink and left the room, leaving her alone with her parents. She faced her father squarely.

"Dad, I'm here because I can't keep on living with Liam's family. It isn't fair. Either I'm coming back here or I'm going to Aunt Sarah's, but if I go to her, I won't be back. So, which is it going to be?"

Her father's eyebrows shot up. "You're talking big all of sudden. What's happened? Has Liam proposed?"

"No, he hasn't. Maybe he never will, but that's not the issue. I need to know whether I'm part of this family or not."

Her father's jaw set. "I said my piece when you walked out of here. As far as I'm concerned—"

Mother's chair scraped the floor as she got to her feet. "Frank, this has gone on long enough. If Alice isn't part of this family, then neither am I. If she goes to Sarah's, then I'll go with her."

Alice stood rooted to the floor in shock. She couldn't remember Mother ever speaking to Dad like that. His eyes flashed with temper.

"Helen—"

"I mean it. We've already lost our son. I won't sit by and lose another child. Alice has a right to happiness if she can find it."

For a moment, Dad looked too surprised to argue, then his tough front crumbled. "Before he went overseas, Liam was on his way to becoming as much of a womanizer as that brother of his. I don't want Alice to get hurt."

Alice swallowed the lump in her throat. If he only knew how hurt she could be – and why. "I'm a grown woman, Dad. If Georgie can take her chances, so can I."

Silence hung heavy in the air. Her father stood. "You've got more spine than I thought, Alice."

She knew him too well to expect him to humble himself by asking her to come back. Not daring to smile, she exchanged a glance with her mother.

"I'll go and give my thanks to the Cochranes. I should be back within an hour."

Liam stopped for a moment on the sidewalk in front of his parents' house. Light peeped around the drawn blinds at the kitchen windows. His boat had left early this morning. The sun wasn't up yet, but it looked like the household was. Picturing Alice's welcoming smile, he hurried around to the back door.

Alice was in the kitchen, but she wasn't smiling. She came to meet him slowly. When he took her in his arms, she felt different. Not as yielding. His anticipation dissolved as he tilted her face up to his.

"What's bothering you?"

She stepped away and lifted a piece of paper from the mail tray on the table. "Liam, I patched things up with Dad this week. I came back here last night so I could be here when you got home this morning, but I've taken my things home." She handed him the paper. "Also, this came for you Thursday night."

He scanned the telegram. *Liam, will be in Hfx on the 24th stop need to see you stop will phone if possible stop Bea*

Bea. Here. The room tilted, the colour of everything in it darkened. Liam let the telegram fall from his hand. Alice's voice barely registered.

"Your mother said Bea is someone you knew in England."

"Yeah."

"You and she—"

"We lived together. For the last year before I was wounded, I stayed with Bea in her sister's flat in London whenever I was on leave."

Alice's face had turned white. Liam restrained an urge to throw something. *Dad's right. You don't get away with anything in this world.* He waited for her to hurl the accusations he deserved. She let out a long breath.

"What happened?"

Liam dropped his duffle bag, kicked it across the kitchen and cursed Bea under his breath. She had a hell of a nerve to show up here and hurt his family and Alice. He sat at the table and shrugged. "I wrote to her from the hospital. She never wrote back. Then I got word that she'd married someone else. I came home and tried to forget her."

Alice stepped up behind him and rested her hands on his shoulders. "Liam, I'm sorry. You must have loved her."

Liam looked up into her eyes. He owed her the truth. "Yeah, I did. I wanted to marry her."

Alice accepted that with the same absence of judgment she'd always shown him. She took a seat across from him and leaned her elbows on the table, her gaze thoughtful. "If Bea married someone else, why do you suppose she's here?"

"Good question." Bea hadn't been the kind of woman to run after a man. She was too pragmatic for that, not to mention too attractive. Liam's face heated when Alice voiced his fear.

"Is it possible she had a child?"

"Of course it's possible. That's why I wanted to marry her, but she wanted to wait. She said her parents weren't keen on her moving so far away, and she wanted to give them time to get used to the idea. But then, less than three months after I was wounded, she married another man. So any child she might have is no responsibility of mine."

While Liam spoke, emotions chased each other across Alice's face – anger, shock, sadness. He saw them as if from a distance. There might be a part of him alive in the world that he didn't even know about.

"You know, I could forgive her for getting cold feet about moving so far from home. Maybe I could even forgive her for marrying someone else so quickly. But if she had my child and didn't tell me—"

Alice laid a hand over his. "I couldn't forgive her for that either."

Out the side window, Liam saw the sun just breaking the horizon. A murmur of voices reached them from upstairs. His parents would be down any minute.

"What do Mum and Dad think of this?"

He rose and stood by the window. Alice joined him. "They don't know what to think."

Liam pushed away his guilt. After all, Nolan had given his parents a run for their money in his day. "No wonder. I haven't told them anything about Bea. I'll have to see her, I suppose. It'll be interesting to see how she explains herself."

Alice spoke with the first anger she'd shown. "It certainly will be."

Liam took her hand. "Yeah. Was your father decent about you going home?"

A sad smile tugged at Alice's mouth. "More or less. Dad doesn't like anyone defying him, but for once, Mother put her foot down. She actually told him that if I went to my aunt's, she'd go, too." She shrugged. "Things will never be much different between Dad and me. We just don't speak the same language." She laid her cheek against Liam's shoulder for a moment before she stepped away. "I'll start breakfast."

Alice took a saucepan from the cupboard and filled it with water for porridge. Liam watched the sun come up and tried to imagine Bea with a baby. If she'd borne him a child, it would have to be close to ten months old now. Otherwise, she would have known she was pregnant when he left her the last time. That day rose clear and vivid in his mind – a misty June morning. Bea waving from the sitting room window. Their goodbyes unsaid, as always. Goodbye smacked of finality. Instead, they'd always parted with some frivolous plan for his next leave. This time, it was a spree on the town.

"Call me from the station when your train gets in." Bea kissed him and gave him a wicked grin. "I'll meet you, and we can start getting drunk in earnest." A joke, of course. They'd have a drink or two with dinner, take in a Vaudeville show and then go home to the flat. Those plans had kept him living from each furlough to the next.

If passion between two people grasping greedily at life could be called love, then he and Bea had been in love.

A few minutes later, when his parents came into the kitchen, Liam told them what he'd just told Alice. It wasn't any easier the second time around. His mother listened tight-lipped, then spoke with more anger than he could recall her expressing before.

"That young lady has a lot to answer for."

Dad fixed a stern eye on Liam. "Yes, she does, but if she wouldn't marry you, you should have been out of there. It takes two to make a mess like this."

"I know, Dad, but she was the only thing that kept me sane. And I didn't run out on her. She knew where to find me."

Dad's expression softened a bit. "I can't really blame you, son. You're only human. Now let's leave it alone until we hear from her."

Liam spent the longest morning of his life, wondering if Bea would suddenly appear on his parents' doorstep. She'd have no choice unless she managed to find Nolan's phone number. After breakfast, Liam crossed the street and warned them to expect a call. Nolan and Ruth didn't ask questions, though they knew about the telegram. The sympathy in Nolan's eyes told him that.

After lunch Drew dashed into his grandparents' sitting room, where the family was doing their best to pass the time. Alice looked up from the music she was copying and dropped her pen. Liam's stomach knotted as he put down his book.

"Call for me?"

"Yes, Uncle Liam."

He glanced at Alice, saw the strain on her face. God, he hated putting her through this.

He followed Drew across to Nolan's and took the phone.

Hearing Bea's voice felt unreal – the English lilt, the well-remembered cadence.

"Hello, Liam." An awkward pause. "I'm glad I managed to phone. It must have surprised you to hear from me."

"Yeah, you could say that. Why are you here, Bea? It's bloody dangerous, crossing these days."

"I'd rather explain in person. Can we meet?"

"Yes, I suppose so. Where are you?"

She gave him the address of a boarding house downtown on Barrington. He gave her directions to his parents' house.

"Thanks, Liam. I'll get a cab and be there in half an hour."

After Liam hung up, Nolan put a hand on his shoulder. "You look like you could use a drink."

"I'm not drinking these days."

"Coffee, then."

"No, I'll have Scotch."

In the front room, Nolan poured their drinks. Ruth had taken the children out to run some errands. Liam sipped in silence, waiting for the whiskey to ease the turmoil inside him. All the memories he'd worked so hard to bury whirled in his mind, the smell of Bea's hair, the taste of her lips, her skin. The rush of making love to her, of feeling alive when they knew life could end tomorrow or the next day or next week. Nolan watched him closely.

"She really got under your skin, didn't she, Liam?"

Liam put his drink down on the coffee table. It wasn't going to help. "Yeah, she did. Nolan, what if there's a baby?"

Nolan leaned back in his chair and grinned. "Then that would make you a father. It happens to most of us eventually, you know."

Liam's stomach lurched. "For God's sake, Nolan, I'm not ready for that."

Nolan sipped his drink, then set it down and fitted his fingertips together. Over them, his eyes looked into Liam's. "No one ever is. I found that out when Drew was born. Being a parent is the scariest thing I've ever done – and the most rewarding."

Liam remembered Drew's birth well. Ruth's labour was difficult, and by the time it ended, Nolan was a wreck. Liam had learned that day how much his brother loved Ruth. Like his parents loved each other. He might not be ready to be a father, but he wouldn't give a child of his any less than he'd been given.

"But you were married and settled when Drew was born. I can't be a father to a child who's in England."

Nolan's brow furrowed the way Mum's did when she was thinking. "Here's how I see it. This girl has come a long way and taken a big risk to find you, so she has a reason. If there's a child, then either she wants to marry you, or she wants to leave the child with you."

Liam choked on a sip of Scotch. "Jesus, Mary and Joseph! What would I do with a baby?"

Nolan chuckled, then sobered. "It hasn't been that long since my kids were babies, Liam. You were good with them, and I'd say Alice would make a good mother. As for ways and means, you know we'd help you until you're earning again. We know you're working hard to make that happen."

Liam tried to picture Alice with a baby in her arms, but he couldn't bring the image into focus. He didn't even know if she liked children. "I couldn't ask Alice to take on someone else's child."

"Your child."

"Still... Besides, Bea has a husband. She married while I was in hospital."

Nolan let out a low whistle. "She did? That changes things, but I still say being a father is like nothing else you'll ever do in life. Don't give it up lightly."

Liam downed the rest of his drink. "I'd better go. She'll be here soon."

He waited in his parents' front room, where he'd see the cab pull up. Alice waited with him. They didn't talk, but just having her there helped, though Liam didn't understand why she hadn't said 'good riddance' and gone home, like most girls would. She sat at the piano, playing snatches of melody. She hit a jarring note when the sound of an approaching car reached them.

Liam moved to the window. The black cab pulled to a stop in front of the house. Bea got out, trim and neat in a plum-coloured travelling suit.

She was alone.

Chapter 19

The same generous curves, the same bobbed, nut-brown curls. Superficially, she resembled Georgie. Strange he'd never thought of that before. He'd spent the morning trying to prepare, but when he stood face to face with Bea, memories overwhelmed him.

Her dark blue eyes held an uncertain light. Her old crooked smile trembled a little as she held out her hand.

"Hello, Liam. It's good to see you looking so well."

He ignored the hand. "Where's your husband?"

Bea didn't flinch from his anger. "Kenneth is dead. He was killed in action, as I thought you were until a month ago."

Oh, Lord. If some idiot clerk mixed me up with Michael-John... Liam stood barring the doorway with his arm until Bea snapped him out of his shocked trance.

"May I come in? I'd rather not discuss this on the doorstep."

Liam took her into the front room. His parents had come in from the kitchen when they heard the door. He showed Bea to a chair and stood behind her.

Everyone, this is Bea Chapman. Bea, this is my mother, Meg, my father, Jack, and this is Alice O'Neill. She and I are keeping company."

He took a seat across the room from Alice. She sat up straight and looked Bea uncompromisingly in the eyes. Bea's face coloured.

"Hello everyone."

Alice only nodded. Mum spoke without her usual warmth. "You've made a long, dangerous voyage, Bea. I'm sure you're not here for a casual visit."

Bea looked down, pulled off her gloves, then met Liam's mother's gaze and held it steadily. "No, Mrs. Cochrane, I'm not. I'm here because there are some things Liam needs to know that I didn't want to tell him in a letter." Bea faced him again. "Liam, last July I got a notice that you'd been killed in action. I had no reason to think otherwise until I got the letters you wrote from hospital – last month."

Alice's face coloured as if from a slap. Mum looked disbelieving – as well she might. It made no sense to Liam, either.

"I sent the letters to your sister's flat. Why didn't you get them?"

By Bea's expression, her answer was as difficult to give as it was for Liam to hear. "After I got the notice, I went back to my parents' house to live. The mail was forwarded, but my mother intercepted your letters. You knew she wasn't keen on the thought of me leaving England. After Kenneth was killed, she finally gave them to me. I don't know if I can ever forgive her."

"Yeah. Did she tell you she sent me a wedding picture?"

Bea's eyes filled with tears. "So that's how you knew I was married. Oh my God. No. No, she couldn't."

A painful knot formed in Liam's chest. It was all plausible. Mistakes happened, and Bea's mother might be that much of a witch, but still—

"The envelope was addressed in her writing. I'd seen it before. So you thought I was dead, and within three months you married someone else. Where did you meet him? Did you pick him up at the same canteen where we met?"

Bea's colour deepened. "No. I'd known Kenneth for years. We were old friends."

Out of frustration, Liam snapped. "Yeah. For all I know,

you were 'friends' while I was at the front."

He saw on Bea's face that he'd hurt her, but her voice stayed firm and quiet. "Liam, that isn't fair. For your information, Kenneth was at the front then, too. I married him quickly because I'd discovered I was carrying your child."

Liam lost his breath as if it had been knocked from him. "You were *pregnant,* and your mother *still* didn't give you my letters?"

Bea pulled a handkerchief from her jacket pocket and wiped her eyes. "I didn't tell her right away. When Kenneth proposed, I told him. He said it didn't matter to him. I knew he'd cared for me for years. When I started to show, I told my parents the child was yours. Kenneth was killed when Nicholas was four months old. He's nine months old now." She blew out a breath and sat up straighter. "He looks like you. When I finally got your letters, I found passage as a clerk on a hospital ship coming to Montreal, and here I am."

"Where's the baby?"

"At my boarding house. The landlady is watching him. She has a little one of her own."

Angry words rushed out before Liam could stop them. "I can't believe you brought a child across the ocean in the middle of a war. Haven't you heard of the *Lusitania*? Why didn't you write?"

She twisted her handkerchief in her hands, lifted a shoulder. "I didn't think you'd write back."

Liam couldn't deny that he probably wouldn't have. He glanced at the others in the room. His mother had tears in her eyes. His father looked angry and resigned. Alice looked as if she'd been punched in the stomach.

Just across town, his son was waiting.

"Maybe I wouldn't have. Bea, if this is your mother's doing I'm sorry, but..." He drew a painful breath around the weight in his chest. "You'll have a widow's pension. You won't be destitute. My pension will be ending soon, but I'm working with my cousin. He isn't paying me yet, but as soon as I'm earning I'll start sending you what I can, when I can, to put away for the boy's education. It won't be much, but by the time he needs it, it'll amount to something, I guess. That's all I can do."

Bea looked slowly from him to Alice and back again, then dropped her gaze. "I understand. Would you like to meet Nicholas?"

Something like panic rose in Liam's throat at the thought. "I don't see any point in that. Is your boarding house all right?"

"Yes, it's fine. I came prepared to stay for awhile, so you needn't worry about me." Bea met his gaze again and gave him a tight little smile. "Don't look so bowled over, Liam. I didn't come here expecting anything from you. If you change your mind about seeing Nicholas, you know where to find me."

She rose. Liam got up with her. "I'm staying with my cousin during the week. There's no phone. If there's an emergency, call my brother and he'll come for me."

He heard how cold he sounded, but Bea showed no sign of noticing. "Thank you. I'd better go." She glanced at the others in the room. "This has upset you all. I'm sorry. Goodbye."

Liam reached for his manners. "I'll call you a cab."

"Never mind. Mrs. Draper told me which tram to take. I - I'll see you, then."

Silence filled the room in Bea's wake. Liam dropped into his chair again and rested his head in his hands.

"Christ, what a mess."

"You can say that again," his father growled. "Do you think she was telling the truth?"

Liam faced him. "I suppose it's all possible, but I don't understand why she's here if she wants nothing from me."

His father snorted. "Neither do I, but I guess you made yourself pretty clear."

Mum looked too overwhelmed to speak. Alice held Liam's

gaze, her voice soft with regret. "Yes, you did."

Her tone flicked on the raw somehow. Liam's temper flared. "What else could she expect?"

"Nothing."

He turned away and glanced out the window. He couldn't pretend to misunderstand Alice, but it was best for all concerned this way. "Bea will marry again. The baby will have a father before he's old enough to miss one."

Mum found her voice. "Probably. She seems like a practical girl, but Liam, she isn't what I was expecting."

"She isn't what I was expecting, either." He'd expected to be able to hate her. Instead, he found himself remembering how it felt to sit with Bea in front of the coal fire in her flat, with the door closed against the world and his mind closed to everything but her. Remembering how it felt every time he had to leave her.

He'd been pretty rough on her. If she was telling the truth, she was no more to blame for what had happened than he, but the fact remained that he'd asked her to marry him, asked her to let him protect her, and she'd refused. "Maybe I shouldn't have been so hard on her, but to come over here with a baby and no one waiting for her – what did she expect me to do, invite her to stay here? What if I'd gone to Celia's? Was she going to drag the kid across the country to find me?"

His mother shook her head. "She probably thought we'd reply to her telegram if you'd moved."

"Nolan said she might be considering leaving the baby with me. I hope I set her straight on any chance of that, anyhow." Unable to sit any longer, Liam got to his feet. "I need some air. Alice, will you come for a walk?"

They put jackets on and started toward Needham Hill. The November afternoon was soft and brooding, all shades of brown under a cloudy sky. Alice walked beside Liam in silence. Though it made no sense, that irritated him.

"You think I should see the kid, don't you?"

Alice looked up at him, took his hand. "His name is Nicholas, not 'the kid.' As for seeing him, I think you think you should, but you're afraid to."

He opened his mouth to deny it, but couldn't. He'd never been a very good liar. "Why?"

Alice stopped and tugged on Liam's hand to make him face her. "Because you might start caring for him."

Sure. That was only common sense, when he'd probably never see his son again. So why did it feel like a cheap excuse? "If I'm not going to be a part of his life, he's better off not knowing I exist."

"But you'll always know he exists." Alice's eyes searched his. "When that telegram came and your mother told me what she knew about Bea, I couldn't forgive her for not being there for you when you needed her, but now I don't know if she's done anything that needs forgiving. I only know that you were with her a lot longer than you've been with me, and now the two of you have a child to consider. I don't want you if you come to me with regrets, Liam – for her or your son."

He read her perfectly. If he wasn't careful, he was going to lose Alice, too. He reached for her other hand.

"I can't help thinking about what Nolan said. If Bea walks away and leaves the baby—"

"If you think she'd do that, then you don't know much about women, or at least about mothers."

Liam took a deep breath, but it didn't ease the cold lump of fear in his chest. "Yeah. Well, I'll have to at least pay a call and make sure she's in a decent place." Alice's face showed that she was struggling with this as much as he – and she hadn't said a selfish word. He swallowed and hoped his tongue wouldn't trip over what he wanted to say, what he should have said last weekend. "I love you, Alice. That isn't going to change."

"And I love you, Liam, but we can't pretend this doesn't change things." She held his gaze with troubled eyes, then stood on tiptoe to kiss him, a kiss full of doubt. "Go and see Bea. Talk to her and figure out where you both stand. I'll be waiting. Right now, I think I'll go home. You'll want to see her tonight, since you have to go back to Prospect tomorrow. I'll see you after church in the morning."

She walked away. Liam went on to the top of Needham Hill and found a sheltered spot to sit. The familiar landscape seemed changed. He looked south towards the spot where The Narrows widened into the Harbour. The ocean of time between his life now and his life with Bea had vanished.

Later, when he was fairly certain the baby would be in bed asleep, he caught a tram downtown. Toward the south end of Barrington he found Bea's boarding house, an unadorned two-story saltbox. It looked respectable enough. A square-built woman in her thirties came to the door.

"Yes?"

"Hello. Are you the landlady here? I'm looking for Beatrice – I'm sorry, I've forgotten her married name."

"Yes, I own this house." The woman looked him up and down, then gave him a businesslike nod. "I'm Mrs. Draper. And you are?"

"Liam Cochrane. I met Bea overseas." He offered his hand, unsure what to expect. Bea had said the baby looked like him. If Mrs. Draper saw the resemblance, who knew what conclusions she'd draw, but after a moment she shook his hand and stepped aside to let him in.

"Come in. You can wait in the sitting room." She nodded toward the first door on the left side of the long, dark hall. "I'll tell Bea you're here."

The landlady disappeared up the staircase. Liam waited on the sofa in the plainly furnished sitting room. He stood when Bea came in.

She'd changed out of her suit from this afternoon and now wore a navy skirt and white blouse, a practical outfit that didn't look plain on her. Bea had always been a girl who dominated her clothes. Whether she dressed up or down, you noticed *her* first – her nicely rounded figure, the animation of her face, the lively play of her blue eyes.

"Hello, Liam. I didn't expect to see you tonight."

Those eyes hadn't lost their punch. When Liam took his seat again and she sat beside him, her perfume triggered an avalanche of memories. He pushed them to the back of his mind and said what he'd come to say.

"I guess I was a little hard on you this afternoon, Bea. I owe you an apology, and I wanted to see for myself that you'd found a decent place to stay."

It didn't help that she seemed uncomfortable, too. "Yes, you were hard on me, but it's understandable. Apology accepted. Nicholas and I are fine here. We're Mrs. Draper's only boarders right now. Her husband is overseas. The place is clean and she's a good cook."

"Good. Are you all right for money?"

"Yes." Bea shifted a little further away and looked him over. "So, how badly were you wounded?"

"Badly enough. I didn't get home until January, but I'm pretty much healed now."

An awkward pause. Was she thinking of his letters? "Your brother – Michael-John – is he still overseas?"

"He was killed in action." Liam had avoided mention of that when he wrote to her, just as he'd downplayed his injury. He hadn't wanted to worry her. Bea's gaze softened with sympathy.

"That's hard. I'm sorry."

"You've had troubles of your own." It was none of Liam's business, but he couldn't help asking. "Were you happy with Kenneth?"

She hesitated before replying. "We were comfortable. We'd known each other well for years."

Comfortable? That didn't sound like Bea. She'd never been

one to compromise for the sake of comfort. "He must have loved you, if he was willing to take on your child."

"Yes, he loved me." Bea flashed her old smile. "And your Alice loves you. I could see it."

"Yeah, she does." Which was one of the reasons he was sitting here. "Bea, tell me honestly. Why did you come over here?"

Bea gave her shoulders a characteristic little shrug and sighed. "For a lot of reasons. I didn't forget you, Liam. I wanted to see you, to see if there was anything left between us. I thought I owed that much to Nicholas. And I wanted to be able to tell him someday about the place where his father grew up."

Liam smothered a pointless pang of regret. "His father will be whoever you marry." Bea squared her shoulders and held his gaze.

"I'm not going to lie to him or hide things from him. When he's old enough, I'll tell him about you. When I do, he's bound to ask questions. I intend to answer them."

Of course the boy would have questions. Liam pictured a gangly kid of fourteen or fifteen, angry and curious about the father he'd never met. Were there any words Bea could use to keep Nicholas from feeling deserted? Of course, her husband would be the boy's father in every way that mattered, but he'd still want to know about the shadowy man who'd sired him. It was only human nature, just like it would be human nature for Liam to see his son in Drew as he grew up, to wonder if Nicholas had his grandfather Cochrane's dogged stubbornness and his father's knack with wood. But that was how it had to be.

Only right now, Nicholas was so close, just upstairs in Bea's room. It might be Liam's only chance to see his son. If he passed it up, would he regret it? He wasn't willing to take the risk.

"Bea, I'd like to see him."

She nodded. "Of course. I'll bring him down."

"If he's asleep—"

"Don't worry, he won't wake. We travelled all day yesterday. He's tired."

Bea left the room and came back with Nicholas in her arms, wrapped in a yellow quilt. When she laid the sleeping baby on Liam's lap it took him right back to the months before he left home, when Emily was a baby. A fissure opened in his heart when he saw the makings of his own features in Nicholas's little face.

"He looks like Dad."

Bea bent to adjust the blanket and brushed a few strands of corn-floss hair from the baby's forehead. "So do you. Nicholas's eyes are blue like mine, though."

Liam brushed his son's cheek with a finger. He'd forgotten the incredible softness of baby skin. The crack in his heart opened wider. "When's his birthday?"

"February 20th. He must have been conceived on your last leave."

One good thing out of those years of hell, and you have to let him go. But not yet. If Nicholas wouldn't remember him, at least Liam could make sure he had some memories of Nicholas, even if it made things more difficult in the end.

"Bea, I'd like to spend some time with him while you're here."

She smiled before she leaned over the baby again. "You can see him any time you want to, Liam."

Chapter 20

Alice put her dust cloth down and picked up the small velvet-covered case on Carl's bedside table. Mother wanted to have his medal framed, but she hadn't gotten around to it yet. Alice took out the gleaming cross and held it in her hand.

Where was Carl now? Far away on western prairies or northern mountains? Or was he farther away still, gone from the world to a cold, empty purgatory where she could never reach him? If so, and if what Father MacManus preached was true, no one would ever reach Carl again.

At the moment, Liam didn't seem much closer.

After church on Sunday, they'd gone for a walk. He'd told Alice about seeing his son. "He looks so much like Drew did as a baby. He has Dad's face."

Alice had no trouble reading the impact of the experience in Liam's eyes. Still, she'd asked. "Are you glad you've seen him?"

"Yeah. He seems real now."

It would hurt Liam deeply when Bea took the baby back to England, more deeply than he knew. For the whole time they were together, she'd sensed that half of Liam's heart was elsewhere. She would have thought less of him if it hadn't been, but she wished she knew where that left her.

She heard footsteps on the stairs. Georgie poked her head in the doorway. "Oh, you're here. I didn't think anyone was home."

"Mum and Dad went out with the Hennessys for supper. I put what's left of the pea soup from last night on the stove. It should be hot by now."

Georgie had just come from work, a bit later than usual. The cold evening air had whipped colour into her cheeks. She sat on Carl's bed, smoothed her ruffled hair and studied Alice's face.

"You've been different since you moved back home. Are you worrying over Carl? He doesn't deserve it."

Alice set the medal, warm from her palm, back in its box. "It's ironic, isn't it? From what Mother read to us in the paper last year, Liam could have brought one of these home if he'd had the rank."

Georgie leaned back on her hands, frowning. "So it's Liam, is it? I wondered. You've seemed unhappy, and you didn't see much of him last weekend."

Alice hesitated. She hadn't told anyone about Liam and Bea, but the family would have to know sooner or later. Georgie might as well hear it first.

"Liam was occupied. An old girlfriend of his from England arrived in town last weekend. She brought their son with her."

Georgie bounced up with a little gasp, mouth open wide. "I hope you told him to take a long walk off a short pier."

Alice paced the room. Somehow, that was easier than facing her sister directly. "Georgie, he didn't know. Until a month or so ago, she thought he was dead. When she found out he wasn't, she came to find him."

"And how does he feel about that?"

"That's what he needs to figure out."

Georgie rose and laid her hand on Alice's arm to stop her. They stood in front of Carl's mirror. Georgie's critical gaze compared their heights, their figures, their faces. A whimsical smile touched her eyes and mouth.

"You know, Alice, I've always wondered why men find you more attractive than me. No—" when Alice opened her mouth to deny it. "It's true. Not that I'm complaining. I've never been a wallflower, but I've never understood it. You aren't any prettier than I am, but there it is. Maybe it's because there's a soft side to you that I don't have."

Alice stood staring at their reflections. "You're being silly. You've had so many more men friends than I have."

"Yes, because you've always been so choosy. So keep being choosy. You don't need a man who comes with a ready-made family."

Choosy. It must have looked that way. Alice hadn't told Georgie that she'd cared for Liam for years. Now she couldn't, until he decided what he wanted. She took Georgie's hand and squeezed it.

"Georgie, I know I hurt you. I'm sorry."

Georgie glossed the moment over with an off-hand lift of a shoulder. "You know, I used to think I knew you pretty well. So did Mother and Dad, but you've surprised us all. There's more to you than any of us thought."

Alice set the box with Carl's medal back on the nightstand, and wished her emotional ground would stop shifting beneath her feet. She didn't know where she stood with anyone anymore. "Maybe none of us have known each other as well as we thought. Soup's on. Let's go down."

Liam paused halfway up the hill from the Harbour, breath smoking in the crisp air. The last day of November. The stores on Hollis and Barrington were decked out for the holidays, but now after dark the blinds were drawn to adhere to blackout regulations. Not very festive, but still, the streets were busy with Friday night shoppers. A pair of young girls walked by, chattering about sealing wax crafts, the latest craze. Liam had one of his feeling-like-a-stranger moments.

Like everything else, Christmas was different now.

He'd gotten an early chance back to the city with Jess's neighbour again. He stood for a moment, indecisive, before turning south on Barrington. Nicholas had been on Liam's mind all week. At odd moments when he was working, eating, relaxing, he'd pictured that little face with its familiar nose and chin.

He'd told Jess and Fanny the whole story. Fanny scorned Bea for not marrying Liam when he'd asked her. Trust a woman to be hardest on another woman. Jess took it more philosophically.

"You can't unscramble eggs, Liam. If it was meant to be, it wouldn't have happened that way."

Maybe. What Liam hated most was how hard this was on Alice. Last Sunday, when he was still bowled over from holding his son for the first time, he'd seen the hurt in her eyes. They'd parted awkwardly because of it. He'd have to try to make it up to her this weekend.

At Mrs. Draper's, Bea opened the door. She was dressed to go out and had the baby ready in the landlady's carriage.

"Liam, you almost missed us. I was about to take Nicholas out for some fresh air. Come along."

They started up Barrington with Liam pushing the pram. He couldn't get used to the way time fell away at the sight of Bea. He half-expected to turn a corner and find himself in Chelsea. She broke into his thoughts.

"So, tell me about Alice."

Where to start? Bea and Alice were so different. If they met by chance, he doubted they'd have much to say to each other. "She grew up a couple of blocks away from me. I've known her all my life, but not well until a few weeks ago."

Bea gave him her patient look. She'd always teased him about how bad he was at characterizing people. "I meant, what's she like?"

"Well, she's a talented musician. She's quiet, a little shy I suppose you'd say, but she's no pushover. She treats me better than I deserve."

Bea slipped her arm through his. "I'm happy for you."

He glanced down at her, but her gaze had been drawn to a

laughing group coming out of a shop across the street.

"Thanks. What will you do when you go back to England, Bea?"

She met his gaze again and shrugged. "I'll be all right. I'll get a job. I worked in an office before the war. I can do that again. My sister has said she'll look after Nicholas when I find something. She and her husband are really quite fond of him."

"Have you considered staying here?" Liam regretted the words as soon as they were spoken. He had no right to ask that of her.

A spark of temper flashed in her eyes as she pulled her arm from his. "Your life is here, Liam. Mine isn't."

"Nicholas is a part of my life, too. If your mother lied to you, that's no more my fault than it is yours. Think about it."

She didn't reply. Liam cursed his lack of tact. Why would Bea want to stay here and see the father of her child with another woman? He stopped and took her hand. "I really know how to put my foot in it, don't I? I'm sorry. I hate the thought of losing Nicholas, that's all, before I get to know him."

"I know."

Her hand was warm, her skin as glowing, her lips as soft-looking as he remembered. Was he some kind of a fool to pass up a woman like Bea, to pass up the chance to make a family for his son? He let her gloved fingers slip from his.

"We're different people now, Bea. Too much has happened to both of us."

"I suppose so." Her mouth curved in a smile tinged with sadness. "But I'm not going anywhere very soon. I've been asking, and it looks like getting back to England is going to be difficult."

At least Liam had that to hold on to. He'd just have to take each moment with Nicholas as a gift, as he had each moment with Bea when they were together. "It should be, with submarine warfare on again. I'm still furious with you for crossing with

Nicholas, but you're here. Stay put until it's safe to go."

They passed a small restaurant. Light poured from the doorway along with the rich, warm aroma of meat, gravy and potatoes as a couple came out. Bea closed her eyes as she breathed in.

"Mmm. That smells like shepherd's pie."

Liam's stomach rumbled. He hadn't had supper yet. "Remember the shepherd's pie at the Black Horse? I haven't forgotten it."

Bea glanced up at him. "You've been working all day and you haven't eaten yet. You must be famished. I haven't eaten either. Mrs. Draper had to go out, so she left supper in the pantry. I was going to have it after our walk."

Their gazes met. Liam swung the pram around. "Might as well stop, then. The food at Sally's is good. I've eaten there a few times."

Minutes later they sat at a table by the window, looking at each other over plates of steaming shepherd's pie. Sally, a middle-aged widow with a sort of ravaged prettiness about her yet, stopped at Liam's shoulder.

"Everything all right?"

"Yes, fine, thanks." But it wasn't. That odd sense of warped time was still with him. How many meals had he and Bea eaten like this on winter evenings, before settling into her bed for the night, between sheets that smelled of her? Back then, those nights had seemed to belong to a different world, separate from reality. So did this.

Bea put down her fork and took a sip from her water glass. "This is heaven. Liam, tell me about your work. You never did tell me anything about that in London."

No. He'd told her a little about his family, but he hadn't said much about home when they were together. He hadn't said much about home to anyone overseas. It only made everything harder.

"Before enlisting, I worked at the rail yard near home. Nothing much to talk about, just labour work. Now I'm learning to build boats. I enjoy working with my hands. I'm with my cousin in his boat shop in Prospect. It's a little fishing village down the shore."

Bea swallowed a mouthful of shepherd's pie and washed it down with tea. "I find that hard to picture somehow. You never seemed to me like the small village type."

"I wouldn't have thought so either. I spent some time out there as a kid and it was too quiet for me, but I like it now. What do you think of Halifax?"

"I don't know." Bea wrinkled her nose. "From what I've seen, it's a little grim."

Now, at the beginning of yet another wartime winter, Liam couldn't deny it. A chilly breath of memory blew over him. This time last year he'd just moved to the convalescent home in Surrey to wait and see if he would walk normally again. And to put the pieces of his mind back together.

"You're seeing it at its worst. It's different in summer. If you could see—" He stopped. By summer, Bea and Nicholas would probably be gone. "It's changed a lot since I left. London's pretty grim in the winter, too."

"I suppose so. I've never thought about it. I've never lived anywhere else."

The voices of the other diners in the restaurant created a bubble of sound, sealing them in from the outside world. Perhaps that was why Liam found himself telling Bea more than ever before about Halifax as he'd known it growing up, and she told him more about parts of London they'd never had a chance to explore.

Nicholas began to fuss as they finished eating. Sally brought their bill. Then they were out on the street again.

Liam still had a slight limp – always would have – and it still got the same smiles from passers-by that it had when he went out with Georgie. *Here's one, at least, who came home to his wife and kid.* Before, the benign looks had annoyed him. Now they hurt him. He couldn't be a father to Nicholas or a husband to Bea. He'd given too much of himself to Alice.

At Mrs. Draper's, Liam carried the pram up the front steps and into the hall, lifted Nicholas out and waited, holding his son, while Bea got out of her coat and gloves.

"Thanks." She took the baby and held Liam's gaze over Nicholas' knitted hat. "This has been a nice, unexpected surprise."

It would be very easy, almost natural after the conversation they'd shared, to kiss her cheek. Liam turned away quickly, pulled his duffle bag from the hall closet and slung it over his shoulder.

Bea took a step forward.

"Goodnight, Liam."

Liam reached out to touch the baby's head. The pain that rose in his throat threatened to choke him.

"Goodbye, Bea."

Out in the darkness again, he headed for the nearest tram stop. While the tram rattled north, he leaned back against his seat. That unreal sense of a shift in time dissolved slowly. It didn't help, it didn't help at all, that he could still feel Nicholas in his arms.

He turned his thoughts to Alice. She wouldn't be expecting to see him until tomorrow, so he had a little time to figure out what to say to her. He hoped it would be enough. If he had to lose Nicholas, he couldn't lose her, too.

Even though half her mind listened for footsteps on the walk, *Moonlight Sonata* flowed from Alice's fingers. She knew how far her playing had come in the few months she'd been studying and practicing. Her reading skills had grown by leaps and bounds as well, but to play a piece like that with ease and expression meant much more. Reading the notes was, to her, a means to an end.

Saturday morning. Liam would be home soon. She'd dreamed last night of seeing him and Bea together on a downtown street, with a child toddling between them. The little boy looked over his shoulder and smiled at Alice before they disappeared around a corner, while she stood rooted in place, unable to follow.

If only she could hate Bea, but instinct told Alice the English girl was telling the truth. She hadn't asked Liam last Sunday what he believed because she was afraid if she brought the subject up, something desperate and undignified would come out of her mouth. If he chose the mother of his child over her, what could she say?

The phone rang in the kitchen. Mother answered it. When her voice rose in concern, Alice left the piano and hurried down the hall.

"Oh, Sarah, I thought you had those steps repaired last fall. How badly are you hurt?" Mother made a shushing motion when Alice raised her eyebrows in question. "You just do what Dr. Mason said and stay off your feet... Probably not. Her young man will be in town today, but I'll catch the eleven o'clock train. I'll see you by noon."

Mother hung up the phone and let out an exasperated sigh. "Your aunt has fallen down her kitchen steps and wrenched her back. I'm not surprised. Those steps have been falling apart for two years. I'd better get some clothes together."

Alice saw her hopes for the weekend going up in smoke. The way things were between them right now, the last thing she wanted was to be away when Liam got home, but she had no choice. "Mother, if Aunt Sarah needs help walking or getting up and down, you can't do it. I'll go."

"But Liam will be home and—"

"You'll have to explain to him."

Her mother held her gaze. Alice had told her about Bea. Though far from pleased, Mother had refrained from saying 'I told you so' and offered what support she could.

"Are you sure?"

"Yes, I'm sure." Alice lifted her chin. "If Liam wants to see me, there's another train to Bedford this afternoon."

She ran upstairs to throw some clothes in a suitcase. An hour later, she climbed the steep slope past St. Ignatius Church to Aunt Sarah's square, two-story brick home. Alice let herself in and found her mother's tall, thin, sharp-eyed older sister sitting stiffly in an armchair in her front room.

Alice and Aunt Sarah had always been friends, in spite of – or because of – the fact that they were as different as black and white. Widowed young, fiercely independent, Aunt Sarah spoke her mind without fear or favour to everyone. Sharp, intelligent and almost as musically talented as her younger sister, she'd always treated Alice with more respect than anyone else in the family.

"Hello, dear. I'm sorry to drag you out here. You've got fish to fry in Richmond, so I hear."

Alice set her suitcase down and bent to kiss her aunt's cheek. "I don't mind in the least, Aunty. How are you feeling?"

"All right, as long as I don't move, but I can if I have to. You don't have to nurse me, Alice, just do the cooking and keep me from going crazy with boredom." A sly twinkle lit Sarah's eyes. "You can start by telling me about your new beau. One of the Cochrane boys, your mother told me last week. Which one?"

Alice forced a smile. If she refused to talk about Liam, Aunt Sarah would only call Mother and ask why. "Well, Nolan's been married for years, so that narrows it down."

"Hmm. I don't know them well, of course, but I spent enough time in Richmond over the years to hear stories about the oldest one." Sarah shrugged. "Doesn't matter. Keeps a woman on her toes. Is your man good-looking?"

"Not as good-looking as Nolan. Liam looks like his father, a little rough around the edges, but..." Alice blushed, remembering their night on the road home from Prospect. Discovering Liam's scars. Discovering how his face looked when pleasure overwhelmed him. Aunt Sarah shook her head.

"You're in love. I've always wondered what that felt like."

Perched on the edge of her aunt's chair, Alice nearly slipped off. Frank as Aunt Sarah was, she'd never said anything like that before. "You didn't love Uncle Daniel?"

Aunt Sarah looked into Alice's eyes, then shook her head. "No, not the way you're in love." When Alice couldn't quite hide her sympathy, her aunt smiled and put an arm around her. "Don't look like that. There's no need. That's why Daniel and I got along so well. No, have your fun while you're young, I say. I've always thought Georgie could teach you a thing or two about flirting."

It wasn't the first time Alice had seen the similarity between her aunt and her sister. Strange that Georgie and Aunt Sarah had never been particularly close. Perhaps they were both too self-sufficient, but did Aunt Sarah really have no regrets about her safe, comfortable marriage?

"I'll bet you could have taught me a thing or two as well when you were younger."

Aunt Sarah snorted. "Still could, Alice. There's a man or two who could tell you that. Now go unpack your things."

Liam didn't get to the O'Neills' until just before lunch. He'd gotten tied up for an hour or so helping Nolan and his father repair Nolan's temperamental furnace. After building himself up to see Alice, it was a bit of a letdown when Georgie answered his knock.

"Hello, Liam. I'm afraid Alice isn't home. She's gone to Bedford to spend a few days with Aunt Sarah."

His stomach sank. He and Alice hadn't made specific plans to meet today, but when they'd parted last weekend, he'd understood – or maybe he'd misunderstood, with half his mind on Nicholas.

"Oh." He stood there in the doorway like a fool, waiting for Georgie to tell him that Alice had invited him to see her at her aunt's. She didn't.

"Sorry. It was unexpected."

Georgie's voice held a decided touch of coolness. Of course, Alice had told her family about the bombshell he'd dropped on her. After he'd promised to treat her with honesty and respect. Liam felt a flush race up his neck.

"Yeah. What's your aunt's address? Does she have a phone?"

"Yes. Just a minute." Georgie hurried from the kitchen and came back with the phone number and address scrawled on a slip of paper. "Here you are."

"Thanks." Before he could make more of a fool of himself, he shoved the paper in his jacket pocket and walked out.

He found Nolan's house empty when he returned. Liam pulled the slip of paper Georgie had given him from his pocket and smoothed it out on the kitchen table. If she was angry with him, he should count himself lucky that her father hadn't answered the door.

He glanced at the kitchen clock. If he was going to make the afternoon train, he'd have to leave in an hour. The evening train left too late to make it worth the trip. He and Alice would just end up sitting in her aunt's parlour, and he couldn't talk to her there. He knew the words would stick in his throat, and what if her aunt were the busybody type? He couldn't afford to bungle this.

He picked up the phone, then set the receiver back in its cradle. Maybe Alice had left the city because she needed some time to herself. She loved him – he believed that – but the way the sparks flew between them whenever they touched, and with Nicholas to consider, could he blame her for pulling back? If only he could write to her, but it wouldn't be a letter he'd want her aunt to read. Nor could he say what he needed to say over the phone.

So he'd write, and next weekend he'd read the letter to her himself.

He rummaged for paper, ink and a pen and took them to his room. Sitting on his bed, he laid a sheet of paper on the nightstand. First, a quick note.

Alice, I'm sorry I missed you. I need to talk to you. I only hope I get the words right. I'll see you next Saturday. I'll be thinking of you 'til then.

Love, Liam

Alice's aunt could read that to her. Liam slipped the note in an envelope and got it ready to mail, then took a fresh piece of paper.

Dear Alice...

His throat constricted and his vision blurred. He was back in his hospital room in England, writing to Bea. *So love, the war is over for me. The doctors have told me I won't ever be quite the same, but my feelings for you aren't going to change.*

Only they had changed. Alice had found a place deep inside him that Bea had never touched. He picked up his pen again.

> *Dear Alice,*
>
> *You said on our first weekend together that you wished we could write to each other, because a letter was something to keep. So, here's a letter for you. I hope you'll want to keep it. I hope even more that you'll believe it.*
>
> *I still find it hard to believe that you've cared for me for years. If I hadn't gone away, I wonder if we would ever have found each other. It almost makes those years apart worth it to think that maybe we wouldn't have.*
>
> *The other thing that makes them worth it is Nicholas.*

Alice, I'll never know how many lives I've taken, but now I know that I've also given life. I can't explain how that feels. When Bea takes Nicholas away, he's going to take a part of my heart with him, but that's how it has to be. Maybe Bea and I could have been happy together, maybe it was never meant to be, but what we had is over.

When I came home I didn't expect to ever have dreams again, but you've changed that. You and Jess. Now I dream all the time, of building something worthwhile with wood, and building something worthwhile with you. Of coming home every day to you and a family I can call mine. More lives that we'll bring into the world together. It'll take a while, but I don't want to waste any more time. It's too precious, and I love you too much for that. More than I thought I had it in me to love. I hope you're reading that in me as I'm reading this to you, because it's true.

He read his words over, tried to imagine what Alice's eyes would look like when he read them to her. Would she believe him? He thought so – she always read him so well – but he couldn't be sure it would be enough.

When the ink was dry, Liam folded the letter and tucked it in his wallet. He took it with him to Prospect the next afternoon and read it over a couple of times each day, until the words came off his tongue without hesitation. He was repeating them in his mind on Wednesday afternoon when Jess's neighbour stepped into the boat shop and perched on a keg of nails. Jess put his chisel down and brushed some shavings from the sleeves of his shirt.

"Afternoon, Galen. I was just thinking about a cup of tea and a bite. Will you come in?"

Galen shook his greying head. "Not today, Jess, too much to do. I just dropped by to tell Liam that if he wants to go to the city with me this week, he'll have to be ready to go tonight. Cora has to see the dentist tomorrow and she wants to do her Christmas shopping, so we're going to stay with her brother and come back Sunday."

Damn. Liam glanced at the stack of deck planking he'd finished. It wasn't nearly big enough, and the boat's owner wanted the work finished by Christmas. "Don't worry about me, Galen. I'll find another way in. Chances are someone else will be going this weekend, with the holidays getting so close." *I'll walk if I have to.*

Jess shook his head. "Liam, what the hell. You can put in some long hours next week. Go."

Liam did his best to hide his relief. "Thanks, Jess. If I have to, I'll stay here next weekend so we can finish on time, but this time... It's important."

He arrived at Nolan's just as they were sitting down to supper. All through the meal, Liam watched his brother's family with new eyes. To love a woman, to see that love reflected in his children – Michael-John would never know how that felt, but if fate smiled on Liam, he'd experience it for both of them. He'd been given his life back for a reason.

Thursday morning, December 6

I walk in the garden alone, while the dew is still on the roses...

The notes of the old hymn drifted out from the front room where Mother was playing. Alice quietly sang along as she finished kneading her bread. She set the dough to rise, washed and dried her hands, then pulled Liam's note from her apron pocket. She'd gotten it yesterday and had come home last night. Aunt Sarah had insisted on it after reading Liam's message.

"By the look of you, you'll be no good to me or yourself here. I can get along well enough now, and you've been in a state since he didn't show up on Saturday, though you've hidden it well. Go on."

Alice couldn't deny it. So, she'd caught the afternoon train, and now she was counting the hours until Liam would be home.

The right words. If what he had to tell her wasn't what she wanted to hear, he would have chosen different ones for his note.

I'll be thinking of you 'til then.

Her happiness shamed her a little. What about Liam's boy? She'd be happy to raise Nicholas as her own, but he also belonged to Bea.

If it's meant to be, I'll have children with Liam. I suppose it's only fair that Bea has his first. He loved her.

To make room for the new bread, Alice cleaned out the breadbox. She gathered the stale scraps and stepped out the kitchen door to scatter them for the birds. When the sunny morning suddenly dimmed, she looked up. An inky black cloud sullied the innocent blue of the sky. An ill-omened thing on such a fine day. She brushed her hands free of crumbs and stepped back inside.

Her mother was still playing *I Walk In the Garden.* Alice called down the hall. "Mother? Mother, look out the window. There must be a fire."

Liam swallowed his last mouthful of porridge as Ruth rose and started gathering the children's breakfast dishes. She took Drew's milk glass and pulled his chair back from the table. "Drew, time to feed Della. Emily, go up and get dressed. You're going to town with Nan this morning, remember?"

Still in her red flannel nightgown, Emily slid from her chair and ran upstairs. Drew put on his jacket and cap, opened the kitchen door and paused on the step. "Mum, Uncle Liam, come see this!"

At the urgency in his voice, Liam and Ruth hurried to join him. Drew's gaze was riveted on a thick column of inky smoke rising in the clear sky above The Narrows. Ruth gripped Liam's arm.

"What do you think that is?"

Drew shaded his eyes and squinted. "I'm getting the binoculars."

He dashed inside. In a moment, he yelled down from his open bedroom window. "Uncle Liam, it's a ship burning! Right down by Pier 6!"

"All right, Drew," Ruth called. "You're letting in the cold. Close the window and come down. Della's waiting to be fed."

Drew ran down and held the binoculars out to Liam. "I saw fuel drums on the deck."

"Are you sure?"

"Of course I'm sure."

Liam didn't doubt it. His heart leapt into his throat, but he didn't want to alarm the boy. He took the binoculars and slung them around his neck.

"All right, you'd better go look after Della."

Drew rolled his eyes and trudged reluctantly to the cow shed. Liam and Ruth turned back to the billowing black cloud. Neither spoke. They didn't have to. Nolan was out there somewhere at work.

A ball of flame soared silently into the air, then another. The lack of sound was eerie. Ruth and Liam jogged around to the front yard for a better view. Dad had already gone to work, but Mum was out on the street, as were many of the neighbours. Almost every household had someone working on or near the Harbour.

Liam's mouth went dry with a sense of déjà vu. Another ball of flame ascended as the smoke column grew. Across the street, his mother hurried back inside, shivering without her coat. A minute later he saw her at her front room window.

A group of small boys dashed by, schoolbags on their backs, going in the wrong direction – down the road toward The Narrows instead of uphill to school. Drew came running from the cow shed, eyes wide.

"Let's go down to the rail yard to watch."

Drew didn't have to go to school until the afternoon. The Catholic boys in the neighbourhood were sharing St. Joseph's with the girls, as the boy's school had burned the previous year and the new one across from the church wasn't quite finished. The girls had classes in the morning, the boys after lunch. Ruth put a hand on Drew's shoulder.

"No. You aren't to go anywhere near the water."

"Aw, Mum, I'll be all right with Uncle Liam."

Liam spoke sternly. "Your mother's right. I might go up the hill to get a better look, but you stay—"

Before he could finish the sentence, a brilliant flash of light blotted out the world. He was picked up and hurled to the ground as if by a giant's hand. His head hit the frozen earth and the light faded to black.

"I walk in the garden alone, while the dew is still on the roses, and the voice I hear falling on my ear the Son of God discloses..."

The old hymn rang in Alice's mind as she regained consciousness. Strange. She must have slipped and fallen. She'd been talking to Mother a moment ago. What had she told her?

Alice tried to get up, but found she couldn't move. She lay still for a moment while her head cleared, then tried again. Something was pinning her down. She opened her eyes.

You must have jarred your brain. This isn't real. It looked as if the back wall of the kitchen lay on top of her. Cold air rushed in through the gaping hole where the wall had been. Dust hung thick above her. That must be why the room seemed so dark.

Alice heard a bewildered little cry and wondered where it

came from. It took her a few seconds to realize she'd made the sound herself. Around the edge of the debris that held her trapped, she saw remnants of shelves and furniture strewn on the floor. The oil range lay on its side, smoking.

God help us, we're under attack.

She listened for sounds of battle, for cries or screams, but heard nothing. The silence frightened her more than bombs would have.

Move, Alice. She started struggling, pushing at the timbers holding her down. She managed to shift them, but not enough to wriggle free. Exhausted, she stopped for breath. Even with the room open to the outside, the smoke from the stove was growing thicker.

Liam was only out for a few seconds, not long enough for the cold to seep through his sweater. Ears ringing, he pushed himself up onto all fours, then to his knees. He nearly blacked out again.

Sweet Jesus.

The slope leading down to The Narrows looked like it had been subjected to heavy shelling. As far as he could see, every house had been reduced to rubble. Oily smoke darkened the sky, like a pall over Armageddon. Liam looked south toward Russell and saw the bulky shape of the new boys' school still standing, but the spire of St. Joseph's was gone. To the north, the familiar tall chimney of the sugar refinery had vanished as well.

He stared across the street in disbelief at his mother's front room curtains, spilling out through the empty hole where the window had been, their deep red like blood on the snow. *Snow? In July in La Boisselle?* He looked over his shoulder for Michael-John, but saw no one. Where were Barney and the rest? Had they left him behind while he was out cold?

A woman's panicked voice cut through the ringing in his

ears. "Liam, can you get up? Hurry. I need you."

What's Bea doing here?

Still on his knees, he turned around and saw Ruth, her face streaked with soot, her eyes dazed. Blood trickled down her cheek from a cut on her temple. Her dress was filthy, and her left arm hung at an awkward angle.

The sight of her jerked Liam back to the present. He staggered to his feet. His body felt battered through and through, but nothing seemed to be broken. The binoculars had disappeared from around his neck. He faced the pile of rubble that had been his brother's home.

"Where's Drew?"

The little boy lay face down in the yard, a pile of roof shingles nearly covering him. Liam stumbled to him, lifted the shingles off and scooped Drew into his arms. He opened his eyes.

"Mum. I want Mum."

The words came out on a sob. Like Ruth, he was soot-smeared and bleeding from cuts and scratches. Liam held him closer.

"She's right here, Drew. You're going to be all right." He carried Drew to Ruth and set him on his feet. The boy was able to stand. Shaking, he buried his face against his mother.

"Is it the Germans? Are they bombing us?"

Ruth gathered him close with her right arm. The left hung useless. "No, Drew. It can't be. Hush now."

Her voice dropped to a comforting murmur. Liam turned to the house again. A curl of smoke rose from the collapsed roof where the kitchen had been. The whole second floor had fallen.

Emily. She's still inside.

He sprinted across the yard and started throwing aside pieces of debris. In a few seconds, Ruth and Drew joined him, tearing their hands on splinters and nails without noticing, working on adrenalin as Liam was.

The smoke coming from the roof became flame. As Liam tried to pull away a shattered wall stud the collapsed upper floor settled further. The roof blossomed deadly orange. Liam grabbed Ruth with one hand and Drew with the other and pulled them away from the house, back out to the street.

Neither of them cried. Their eyes were blank, their faces pale under a coating of soot and blood. Liam had seen that look on women's and children's faces too many times before. Their minds had shut down, unable to process what had happened.

He took Ruth's hand. "Wait here. I'm going to see if I can find Mum." Ruth didn't seem to hear him. He left her standing there in dazed silence beside Drew, and crossed the street.

The front half of his parents' house leaned at a sharp angle, but it hadn't fallen. The back half had been blown away. Liam peered in the empty front room window. Through a haze of smoke, he saw his mother lying on the carpet, surrounded by shards of glass. He scrambled through the opening, picked her up and carried her to where Ruth and Drew still stood rooted, watching fire engulf their home. Liam laid his mother on the ground and knelt beside her.

Small shards of class protruded from her face, her arms, her chest. Blood seeped from under the lid of her left eye. Liam began picking away the glass, all but a couple of pieces that seemed more deeply embedded. As he finished, she moaned and half-opened her right eye.

"Liam... is that you?"

"Yes, I'm here." He wasn't sure if the blood on her face was from her injuries or his lacerated hands. He reached for a handful of snow and tried to wipe her clean, without much success.

The cold revived her. She reached for his hand.

"Your father and Nolan..."

"I'll look for them, Mum, but first you and Ruth need help." Liam got his arm underneath her and helped her stand. Holding her up, he looked around him.

Neighbours straggled up the hill, many blackened almost beyond recognition, some with injuries that sent Liam's mind reeling back to his worst nightmares. Many were half-clothed and shivering. Most wore the same dazed look as Ruth and Drew.

Without speaking or looking back, the Cochranes followed them.

Chapter 21

Choking on the thickening smoke in the kitchen, Alice strained against the imprisoning section of wall with the strength borne of desperation. The wall shifted to one side, enough for her to pull her legs out from underneath it, scraping her shins in the process. She got to her feet and staggered into the hall.

A pile of broken roof trusses blocked her path. She turned back and grabbed her coat, which still hung on the coat rack by the hall doorway. Then she climbed through the gaping hole in the kitchen wall and stumbled through snow and debris to the front yard.

The front of the house lay flat. What had been the front room lay buried under the collapsed wall. Alice clambered over the rubble, pulled away some siding and shingles until her fingers hit something smooth and polished – a piece of the piano's top. Next to it, she glimpsed a patch of coloured fabric. Her mother's dress. She dug toward it.

"Mother..."

Alice tossed aside the last piece of wood. Her mother's face was still, her eyes closed, as they often were when she played pieces she knew from memory. Alice knelt and felt her neck for a pulse.

There was none.

Liam kept the family moving along with the stream of battered humanity heading south. He took off his sweater and tied it around Ruth's shoulders. His arm gave his mother some warmth as he helped her along. Drew trudged beside Ruth, tearless and silent.

They met a group of soldiers marching north at double-time. One of them paused to give Mum his great-coat. "That ship was loaded to the gunnels with explosives. A collision with another ship started the fire. There's going to be hell to pay all the way up the line of command, I'll tell you that."

Liam didn't care about hows, whys or consequences. All that mattered was getting Mum and Ruth to a hospital, then finding his father and Nolan, Bea and Nicholas, and Alice.

Alice. They'd passed Russell Street on their way, seen the ruins of the church, the girls' school, the houses. The damage was even worse than on Kaye. Liam shut off his thoughts and his feelings as he'd learned to do overseas. He couldn't afford to think or feel right now.

They kept putting one foot in front of the other until they reached the veteran's hospital. Already the corridors were filling with the injured. People sat or lay wherever they could find space, waiting for care. The pervading smell of blood made Liam's stomach turn over.

There wasn't a doctor to be seen – they were all busy – but nurses and volunteers moved among the casualties, and the less seriously injured were doing what they could for others. No one complained. Most were still in shock, like Ruth and Drew.

Liam found room for Ruth and his mother in a side corridor. As they settled on the floor, a man came down the hall, a patient Liam recognized from his stay here. Nelson Chase had lost a foot overseas. He was hobbling about on his new prosthesis, doling out tea to the injured.

"Liam, what the hell happened? There are all kinds of crazy rumours floating around."

Liam told him what little he knew. Nelson was about to hurry away when Liam thought of something.

"Nelson, you're about my size. Do you have a uniform I could borrow? I'll be able to get around town with a lot fewer questions if you do."

Nelson handed his tray of cups to Liam. "Yeah, I do. I'll be right back."

Liam passed out the rest of the tea in his absence. No one seemed to notice his bloody hands, but Nelson had. He returned not only with a uniform and great-coat, but torn strips of cotton from a pillowcase. "Filched this from a linen closet. You look like you could use it." He quickly wrapped Liam's hands. "Now I'd better go see what else I can do."

Without waiting for thanks he hurried away. Liam used the remaining cloth to fashion a sling for Ruth's arm, then tucked the coat and uniform behind Ruth and his mother.

"As soon as you two see a doctor, I'll start looking for Dad and Nolan."

His mother was only semiconscious. Ruth looked up at him and shook her head. "Go now, Liam. There's nothing you can do for us here."

"No. If it were only you and Drew, maybe – I know you're going to be all right, but—" He glanced at his mother, took a breath and steadied his voice. "I'm not leaving her."

Alice backed away from the ruins of home. For a moment she stood on the road, paralyzed with indecision. Then, following blind instinct, she started up the hill toward the church.

She found no comfort there. St. Joseph's had been reduced to a broken shell, as had the girls' school. Only the unfinished building across the street stood more or less intact. Alice recalled the nip of the pointer across her knuckles, the smells of chalk and damp wool on winter mornings, the taste of bile in her throat as test papers were passed out.

A few bewildered children passed her on their way downhill

to look for homes that no longer existed. One of the Sisters standing in the schoolyard had been Alice's teacher in her last humiliating year. Huddled in her soot-streaked coat, Alice shivered and hurried on before the woman could recognize her.

Still she saw no signs of battle, only destruction. With thought suspended, no goal in mind but to move, she started south along Gottingen Street. She saw the people who straggled along with her, but their faces didn't register. And so many dead…

Her mother, Carl, for all she knew Georgie and Dad. She might be utterly alone in the world, except for Liam. Thank God he was safe in Prospect. Surely he'd come when he heard – but she couldn't expect to be his first priority, not any longer. Nicholas and Bea would come first, then his family. She thought of his parents, Nolan and Ruth, the children. Had any of them survived?

Alice wasn't sure how long she'd been walking, didn't really remember the route, when she found herself looking across Halifax Common toward the white bulk of Camp Hill Hospital. To the south, the buildings she saw looked whole. Whatever had happened, it seemed that Citadel Hill had shielded the South End from disaster.

A knot of people stood on the Common, surrounding a group of soldiers. The sight of the uniformed men got Alice moving. Perhaps they could tell her what had happened. Feet numb with cold in her indoor shoes, she started across the field.

Liam shrugged deeper into Nelson's great-coat as he descended the hospital steps. The clear, mild day had dimmed to a starless, cold twilight, with flakes of snow in the air. He moved stiffly, cramped from the hours of sitting on the floor with his mother and Ruth, alternating with doing what he could for others nearby.

Ruth's arm had been set. The doctor said it was a clean break. Drew's cuts had been dressed, and Mum had been taken to surgery. They were going to remove her injured eye.

"Don't worry about me, Liam," she'd whispered in his ear before going. "Look after Ruth and Drew." But Ruth gave him a weary smile. Emily's loss still hadn't registered.

"Go. We'll wait here."

Liam had knelt and put his hands on Drew's shoulders. "Drew, I have to go out for awhile to look for your dad and Gramps, but I'll be back. You take care of your mother for me, and give my love to Nan when she wakes up."

Drew nodded, but he didn't speak. He'd hardly said a word all day. Liam didn't wonder. The boy had seen sights today that would turn a hardened Army surgeon's stomach.

From the steps, Liam saw campfires flickering on the Common through the thin veil of falling snow. A tent village had sprung up. That would be a logical place to start looking for his father, Nolan and Alice, but Bea's boarding house was far enough south that it might have escaped damage. He'd go there first.

Dressed as he was, the soldiers and policemen he met didn't question Liam as he walked south along Barrington. Here the buildings were standing, though hardly a window was intact. Everywhere people were sweeping up glass and nailing wood or blankets over window frames, questioning and speculating about the cause of so much destruction…everything from an air attack to enemy sabotage.

He found Mrs. Draper leaning out an empty upstairs window with a patchwork quilt in her arms. She waved when she saw him, came down and met him at the door. "Going to storm by the look of it. Bea isn't here. She caught a tram at eight-thirty this morning. Said she was going to see someone about a job."

Dread shot through him. Bea would have returned long before now if she could. If she'd taken Nicholas –

"Where?"

"She didn't say." Her gaze shifted to Liam's bandaged hands. "You're hurt."

"Not badly. Is Nicholas here?"

"Of course he is. He's upstairs in her room." Mrs. Draper gripped the doorframe so that her arm barred Liam out. Her mouth tightened as she looked him up and down. "Mr. Cochrane, there's something I want cleared up. I'm choosy about the boarders I take, and I've nothing to say against Bea – she seems decent enough and she takes good care of her baby, but she told me she was a widow. She wears a wedding ring, but she doesn't use your name, and anyone with eyes can see how much Nicholas looks like you."

Liam took a deep breath. He'd expected this before now. The woman was no fool. "Mrs. Draper, can we talk about this inside?"

A little grudgingly, she removed her arm. He followed her into the small parlour where he'd sat with Bea – could it have been only last weekend? Reality began to seep in. Little Emily was gone. Nolan and Dad might be, too, and so might Bea and Alice.

He couldn't start feeling. Not now.

With adrenalin spent, exhaustion took over. His hip ached and his legs turned to lead. Afraid they'd buckle, he dropped on the sofa.

"Mrs. Draper, you're right. I'm Nicholas's father. Bea didn't lie to you. Her husband was killed in action. She and I knew each other before her marriage. She came over here to find me."

Mrs. Draper gave him a hard, appraising look. "I see. Wait here a minute."

She left the room and returned with an envelope. "This is Nicholas' birth certificate. When I checked on him after Bea left, this envelope was on her dresser. Why do you suppose that was?"

Overwhelmed as he was, Liam could only shrug. "I don't know. Maybe she was tidying up."

Mrs. Draper's gaze met his, hard and direct. "Maybe."

He understood her plainly enough, but his instincts rebelled at what she was implying. "Mrs. Draper, Bea loves Nicholas. She wouldn't—"

"I'm not saying she would, but I need to know what's to become of him if she doesn't come back here."

Liam answered without a second's hesitation. "You've got no worries there. If Bea doesn't come back for Nicholas, I'll be taking him."

Mrs. Draper glanced down at her feet. Her face coloured a little, perhaps a touch of shame. "All right, then. Do you want to see him now?"

Liam's heart squeezed. The first sign of feeling, of life, since this morning. "Yes. I want to be sure he's all right."

Mrs. Draper fetched Nicholas and sat him on Liam's lap. The baby looked up at him calmly with Bea's dark blue eyes. From the first, Nicholas hadn't been strange with him.

"He isn't that kind of baby," Bea had said. Liam held his son close while his heart tore. If he took Nicholas and learned to love him, then Bea took him away... Liam looked down at the boy and knew he had no choice.

"Mrs. Draper, right now I don't even have a place to spend tonight, but within a day or two I should be able to take Nicholas to my cousin's in Prospect, if Bea doesn't turn up. Will you keep him 'til then?"

"Yes, I'll keep him, if you'll give your word you'll be back for him."

"I will."

Liam sat there holding the baby for a few more minutes, while he gathered his courage. Then he gave Nicholas back to Mrs. Draper. In her arms, the boy watched Liam leave the room. He held the thought of his son close on the long walk back across town.

When he reached Camp Hill the snow was thickening, obscuring his view of the tents on the Common, casting a merciful veil over the ruins of Richmond. But there was nothing merciful in the frigid wind kicking the snow up in swirls. He pushed away an image of Alice lying in the rubble of her home and stepped into the warmth of the hospital.

Things there had settled into a semblance of order. Casualties still lined the hallways, but the worst had been placed in wards – or had died and been removed. Rather than bother an exhausted nurse or orderly, Liam decided to find his mother and Ruth himself. Others were doing the same, walking the wards looking for family members.

He peered in a doorway and spotted Ruth's bright head. She was sitting on a little stool beside a bed, holding the occupant's hand, while Drew sat cross-legged on the foot of the bed. Assuming the patient was his mother, Liam hurried to them. His heart turned over when he got closer.

Nolan. His head was bandaged, his eyes closed. Ruth looked up at Liam with a teary-eyed smile.

"He has a broken leg and head injuries. We don't know how bad. Some men brought him in about an hour after you left. They said the wave from the explosion swept him off the deck of their ship, then picked him up and dropped him on deck again. Dr. Gregg – he was your doctor, wasn't he? – said his skull isn't fractured, so we're just waiting for him to wake up."

Liam swallowed hard. If – *when* – Nolan woke, worse pain than what he'd suffered waited for him. Emily had been his princess. Liam lowered his voice to a whisper.

"Where's Mum?"

"She's in the ward across the hall. She's asleep."

Before Liam could reply, Nolan began to stir. Ruth leaned over him. "Welcome back, love."

"Ruth... where are the kids?"

His voice sounded normal, only very quiet. He was aware. Liam clung to that fact as he braced himself for what was coming.

Drew reached for Nolan's other hand. "I'm here, Dad." Tears streamed down his cheeks, the first tears Liam had seen him shed today. Nolan squeezed his son's fingers.

"Good. Where's Emily?"

Ruth leaned closer, stroked his hair. "Nolan, Emily was upstairs when that ship exploded. We couldn't get her out of the house."

Liam watched his brother's face crumple with grief. He knew now what it would mean to him if he lost Nicholas, even after such a short time. He couldn't imagine Nolan's and Ruth's pain.

He came forward and stood at his brother's other side. "She didn't suffer, Nolan. We never heard any cries."

Ruth rested her head on Nolan's chest, reached for Drew's hand and began to sob. Liam backed away from their sorrow. He wasn't a part of it, had no right to be. He'd been away for most of Emily's short life.

He squeezed his eyes shut against the fierce burning behind them. Christ, was he going to break down here in the middle of a crowded ward? He took a couple of deep breaths, steadied himself and crossed the hall.

He found his mother's bed and stood beside her. Her eyes were bandaged, but she appeared to be asleep. Very gently, he took her hand.

She and Dad had always been there for him. Liam had taken that solid foundation for granted before he went away. He never would again, not for himself or Nicholas.

If Bea takes him back to England, I'll keep in touch. I won't be just a name to him.

"Sleep well, Mum. Tomorrow, if I can manage it, you're going to meet your youngest grandchild."

He left the hospital and headed for the tent village on the Common, trudging through the snow that was beginning to settle thickly now. The smell of campfires and too many bodies crammed into too small a space came to him on the cold air. Liam walked the paths between the rows of tents, limping badly now, peering at faces in the firelight. An old man sat huddled with a blanket over his shoulders, a tabby cat in his arms – perhaps all he had left in the world. At the far end of the camp a baby was crying. Closer at hand, someone was singing softly.

I walk in the garden alone...

Alice's voice. The words of the old hymn blended with the wind so that Liam wasn't sure it wasn't just a trick of his mind. He followed the sound to its source, in a tent further along the row, knelt and looked inside.

"Alice."

She rocked slowly as she sang, a dim shape against the faint glow of firelight on the tent wall. She flinched when he spoke. He eased himself into the tent. "Alice, it's me. It's Liam."

She stopped rocking, but didn't speak. On his knees, Liam crawled to her, gathered her in his arms and pulled her onto his lap. She was wearing a coat, but he unbuttoned his, drew her against his chest and wrapped the thick wool around her. For a long time, he just held her, while the numbness in his heart gave way to waves of relief and pain. There was so much he needed to say, and he had no words.

After a while Alice spoke, her face buried against his shoulder. "Everything's gone, Liam."

He kissed her hair and got a taste of soot. "Not everything. I'm here. I always will be."

Wool rubbed Alice's cheek, waking her from a sound sleep. Her nose tingled with cold but her body was warm, though it ached everywhere. She lay with her head on Liam's chest, her legs entwined with his, her coat beneath them, his over them. The buttons of his uniform dug into her breast, the small hurt an anchor when she remembered what had happened.

I'm here. I always will be. Clinging to his promise, Alice lay still, listening to the rhythm of Liam's heart – the only thing that kept hers beating.

Through yesterday, as she helped to set up tents and did whatever else she could while the makeshift camp filled, the truth about the explosion had filtered in. A ship, the *Mont Blanc*, loaded with explosives, had collided with another vessel, the *Imo*, then drifted into Pier 6 in Richmond – and detonated. No one knew the details, but there was no enemy attack. Rumour gave way to facts. Through it all, as she bandaged minor wounds and passed out blankets and food, she'd searched for Liam, though she hadn't dared hope he'd come to her so soon, if at all.

Only he had.

She raised herself on an elbow to see his soot-smudged face. They'd both been so exhausted they'd fallen asleep in each other's arms with barely a word. She didn't even know who, if anyone, he'd lost. When he woke, she lifted one of his bandaged hands to her cheek.

"Liam, your family –"

Grief darkened his eyes. "Nolan and Ruth and Drew and Mum are at Camp Hill. Emily didn't make it out of the house. I don't know about Dad. What about your family?"

Alice swallowed scalding tears. "Oh, Liam, that beautiful little girl. Poor Ruth. My family... Mother is gone. I haven't seen Dad or Georgie. Where are Bea and Nicholas?"

Liam ran his thumb along her jaw line. It came away black. She hadn't had a chance to look, but her face must be as filthy as his. Alice didn't care. All that mattered was that his sadness seemed to lighten. "Nicholas is fine. I saw him last night. Bea went downtown yesterday morning and didn't come back." He drew Alice back down against his chest and wrapped her tightly in his arms. "Did you get my note last week?"

She nodded, rubbing her cheek against his shoulder. "Yes. Did Mother tell you why I had to go to Aunt Sarah's?"

"No. I didn't see your mother. When I showed up at your house on Saturday, Georgie told me you'd gone to visit your aunt for a few days."

Alice lifted her head. "She didn't tell you Aunt Sarah had fallen and hurt her back, or that I said to come out to Bedford to see me?"

"No. If she'd told me that, I would've been there. The last time I saw you, I was pretty much distracted. I knew I'd hurt you. I thought you probably wanted some time to think."

Liam's eyes kindled with anger. Alice's misted over, recalling her last conversation with Georgie. *You don't need a man who comes with a ready-made family.* It hurt less to believe Georgie's motives had been good.

"Maybe she was trying to protect me. Anyway, it doesn't matter now."

Liam shifted beneath her, locked his gaze on hers. "Alice, remember when you said you wished we could write to each other? I wrote you a letter. I was going to read it to you. It's lost – it was in my room at Nolan's – but I know it from memory. I'll tell you what was in it."

Alice watched his face as he recited his letter to her, every word straight from his heart. By the time he finished, tears streamed down her cheeks. She wiped them away with her sleeve, dirtying her coat beyond hope, and kissed him. Slowly. Tenderly.

"I believe you, and I would have kept it, Liam. I would have kept it forever."

The sudden glow in his eyes started fresh tears in hers. "I'll write it out again for you. Alice, if Bea doesn't come back for Nicholas of course I'll be taking him. If she does come back, I'm going to ask her to leave him with me. With us. If you aren't interested, I understand."

Her tears had fallen on his face, washing clean spots in the grime. Alice dabbed at one and smiled. "There's nothing I'd like more. Do you think she'd consider it?"

"I don't know, but I'm going to find out. Before I knew I had a son, I wouldn't have had any idea what Nolan and Ruth are going through now. I may have to let Nicholas go, but I'm not going to let him go completely. I'm going to write to him. I'm not going to be a complete stranger to him, and I'll see him again someday."

A promise. Life still held promise. Alice touched her lips to his. "Of course you will. *We* will."

Liam tangled his fingers in her hair, held her still and kissed her, as thoroughly and passionately as he'd ever kissed her. The surge of life in him called to the life in her. One hungry kiss led to another, and another. When they had to breathe, he pulled her down beside him and leaned over her. Even with them both fully dressed, his gaze scorched her skin.

Alice touched his cheek and nodded. They didn't speak again, tried not to make a sound that would carry through the ten's thin walls as they undressed each other, but when they came together, skin against skin, someone must have heard them.

Alive. With every nerve firing, palms burning, bodies straining for each other. This was what it meant to be alive. When Liam pushed his way inside her, Alice's teeth found his shoulder. He gasped and plunged deeper. Pain and pleasure – both were life.

One day soon, there would be time to go slowly, to explore all the ways they could please each other, but now, this was what they both needed – a fast, heart-pounding, soul-splintering joining. Alice breathed Liam's breath, moved to his rhythm, until he poured himself into her and sank down into her embrace.

For a long while they lay there, still one, while around them the tent camp stirred with people waking to face their shattered world. Alive.

Epilogue

Lunenburg, Nova Scotia
March 26, 1921

Cheers rang along the harbour front, echoing off the rocky strand into the still air. Slowly, gracefully, the dark-painted hull of the new schooner eased from her slip at the Smith and Rhuland shipyard and into the glassy water, creating a wake of ripples as elegant as the lettering on her side. *Bluenose.* The sun shone brightly on her christening.

She took to her element as easily as the seagulls that circled above her. A glow of satisfaction spread in Liam's chest as she bobbed and curtseyed with the gentle swell. Built to challenge the American schooners out of Gloucester for racing supremacy, *Bluenose* carried a full cargo of expectations. Time would tell, but as he'd helped close her in, Liam had felt speed in her, in the oak he shaped to fit her keel. Everyone at the yard believed she would be special.

Nolan turned from the schooner to face him. "What do you think, Liam?"

"She'll be all right, but she's a bit different from other vessels." Narrower. Sleeker. More like the Gloucester schooners. *Bluenose's* designer had spent a lot of time and thought on that, but Liam only knew what his instinct told him. She would fly.

He lifted Nicholas from his shoulders and set him on his feet. Four last month, the boy dodged between two of the other shipwrights and ran to the very edge of the water for a better view. Liam let him go. Nicholas knew the shipyard as well as he did home.

Alice held two-year-old Katie in her arms. With her

grandmother Cochrane's black Irish looks, Katie's resemblance to Emily tugged at everyone's heartstrings, but the birth of Ruth and Nolan's daughter last fall had blended joy with the pain. They'd named her Hope, and hope was what she'd brought to her parents and Drew. It was good to see them smiling again.

It was Saturday, and the whole family had driven down last night for the launch. Mum and Dad stood together beside Nolan and his family. With her glass eye, Mum appeared unchanged unless you watched her carefully. The long scar on Dad's face showed faintly blue in the sunlight. He'd been found in the wreckage of the dockyard, badly cut and close to hypothermia, but alive.

Frank O'Neill had survived as well, though he and Alice were no closer than they had ever been. Like Nolan and Ruth and Liam's parents, Frank lived in one of the new Hydrostone houses where Richmond used to be. Alone by choice. Or perhaps his nature gave him no choice. They'd stopped trying to figure that out years ago. Liam did his best to make sure Alice had no regrets. She taught music, performed at concerts here in Lunenburg and occasionally in Halifax, and made their home a place where love and laughter lived.

It helped that they'd heard from Carl. He'd settled in a small town out West, and judging from his letters he'd found himself, with some help from a special woman. He'd married her, and they were planning a visit home this summer.

Georgie had turned up the day after the explosion, with only minor injuries. She lived in a boarding-house downtown with three other young women, having flatly refused to keep house for her father. She still worked at the paper, and the family was starting to believe she'd never marry. She came out to Lunenburg two or three times a year, but never stayed long. She had too many irons in the fire in the city.

Bea had never been found. Perhaps she had been among the spectators on the waterfront who were lost when the *Mont Blanc* exploded. Liam had never told anyone that she might have deliberately left Nicholas behind. There was no point. In Alice, the boy had a mother who loved him as her own.

I'd rather be dead than old and stodgy. Georgie's words suited Bea, too. Liam chose to remember her laughing.

Three years. Liam took Katie from Alice, reached for her hand and called to his son. The trenches in France and the destruction of Richmond still shuttled between the background and foreground of his mind, as they always would, but as he and Alice started up the steep hill from the shipyard toward home, the strongest and brightest threads in the fabric of his life were beside him, woven through his heart.

I'm here. I always will be.

Historical Note

The Halifax Explosion of 1917 remains the largest non-natural, non-atomic explosion in recorded history. It was used as a case study for the Manhattan Project. It occurred on the morning of December 6, when the *Imo*, a Belgian relief vessel, collided in The Narrows with the French vessel *Mont Blanc*, bound for Europe with a cargo of explosives and airplane fuel. The collision started a fire on the *Mont Blanc* that touched off the volatile cargo. Blame was never clearly established.

The community of Richmond in Halifax's North End was obliterated. Approximately 2000 people were killed and thousands more injured, many blinded by flying glass as they stood at windows watching the *Mont Blanc* burn. The tragedy lent impetus to the development of safety glass. The Catholic parish of St. Joseph's, in the heart of Richmond, lost half its members that day, along with the church itself and the girls' school next door. Rebuilding took decades.

In the aftermath of the Explosion, one saving grace was the presence of the military in the city. Crew members of the Royal Navy flagship HMS *Highflyer* sacrificed their lives trying to prevent the *Mont Blanc* from exploding. Soldiers and sailors rescued countless people from collapsed buildings, kept order, and helped oversee the distribution of the relief supplies that quickly poured in from far and wide.

One of the first responders was the state of Massachusetts, where so many Nova Scotians had family ties. To this day, the Christmas tree that glitters each year in Boston's Prudential Square is a gift from the people of Nova Scotia in remembrance of help provided in time of need.

Stories of the Explosion are woven into the fabric of Halifax's culture. We remember 'Ashpan Annie', a toddler who was found in the rubble of her home days after the blast, lying in the ashpan of the kitchen stove. The warm ashes had kept her from freezing. She died last year. We remember the recuperating soldiers at Camp Hill Veterans' Hospital who gave up their beds to those more seriously injured. We remember Vince Coleman, a telegraph operator who, when he realized the *Mont Blanc* was likely to explode, stayed at his post to send a warning message to an incoming train. Coleman's bravery saved dozens of lives, but cost him his own. His message ended with a simple 'goodbye.'

Needless to say, ghost stories of the Explosion abound. A friend of mine who lives in the North End told me that one day she arrived home from work, glanced in her kitchen window and saw a man in old-fashioned clothes sitting at her table. While she was looking at him, he vanished. Her 'visitor' became my inspiration for Liam Cochrane.

I taught for ten years in one of the few North End buildings to survive the Explosion, the school directly across Russell Street from St. Joseph's Church. Originally a Catholic boys' school, the building was still under construction in December, 1917. Climbing the main stairs in the dark early on winter mornings, I often felt that if I listened carefully enough, I'd hear echoes of children's laughter from ninety years ago.

Enjoy the following excerpt from Carl O'Neill's story,

DELIVERANCE

Coming Soon

DELIVERANCE

Chapter 1

Mackenzie, Saskatchewan
October 1917

The whisper of the approaching train grew to a rhythmic pulsing in her ears. *Three more days. You'll have his worthless seed scraped from your body and it will be over. Three more days.*

Naomi Franklin's eyes watered in the cloud of dust that blew up as the train came to a stop by the platform. Only two passengers got off; Mrs. George MacPherson who'd been to Regina to see a specialist about her heart – she'd been one of Dad's patients for years – and Trish Harris, who'd spent the last month in Regina helping her sister with a new baby. There was the mail, of course, the real reason the train stopped at Mackenzie.

Naomi picked up her suitcase and stepped forward to board the train, then halted as two porters staggered down the steps carrying a man between them, fireman style. They tried to set him on his feet, but his legs buckled. The older of the porters, a thin, stringy middle-aged man, swore as he struggled with the burden. When his gaze met Naomi's, he flushed with embarrassment.

"Pardon my language, miss. Is there a doctor in town?"

"No."

"What about a jail?"

Naomi's stomach rolled at the reek of stale alcohol and sweat coming from the man the porters carried. Not only was he drunk, he looked so ill her mind clicked into triage mode. Shallow, labored breathing, obvious fever, but no rash or jaundice. Fading bruises on his flushed face, but no other visible signs of injury.

"Why? What's he done?"

The middle-aged porter grimaced as he got a fresh grip on the man's dead weight. "Public intoxication should do it. We knew yesterday that he was drinking on the sly, but he wasn't bothering anyone so we left him alone. This morning we found him like this. All I know is we aren't going to have him dying on our hands."

Naomi stifled a pang of pity. *This one isn't your responsibility.* She'd carried the weight of Dad's work as well as the weight of her grief since he died, but not now. Right now, one more straw would break her.

"There's a doctor in Donwell, an hour down the line."

The older porter shook his head. "And what if he's out on a call? We aren't taking this one any further on the train. If you'll tell us where the jail is we'll be grateful, miss."

Naomi's fists clenched with futile anger. There was nothing to stop the porters from simply dumping this man on the platform and leaving him there. If they took him to the jail, Constable Walters would come for her – but she'd be on the train, on her way to take care of her own problems. And this man would join the others who haunted her when she woke in the night – only she'd done her best to help *them*.

"The doctor here was my father, and I nursed overseas for two years. I'm pretty sure this man has pneumonia. Bring him to my house. It's only five minutes from here." The younger porter had the sick man's duffle bag over his shoulder. Naomi took it and led the men off the platform.

Mackenzie had a way of blending in with the surrounding open prairie. The browns and whites, yellows and greys of the buildings had bleached or darkened with the years, until they became as subtle as the colours of dry grass and shorn wheat fields. Since returning from France, Naomi found the town even quieter than she remembered it. Not surprising, after seeing London and Paris. Of course, almost all of the men her age were overseas and the women – the girls she'd grown up with – were married, running farms in their husbands' absence, and raising babies.

Home was a faded yellow Victorian. Naomi dropped her suitcase on the porch, unlocked the front door and struggled with it when it stuck. She always used the kitchen door. She switched on the hall light and led the way upstairs to her father's room.

The porters laid the stranger on the bed and pulled off his jacket. Naomi ran down to Dad's office for his medical bag. When she returned, they had the sick man's shirt unbuttoned.

Stethoscope in hand, Naomi froze in place. His ribs were strapped, the remains of heavy bruising showed along his clavicle, and he had a healed bullet scar on his right shoulder. The younger porter let out a low whistle.

"Looks like he was in quite a scrap not too long ago. I'd say he's been overseas, too."

"So would I." Naomi fished a pair of scissors from the bag and cut the wrappings on the stranger's torso. Yet more bruises. A scrap? Someone, or several someones, had beaten the tar out of him. He would have been in no condition to travel even before he took ill. When she listened to his lungs, her stomach clenched at what she heard. "He's got a fine case of pneumonia, all right." She straightened up and laid the stethoscope in the bag. "What's his name?"

"He never said. Didn't say much of anything to anyone. He made it clear he wanted to be left alone."

"Did he have any luggage?"

"Nothing but the duffle bag."

Naomi looked down at the stranger's battered face and torso. A derelict? If so, he hadn't been one for long. He was thinner than he should be, but his body was firm and solid, not the body of an alcoholic vagrant.

"Will you get him undressed and into bed for me? Then you might as well go back to the train. There's nothing more you can do, except send this telegram for me."

She pulled a sheet of paper from her father's desk and scribbled a message to Dr. Robertson in Vancouver, postponing her appointment and telling him she'd be in touch in a few days. By then, this man would be on the mend or dead.

She swallowed against the nausea that rose in her throat. At this early stage in her pregnancy, the time wouldn't make much difference. Dr. Robertson was an old friend of Dad's and she trusted him to perform the procedure safely, but it meant a few more days of carrying the memory of violation inside her.

She gave the porters the money to send the telegram and saw them to the door. Fifteen minutes later, Naomi heard the train whistle as she leaned over her unconscious patient. She swallowed bile again and shuddered. Morning sickness. She'd seen too many young men die to have her stomach turned by the possibility of one more.

With his black hair and fair skin, he likely had blue eyes. Scottish or Irish descent, probably. A few days' growth of beard darkened his jaw. No one feature set this stranger apart from the hundreds of other men she'd cared for, but something about his face drew her.

She took a deep breath, laid a hand on his bruised ribs and pressed firmly. The bone shifted. The stranger groaned and opened his eyes. As she expected, they were a deep Celtic blue. She leaned closer and waited for him to focus on her.

"I'm sorry. I had to find out if your ribs were broken."

An ironic glint cut through the glaze of fever. "Could have told you."

His voice was gritty with pain. Naomi ignored the tug at her heart and put on her professional mask. Feeling too much had always been her weakness as a nurse. She'd been told so more than once in the beginning, before she'd learned to shut her emotions off.

"You weren't awake to tell me. What's your name?"

"Carl O'Neill."

"Mine's Naomi Franklin. Mr. O'Neill, you have pneumonia. You shouldn't have been travelling in your condition."

"You sound like my mother."

Naomi almost rolled her eyes. One of the hardheads. "Probably. I'm going to take your temperature and give you something for your pain and fever, and then I want you to rest."

The thermometer registered a hundred and four. Heart racing, Naomi set it on the nightstand and ran down to Dad's office. She didn't know how much longer she'd be able to keep ordering drugs in her father's name, but so far she'd managed to keep a small supply in stock. She mixed a dose of laudanum in a glass of water and found some aspirin, then filled a basin, added ice from the icebox and headed back upstairs. O'Neill lay still, eyes closed. Naomi set the basin on the wash stand and touched his shoulder. "Stay with me for just another minute. This will make it easier for you to rest."

A flicker of black lashes, a flutter in her belly as she looked into those blue eyes again. Naomi supported him with her arm, gave him the aspirin and held the water glass for him while he drank, then lowered him back onto his pillow and dipped a washcloth into the basin. She ran it lightly over O'Neill's bruised chest and ribs, then wet the cloth again and washed his face. He didn't stir. The laudanum had already pulled him under.

It looked as if he'd been punched to the ground and then kicked. A fading ring of yellow and purple circled one eye, his lower lip had been split and was still a little swollen, and another healing cut ran across his cheekbone. A tough face at the best of times, but right now Carl O'Neill looked like a bare-knuckle boxer – a very sick bare-knuckle boxer. Naomi dropped the washcloth in the basin and laid her fingers against his neck. His pulse was fast and thready.

"A fighter, are you? Well, you've got another fight ahead of you now."

She left the covers down around his waist, drew the blind and left him to sleep. Downstairs in the kitchen, she filled the kettle and put it on to boil. She hadn't been able to eat breakfast, but she thought maybe now her stomach would hold tea and some lunch.

Naomi walked through Dad's office to the examining room and cleaned the thermometer with spirits. She never used this room now; it just didn't feel right. She saw her patients in their homes. Back in the office, she sat at the desk. The worn leather chair creaked under her weight. She leaned back, closed her eyes and breathed in the familiar scent of books, ink and a tinge of antiseptic.

I'm doing my best, Dad, but it isn't enough. These people need a doctor. None more than the man upstairs in her father's bed.

Not that a doctor could do much more for Carl O'Neill than she'd done. With pneumonia, it was more or less a matter of luck and a strong constitution. She guessed he had the constitution. As for luck, time would tell.

Six months. It didn't seem possible that Dad had been gone

that long, but Naomi's sense of time had been warped since she got home from France last Christmas. Where had the last three years gone?

The kettle whistled. She made a pot of tea and a ham sandwich, ate, and then, in the middle of washing her dishes, had to run to the bathroom to be sick. She rose from her knees cursing.

A few more days, and it will be over.

But would it? Wouldn't she always feel the splintery floor of the Grangers' barn bruising her back, Mark Granger's rough hands groping and pinching her, the searing pain when he forced himself into her?

She rinsed her mouth, poured another cup of tea and managed to keep it down, along with a piece of toast. When the silence in the kitchen began to weigh on her, Naomi returned to her patient. He slept soundly. She touched her palm to his forehead. His fever seemed to have come down a little. She'd take his temperature again when he woke. When her fingers slid into his damp hair, she pulled her hand away.

Asleep, with his pain eased by medication, Carl O'Neill's features didn't look quite so hard, but Naomi had learned enough about men overseas to recognize a tough one. Why had he travelled half-way across the country with injuries that should have kept him in bed? Trouble of some kind, no doubt. He might be as bad as Mark Granger – No. Mark was weak and despicable. Carl O'Neill might be a thorough bad lot, but instinct told her he was no weakling.

She'd dropped his duffle bag on the floor in front of the oak highboy. Naomi opened it and found only a couple of changes of clothes. The jeans and shirt he'd been wearing lay on the desk chair where the porter had left them. She picked up the jeans and pulled a wallet out of a back pocket. Feeling unforgivably rude, she went through it.

It contained nothing but his train ticket. No money, no

identification, no photos or letters. No military discharge or leave papers. If O'Neill had been in the service, he didn't want it known – or perhaps he'd been shot in some kind of criminal activity, not in battle.

You have your secrets too, Naomi. And he's hardly in any position to hurt you now.

Answers could wait. For now, she just didn't want to have to close the eyes of another man whose life had ended far too soon. She dumped the clothes on the desk, pulled the chair over to the bed and sat beside him, sharing his struggle in silence, until the afternoon shadows grew long.

About the Author

Jennie Marsland is a teacher and an amateur musician as well as a writer. She fell in love with words at a very early age and the affair has been life-long.

Jennie has always been fascinated by history. Glimpses of the past spark her imagination. She finds her inspiration in the beauty of Nova Scotia's landscape and in family stories about earlier times, passed down from her parents and grandparents.

With a background in Biology and a degree in Agriculture, animals have always been a big part of Jennie's life. Her household includes a cranky elderly cat, Emily, and two Nova Scotia Duck-Tolling Retrievers, Chance and Echo, who are without a doubt the most spoiled creatures on the planet. When she isn't writing, she gardens, plays guitar, dabbles in watercolours and caters to the needs of the four-footed tyrants of the house.

12228279R00171

Made in the USA
Lexington, KY
30 November 2011